UNDER CONTROL

Also by Mark McNay

Fresh

UNDER CONTROL

MARK MCNAY

CANONGATE
Edinburgh · London · New York · Melbourne

First published in Great Britain in 2008 by
Canongate Books Ltd, 14 High Street,
Edinburgh EH1 1TE

British Library Cataloguing-in-Publication Data
A catalogue record for this book is available on
request from the British Library

ISBN 978 1 84767 052 6

Typeset in Bembo by
Palimpsest Book Production Ltd,
Grangemouth, Stirlingshire

Printed and bound in Great Britain by
Mackays of Chatham

This book is printed on FSC certified paper

www.meetatthegate.com

For Mathew

Acknowledgements

Thanks to The Arts Foundation for financial support.

Thanks to Gemma Knock and Sarah Howard.

Thanks to Kelvin Jackson, Steve Lewis, Harry Lippett, John McGinn, Tom Murfitt and Paul Rossetti.

Thanks to Francis Bickmore and Georgia Garrett for reading my drafts and helping to make them better.

Monday, 10th May 2004

The living room was packed out with furniture. Gary's bed was pushed against the wall under the window. He'd made a little alcove using the wardrobe and chest of drawers.

'What's going on?' asked Nigel.

'I've brought everything in here to make the decorating easier.'

'Let me see the building site then,' said Nigel.

He trailed Gary through the hall and into the empty bedroom. He noticed the curtains had been taken down. A stepladder leaned against the window frame. There was a bin bag in the middle of the floor. It had wallpaper scrapings coming out of the top.

Nigel walked to the far corner and picked up a can of paint. It had been sitting next to a roller and tray and some brushes.

'So it's going to be white?' he asked.

'It sure is,' said Gary with a nod. 'And,' he added, 'I got this to finish it off.' He pulled a giant paper lantern from the cupboard. It was folded flat in a clear plastic bag.

'Classy,' said Nigel, with one hand on the windowsill.

'Superior decorating is about accessories,' said Gary,

like he'd heard it on the television. Nigel rested his hands on his hips.

'True,' he said.

Gary put the lantern away and walked back to the living room.

'So when do you expect to be finished?' asked Nigel to Gary's back.

'I don't know. A week or something.'

'This place is coming on,' said Nigel, 'You're doing fantastic when you think that this time last year you were sleeping in a car park.'

'You've helped me a lot,' Gary said, looking into Nigel's eyes.

'I'm just doing my job,' said Nigel to the floor. 'You've done most of the work yourself.'

'It's good to have you though.'

Nigel swept a cushion on the couch with his hand, and then sat down. 'So is everything else all right?' he asked.

'Yeah,' said Gary.

'Are your tablets suiting you?'

'They're OK. I'm finding it hard to read though.'

'Seems like you're doing all right to me,' said Nigel, pointing to a pile of broadsheets in the corner. 'I struggle to work my way through those papers.'

'I can read,' said Gary as he scratched his chin, 'but I find it difficult to concentrate.'

'That's an unfortunate side effect.'

'It's more than that,' said Gary, eyes angry.

'It could be worse,' said Nigel in his calming voice. 'Remember how you felt when you stopped taking them?'

'I went a bit mental,' said Gary, laughing. 'I thought the whole world was against me.'

'It wasn't so funny at the time.'

'It is now though,' said Gary. His eyes tried to pull Nigel into complicity, but Nigel avoided it by adjusting the straps on his bag.

'Do you want a fag?' asked Gary, nodding at his tobacco.

'I need to get going,' said Nigel.

'You're a busy man.'

'I'll come and see you on Wednesday.'

*

When he left I went to the window and watched him walk down the garden path. He opened his car and dropped the bag onto the passenger seat. Then he got in and pulled the door closed. He looked up and I waved to him, but I don't think he saw me because he didn't wave back.

I went into the kitchen where I had some sheets of cardboard. I dragged them through to the bedroom. I got the net curtain and hung that back up. Then I tacked the cardboard over the window, flush with the wall. It took all three sheets to cover it.

When it was done I went outside to the garden. I looked up to my window and all I could make out was the net curtain, nothing looked unusual. I nodded to myself, satisfied the neighbours couldn't see what I was up to.

*

Nigel pushed through a pair of double doors into the office. Along the edge of the wall stood banks of filing cabinets. He drew his fingers along them as he walked to his desk.

Wendy looked up as he approached. 'Morning,' she said. 'Did you have a nice weekend?'

'Not bad,' he said. 'Sarah took me out for dinner yesterday. How was yours?'

'Over too quickly.'

'What did you get up to?'

'Just spent time with the kids,' she said as she thumbed through a service directory. 'Had much on this morning?'

'Just a visit with Gary.'

'How did it go?' she asked.

'Really well,' said Nigel as he pulled his diary out and opened it on his desk.

'I'm glad,' she said with a nod.

'He's starting to put a lot more work into his flat.'

'That's good,' she said.

'He did seem kind of intense,' he said and Wendy looked up from the directory.

'Do you think he's complying?'

'I hope so.'

'Remember the last time?' she asked, chewing on her pencil. 'You should inform Probation if you've got suspicions.'

*

I took a breath and opened the airing cupboard. It was filled with books and bits of notepad. It was even more stacked than what I thought it would be.

I get most of my books from charity shops. There were piles of them in there. All at odd angles with bits of paper flopping out between them. On the top shelf my folders were stacked neatly. Three of them had a title on the spine. Philosophy, Politics, Psychology. The three Ps, my fields of interest.

I'd leave them out on shelves but sometimes it's best to keep that sort of stuff hidden. Sometimes they take it as an excuse to nut you off.

Mr Johnson's lack of acceptance with his current living situation was reflected in his grandiose attempts at self-education.

The other folder was black. It had nothing written on the spine. I pulled it out and sat with it on the couch. I opened it on my lap and flicked through until I came to the page with the finished diagram of the model. I tried to work out exactly how I was going to build it.

★

Nigel bent over the application form on his desk. It was to fund a new bed for Gary. He wrote an accompanying statement saying a grant would greatly increase his patient's quality of life. Then he finished by ticking a confidentiality box and signing on a dotted line. He stood up and put it in a brown envelope. He walked to the end of the office and dropped it in the mail bin.

He looked at his watch. Ten o'clock. He went back to his chair and picked up his bag.

'You off?' asked Wendy.

'I'm afraid so,' he said with a smile. 'Sorry to leave you on your own.'

He started his car and clicked a tape into the machine. As he drove through the city he passed an old man pushing a shopping trolley. It was filled with plastic bags, all his life in a wire cage. There was a broom handle sticking out of the corner with a pair of underpants on it like a flag.

'Where will it end?' asked Nigel as he looked at the man.

He came to a hill with a block of flats at the top. It looked like the mansion of a Transylvanian count, waiting for the night to disgorge its inhabitants onto the world.

Nigel pulled into the parking bay. He clicked the stereo off and took a few breaths. He could see Ralph at his window with a cigarette in his hand. Nigel entered the hallway and climbed the stairs. When he got to the top, he knocked on the door. Ralph opened it. 'Come in,' he said.

'How are you?' asked Nigel as he followed Ralph inside.

'Not good.'

'What's happened?' asked Nigel as he sat on the couch. He crossed his legs. He placed his hands together on his knee and looked around the living room. The place had the overcrowded feel of a pensioner's. Someone who once lived in a big house but due to the departure of children and the financial constraints of old age had moved somewhere smaller. Only this was the largest flat Ralph had ever lived in.

Everywhere was tinted orange from nicotine. The smell of cigarettes vied with the aroma of meat fat but neither was dominant. Ralph smelt of unwashed clothes. His fingers looked dirty.

He took a while to compose himself. He arranged the ashtray on the arm of his chair. He opened his pouch and started to roll a fag. In between these movements he looked at Nigel as if he was about to say something then he resumed his actions. Nigel expected this so took his time to relax and scan the flat for signs of difference. Finally Ralph lit his cigarette.

'I've got a confession to make,' he said through an exhalation of smoke. Nigel nodded and made an encouraging noise. Ralph continued.

'I've been using again.'

'That's a shame,' said Nigel as he watched the changing expressions on his patient's face. 'You must be in a lot of pain,' he said and Ralph nodded through watery eyes. Nigel brushed a speck from his jeans. 'How did it happen?' he asked.

Ralph looked at the Famous Grouse Whisky mirror then at the window. 'I don't know,' he said in a rush. 'I just bumped into a guy and we bought some gear.'

'Have you got a habit again?'

'Just about.'

'What am I going to do with you?'

'I don't know,' said Ralph through trembling lips.

'It's not too late if you want to stop,' said Nigel.

'Easy for you to say,' Ralph sneered.

'Maybe it is,' said Nigel. 'But I am here to help,' he said in a half whisper.

'How?'

'What do you want to do about it?' asked Nigel, drumming the arms of the couch with his fingers.

'I don't want to end up back on the streets.'

'We should get you in to the drug counsellor.'

'That sounds like a good idea,' said Ralph as he sucked on his cigarette. He sat up like he'd just remembered something. 'Do you want some tea?'

'No thanks,' said Nigel. 'But you get one if you want.'

Ralph went through to the kitchen. Nigel stayed in the living room. There wasn't a book in this house. Just videos. There was a pile of drawings on a table in the corner. He walked over and glanced through them. They were like the heavy-handed work of an earnest youngster wanting to do well in art.

Ralph joined him at the drawing table. 'What do you think?' he asked. Nigel picked up a picture and examined it.

'They're really well done.'

'Yeah, I've always been good at drawing,' said Ralph. Nigel put the pictures down.

'You never said.'

'My mum bought me the art stuff last week. Reckoned I should have a hobby.'

'That's an idea,' said Nigel. 'A lot of people use drugs because their lives feel empty, so doing something constructive, like drawing, can help.'

'That's what she told me,' said Ralph. He flicked through his pictures. 'My aunt's dog.'

'I like the way you've done the eyes. He looks like a handsome beast.'

'I'm taking him for a walk next week.'

'Good stuff.'

They were silent for a bit. But still standing together. 'So how long have you been using?' asked Nigel. Ralph turned slightly but didn't look up.

'A couple of months.'

'Why didn't you say anything before?' asked Nigel, walking to the couch. He sat down. Ralph followed and slumped into his chair.

'I don't know,' he said and put his head in his hands. Nigel wanted to touch him. Put a hand on his shoulder to reassure him. But he'd found it was better to give people space. And touching sometimes made them flinch. So he stayed still and thought about the plants Sarah had bought.

Their back garden was more of a yard. It was a bit sterile out there. Summer would be here soon and they wanted a place to sit and catch the last of the day. A lovely spot to have a glass of wine or fruit juice and read a magazine. Trouble was it looked like the bin area from a block of flats. They needed to get some garden furniture and some wooden stands for the plants. Make the scene more pastoral.

Ralph stirred and raised his head. 'Will you come to the clinic with me?' he asked. Nigel responded by opening his bag and pulling out his diary.

'Of course I will,' he said as he marked down a reminder. He looked up from the pen. 'How are you getting on at the support group?' he asked.

'Good,' said Ralph with a nod.

'Done anything interesting?' he asked and Ralph frowned in concentration.

'I went for a game of snooker with Chris,' he answered.

'He's a nice man.'

'Yeah, I like him. I've also been out with another guy called Gary,' said Ralph. He spoke with more confidence. 'I went round his house to watch telly.'

'Does that not help, meeting other people?'

'I suppose it does help, but not everybody wants to stay clean,' said Ralph as he arranged his tobacco.

Nigel wondered who else in the group was using drugs, but he didn't say anything. It wouldn't help their relationship if he tried to get him to inform on the others.

He hoped it wasn't Gary. 'Have you done much art at the group?'

'Yeah. They've got paint now,' said Ralph, relaxing back into the chair. 'Before it was just pencils.'

'I've not been in for a while. Maybe it's time I showed my face.'

'Maybe,' said Ralph.

Nigel looked at his watch.

'OK, I better be going,' he said as he gathered up his bag and stood up. Ralph followed him to the door. Nigel waited for him to open it then he stepped out into the close. 'See you next week,' he said as he turned and watched Ralph disappear back into his flat.

*

I packed the last of the wallpaper into the bin bag and put it outside. I walked back into the flat and thought about the decorating. I had already scraped the walls. They seemed sterile but it wasn't enough. To make the best setting for my model it had to be a complete cell, like a dead zone.

I stripped my clothes off and put them on the couch. I went into the bedroom and rolled the carpet up. It raised a bit of dust and my nose got itchy. I dragged it through to the living room. Then I got the Hoover out of the cupboard and used it to suck up all the shit and crumbs left over.

When that was done and the place was as clean as it was going to be, I opened the big can of emulsion. I started with the ceiling, creaking up and down the stepladders. I wanted to do a proper job and took my time. I dipped the brush into the paint and scraped the excess on the edge of the tin. Then a few strokes of lovely white spreading into the world.

I could see the future in this room. A fresh start away from all the shit I'd had before.

When I was finished the ceiling and the walls I started on the floor. I had over half the can left, so I spread it on thick. From the far corner I worked my way to the door. When I got there I looked into the room and it was an empty shell. Totally white.

It was as pure as I could make it. The model I would build inside this space would have an environment almost untainted by the ideas of others. A context constructed by me. It was like an empty piece of paper ready for the scribbles of a crazed genius, a man with straggly hair, rough-shaven and hungry. A man who lives outside the world of others, who shakes his head and scratches his scalp at what they take for truth. He lives in a cave, dipping his pen into ink and scraping his thoughts on the surface.

They form a pattern, preset but original, and the witchdoctors stand over it and see the future. They speak to each other in strange tongues no one else can understand, the secret codes they use to hide in.

*

Nigel started working on his timesheets. He had to account for all of his day. He wrote in the length of the visits, how long it took to get there, any phone calls he made. He also included letters he wrote, and meetings with doctors and other health professionals. The pencil squeaked and rasped as it moved between the lines. After a couple of minutes he lifted his head and watched Wendy work. He coughed and she looked at him.

'Do you want some chocolate?' he asked, reaching into his bag. She nodded and climbed out of her chair. He unwrapped the bar and broke a piece off. She came over with bright eyes and outstretched hand.

'Hand it over then,' she said.

'There you go,' he said and dropped it in her palm. She put it in her cheek and sighed as she sat back down.

He shared the rest of the chocolate with her as he told her about Ralph.

'You've had a rough morning, haven't you?' she asked.

'I'm gutted actually,' he said as he nodded. 'I really thought he was on the mend.'

'You win some and you lose some,' she said. 'Hard but true.'

'He's not gone yet.'

'Maybe not,' she said as she stood up. 'But he has a long hard journey ahead. In my experience, once they start back on heroin, they don't usually stop till they've lost everything.' She picked up her mug. 'Do you want a cup of tea?'

'Yes please,' he said and the door closed behind her.

He got back to the timesheets. He came to the section about Gary and an estimation of his mental state. He couldn't think exactly what to write so he put in a question mark and decided to have another look later.

He was re-sharpening his pencil when Wendy came through the door backwards. She turned as she entered and Nigel saw that she had a tea in each hand. She smiled as he held one out to him.

'Thanks love,' he said. 'I need this.'

'I'm going for a fag,' she said. 'Do you want one?'

Nigel thought about it. He'd not had one all day. He wasn't much of a smoker really. Usually just had them with a drink in the evening. But he did have the occasional roll-up in the daytime. It was stupid really because it just kept him in a constant circle of need.

'Yeah go on.'

TUESDAY, 11TH MAY 2004
MORNING

Nigel made porridge and a pot of coffee. He sliced an apple and placed it on a tea plate. He put the lot on a tray and took it upstairs. As he opened the bedroom door Sarah pulled pillows behind her back and sat upright. He put the tray on her lap.

'Thanks love,' she said and reached her face up to kiss him. 'Just what a girl needs before a trip into the country.'

'Looking forward to going away?' he asked.

'You make it sound like a holiday.'

'Well, it is really.'

'It's a training course,' she said with the spoon poised, dripping over her plate.

'Excuse to get drunk and pat each other on the back.'

'Whatever, Nigel,' she said with a smile.

'It's a nice day for it anyway,' he said as he opened the curtains and looked out the window. He sat on the edge of the bed. 'The weather reckoned it was going to be dry till Friday,' he said.

'Good,' she said. 'I don't fancy wandering the moors in the rain.'

He watched her spoon porridge into her mouth. As

he stepped away from the bed he turned to face her. 'I'll miss you.'

'I'll leave Teddy so you'll have somebody to cuddle,' she said. 'Now go and get washed.'

He went into the bathroom and closed the door. He rubbed some foam into his chin and scraped off his bristle with a razor. Gentle strokes along the neck, taking his time with the Adam's apple.

*

Ralph was lying on my couch. He was nuzzling my cushion like a fucking pervert. I jumped out of bed and gave him a nudge with my foot.

Come on you lazy fucker.

He looked at me, blinking through eyelids half stuck together.

What?

Get up.

What for?

I showed him my clenched fist.

Just get fucking up or I'll give you some of this.

He got up quick. I wanted to give him a punch but was scared to in case I couldn't stop. He moved towards the door and stood there staring at the carpet. I poked around the papers on top of the mantelpiece.

Where are my keys?

I don't know.

Well fucking look.

He crawled on the carpet and I went into the bedroom.

They were lying next to the bed along with the other stuff from my pockets. I picked them up and counted the money. Thirty quid. I went back into the living room.

Have you been in at my dosh?

No.

Are you fucking sure?

I never touched it.

You fucking better not have.

Ralph moved back to the door.

Right I'll go now, he stuttered.

Fed up with me, are you?

No.

Well why do you want to go?

I thought you said I had to.

Sit down you stupid cunt.

He sat on the couch.

Do you want some tea?

He nodded so I went into the kitchen and put the kettle on. Then I grabbed a mug out of the cupboard and as I put it on the worktop it slipped and smashed on the floor. I shouted to Ralph.

Do you still want tea?

He shouted back.

Yes please.

Well get in here and clean up this mess.

He came in and I gave him a dustpan and brush. He got on his knees and started to pick up the bits of mug. I got another one out of the cupboard and waited for the kettle. I looked at Ralph and had the urge to boot him to fuck and back. A hard one for starters to send him rolling into the corner of the room, holding himself and groaning. Then just kick and kick till he stops screaming and lays still. Leave him with blood coming out of his ears, and legs so fucked up he'll always have trouble walking.

It was a strong urge.

Ralph, I said.

What?

Best you get out of here.

He stood up and put the dustpan on top of the bin.

But the door's locked.

I held the keys out.

Just go.

He grabbed them and I heard them rattle as he struggled with the locks.

See you later, he called.

The door slammed shut and I went into the living room and locked up. Then I sat on the couch and put my head in my hands.

It was starting again.

*

Legionnaire Galileo grabbed bamboo handrails as he passed the whorehouse. He licked his lips as he looked inside. A group of soldiers held drinks aloft to a television above the bar. Ronald Reagan smiled back at them from the flickering screen.

Galileo wiped his face as he straightened up and pulled himself towards the barracks. He walked through the paradise of the South Pacific, the smell of fish and sewerage, the piles of rusty tins and the fantastic greenery that eats everything up. He climbed from the verandas and back onto the road. He kicked at the red earth as he walked. In the distance was the atoll from where all this activity was centred.

He looked at his watch and started to run. When he got to the gate, other Legionnaires were barging through. He joined the squad that paraded in the middle of the square. Two sergeants ducked their heads as they appeared from the hut at the corner of the parade ground. The big one was called Gaston, the other Betts. Gaston swaggered to the head of the squad and shouted the men to attention. There was a clatter of heels hitting the ground. Then Betts told them what he had told them many times before.

There will be another test at midnight. The bomb will be moved from the laboratory this afternoon and we will accompany it across the sea and onto the atoll. We will stand guard as the scientists place it 3000 metres below the surface. It will be exploded at midnight. The code word is Shark. If you come across anyone who doesn't know this word, you will shoot them. Am I understood?

★

Charlie brushed her teeth and gave her face a wash with coal tar soap. She tied her hair up and looked in the mirror. She got some moisturiser and rubbed it into her palms before spreading it and working it into her face and neck. She put on some eyeliner and lipstick. By the time she left the bathroom she felt pretty foxy.

When she was dressed she let herself out of the flat. She shouldered her bag as she reached the bottom of the stairs. She felt like something out of a clothes advert as she pushed open the door and, heels clicking, walked into the street. A van passed her. The driver peeped his horn and shouted something out of the window. She smiled and waved and felt the power of her body radiating into the world.

In the distance an old lady stood on the pavement. She was laden with shopping, looking up and down the road. Charlie quickstepped till she was next to her.

Do you need any help?

The woman looked at her and smiled. She gestured to her bag.

I've bought too much shopping.

Do you live far?

The woman nodded across the road.

No. Just there.

Charlie took the weight of the bag in her right hand and the old lady's arm in her left. She held her hand up to the traffic and a car slowed and stopped. Charlie nodded to the driver and stepped into the road.

That's the advantage of beauty, said the old lady. Nobody would stop for me.

Charlie felt guilty for being young.

Yeah. It's tragic.

She glanced back at the driver and he was staring at her. She was locked in his eyes for a couple of seconds before she could pull herself out of it. The guy seemed familiar, but that happened to her a lot. Usually she could bounce them off with a cold gaze.

But this one jarred her and she felt a blush as she realised who he was. She couldn't even smile. She tore away from the face and forced her senses on crossing the road.

The old lady stumbled as she climbed back onto the pavement. Charlie steadied her.

I've got you.

They crossed a grass verge and into a quadrant of granny flats. Two pensioners were sitting on a bench near the door. One of them had feet too swollen for the shoes she had on.

Is that her at it again?

Charlie turned to her.

What was that?

Swollen Feet looked unsure and laughed.

She's always getting somebody to carry her shopping.

I don't mind. I hope somebody carries mine when I'm this age.

They got to the door and the old lady turned to Charlie.

Thanks lovey.

Charlie handed her the shopping.

No problem. You take care.

As she stepped back to the street, she thought about the driver. She hadn't realised before how handsome he was. Dark-skinned and brown eyes. Maybe a hint of Italian or something.

Charlie walked along the pavement. She passed a warehouse-like building with a huge glass front. On the first floor people were doing exercises. Some of them walked on treadmills while watching a plasma screen so big she could make out the BBC news from the road. There was a huge car park. Charlie wondered why people would drive to a gym to stride on a machine rather than just having a stroll in the park or something.

No money in people taking a walk, she said to herself.

The university lecturer she'd once had as a punter used to bang on about the evils of capitalism. Everything in this society is geared so the boss class can make money, he'd said. And she could see he was right.

They used to have some interesting chats in his car, after he'd fucked her. A cigarette each, and sometimes an extra twenty quid, and he'd settle back in his seat and tell her how the world was organised. He'd encouraged her to apply to college. A clever woman like you is worth more than this, he'd told her and she'd seen herself in his eyes. She was a hole he could pump, then walk away without any attachment.

But with all his knowledge about politics and exploitation, what business did he have paying for sex, she'd asked him. He hadn't liked that question. He stopped coming round after that. Some people can't face their own shame.

*

At lunchtime Nigel drove to the Heath. He parked up next to the jail where he could get a view of the cathedral and part of the city. He liked to come here for his lunch. It was a restful spot ideal for listening to the radio while a beautiful part of the world got on with its life.

He picked up the plastic bag with his lunch in and had a look inside. He pulled out a sandwich and thought about the woman he saw crossing the road. He knew her, that was for sure. But where from? Maybe it was just the eyes or lips of someone he'd kissed as a lad. Maybe she was a woman he'd stood next to in a queue, or bumped trolleys with in a supermarket, or overtook him on the motorway. Whoever she was, her blue eyes had caught his and got locked in a box deep inside his head.

As he munched he watched the birds flying from one tree to another. It was like they were playing a game, backwards and forwards, always onto the same perch. Then, when it drooped from the weight of too many sparrows, one by one they flew back to the other tree.

It suddenly came to him who the woman was.

'Gary's girlfriend,' he said with a mouthful of bread. He hadn't seen her for months and she'd lost a lot of weight. But he was sure it was her.

He ate the rest of his lunch and got out of the car. When he stood up he brushed the crumbs from his clothes. He stretched and twisted his neck this way and that. He looked at the birch woods that edged the Heath. The trees were covered in the fresh leaves of May. As he walked towards them his shoes got wet from the grass.

He followed the path until he was enclosed in green. His mind relaxed as he moved. Sometimes he didn't even know he was tense until it eased like this. He breathed deeply. The air smelled so clean, it was hard to believe the Heath was in the middle of the city. The only clue was the noise of cars.

He pushed through some bushes and had a piss against a tree. He liked doing this, the animal equivalent of carving his name on the bark.

Nigel woz ere.

He walked until he came to an old gravel pit. He sat on his haunches at the edge and watched the movements in the water. He wandered if they were caused by frogs hunting for food.

He looked at his watch. He stood up and walked back to the car. He passed a woman in green wellies walking a dog. He smiled and said hello. He thought of stroking the dog but it was a bull terrier so he decided not to. It seemed friendly enough though. In and out of the bushes it was, sniffing at things and wagging its tail. Nigel kept walking. When he got to the car he checked his feet for shit before getting in.

*

Charlie stood on the street corner, her long legs poking from beneath her miniskirt. She tried to show them at their best advantage. They were her saviours. Guaranteed to attract a punter when all else failed.

A car drew up. A man in his fifties was driving. He had red hair and long sideburns. Obviously a father, so she rubbed her knees together like a young girl needing a pee.

Do you want business? she asked.

He looked at her with nervous lust.

How much?

She sized him up like a butcher buying a steer.

Thirty. Or twenty for oral.

Get in, he said as he unlocked the passenger door.

She directed him to the wood yards. He pulled the car into some shade by a railway arch and switched off the engine. He turned and went to grab her. She pulled away and put her hand out.

Money.

He reached into his back pocket and got his wallet. She took the thirty and put it in her bra. As she did this he pulled his trousers and pants down to his thighs. His cock sprung out. She stretched a condom over it with a snap. She leaned back the chair and pulled him between her legs. She gripped his hips with her calves and worked him in and out hard.

That's it baby. Oh that's nice. Yeah baby just like that. And he was done and wheezing and back at the wheel. He patted his face with a hanky and started the car. Then they were off back to the city.

Where shall I drop you? he asked, without catching her eye.

Right where you found me.

He drove back to the block and she spoke as she opened the door.

I'm always here early if you want some company.

That wasn't so bad, she thought as she quickstepped to the phone box. The hinges banged as she opened the door and slammed out the number.

It's Charlie.

Come round.

Clive lived in a block of flats round the corner. Handy enough because most of his punters were girls like her. The lifts never worked so she didn't bother trying. Just ran up the stairs with an energy she couldn't muster till after the phone call. She was dripping with sweat by the time she knocked on the door.

The wife answered. Charlie went into the living room and sat on the edge of the couch.

All right? she asked.

He reached under his chair and pulled out a mirror with some freshly cut heroin on it. She didn't take her eyes off the drugs. He sliced a line off the pile and was going to wrap it for her. But she wanted it now. She glanced at the wife.

Have you got any foil?

The wife tutted and looked at Clive. He nodded his head. Charlie smiled at her as she brought the roll through from the kitchen. It didn't take long to sort it out. She held it to the edge of the mirror and he swept the heroin into her possession. Her mouth watered as she lifted it to her face. Lovely lovely lovely. She flicked the lighter and moved the flame under the brown powder. It melted and moved and she sucked in the smoke through a foil tube.

The drugs tasted strong. She smoked and smoked till she wasn't sore any more. Then she lifted her head and smiled at the dealer.

That's better.

The dealer smiled back.

Glad you're enjoying it, he said.

Charlie sucked on the tube till the last of the smack disappeared. She held it in her lungs till there was only a whiff when she exhaled.

She stood up.

Right I better get back to work.

The dealer picked up his remote control and flicked the sound up on the telly.

Let her out, he said to his wife.

Charlie piled down the stairs. She felt good now. Like Hendrix was playing Hey Joe in her head.

How you feel baby?

I feel fine daddy.

*

I locked the door and went down the stairs. When I pushed into the garden the sun hit me and I felt good. I strolled down the path, under the trees, and I whistled a blues tune as I put my hand on the gate. I opened it with a squeak and I was onto the pavement, moving along.

I felt kind of cool as I sauntered down the street. A woman walked past and she gave me the eye. I'm a big guy and with the shades on I can look fearsome. And women like that sort of stuff. They say they want equality, and maybe they do, but at the same time they love the feeling of being curled up in a big man's arms, somebody that'll take control of their bodies and give them the razzing of their lives.

It didn't take me long to walk to Probation. It's got a lovely setting, like a lot of things in this city. It's part of the buildings that surround the cathedral. Old flint walls topped with red bricks, and sagging with age. The Probation office is in a converted church. Outside it seems old and chilly. It's blackened by the soot of cars and buses. But when you get inside the offices are warm and airy and smell of something new.

I took my shades off as I approached the reception desk. I didn't want the fuckers thinking I'm too cocky. Might give them a reason to spy into my business a bit further than I want them to, and that could be messy. End up back in the jail or even getting nutted off.

The bird on the desk looked into my eyes and smiled.

Can I help you?

I've got an appointment.

Her forehead crinkled.

Who with?

Margaret Best.

I'll just see if she's in.

She pulled her machine about and it made some noises.

Yes?

Your three o'clock is here.

I'll be right out.

I sat down and waited. The receptionist got on with writing something and I watched the traffic outside. A bus stopped at the end of the path and three guys got off. One of them had a Chelsea top on and a can of beer in his hand. He was saying something to his pals and making his point by swinging the can around. The other two nodded. They looked like they were plotting some sort of villainy. They stepped from the pavement and moved towards the Probation office. I didn't really want to talk to them or listen to their half-arsed plans for robberies or drug deals.

They were drunken idiots telling the world what they're up to then looking for someone to blame when they get caught. In a previous life they were probably crustaceans. And they will be in the next too. The great god of re-incarnation, who watches all of our lives with a clipboard in his hand, will have them marked down for more pond-life on their next trip to the world. Maybe the next time they're human they'll fucking well act like it.

The guys were just pushing through the door when Margaret appeared. She's a tasty bit of fluff. Late twenties, nice face and a slim body. But not one of them skinny model types. She's got tits and arse. I like that in a woman. She had a white shirt on and you could just see the dark of her nipples.

The guy in the Chelsea top let loose a low whistle. I turned round and stared at him. I didn't say anything. The guy smiled at me. I didn't smile back. Just gave him my dead eyes until his body sagged and he looked at the floor.

I turned back to Margaret. She glanced back and forward between the crustaceans and me. She had the edge of a blush on her cheeks. She stuck her hand out and tried to smile.

Gary. Good to see you.

I wondered if her husband was up to the job.

Hiya, I said.

She turned around and walked back into the offices. I followed. Her arse moved around in her trousers. As she opened her door I felt like pushing up behind her. Manhandling her to the desk whilst rubbing my cock against her bum. She'd wiggle and say stop it, but giggling like a horny girl. I'd grab her neck and force her face onto the desk. She'd say stop it again and I'd stroke my cock between the cheeks of her arse.

How are things with you?

It took me a second to focus.

Yeah, I'm all right.

She sat down next to her desk and pointed to the other chair.

What have you been doing with yourself?

She leaned back as she said this and I thought of biting her neck and her moaning.

Suck my titties baby.

I sat down.

Not much really.

She shuffled some papers on the desk.

What about the support group?

I thought of getting on the floor and pulling her foot between my legs and kissing her knee, her grabbing my hair.

I want you now.

I looked at her and thought what to say.

It's all right I suppose.

She frowned.

Don't you like it?

It's full of idiots. What have I got in common with them?

Loneliness?

I looked into her eyes.

Have you had your hair done?

She touched the ends of it and I saw a flash of pleasure twitch her lips.

I washed it last night.

Smell nice, does it?

She frowned.

So the support group. Are you going to continue to attend?

Yeah.

She got a sheet of paper and wrote something on it.

I thought of running my hand through her hair and her lifting her neck and sighing.

Oh that's lovely.

And the gasp of her breath as I feed her my length.

Do you like that you dirty little whore?

Fuck me Gaz, fuck me.

★

The car bounced over potholes and threw puddles of water through a fence and into the adjacent field. Nigel looked at the house. It had a bit of smoke coming out of the chimney. The walls were pink stucco that had a diagonal crack travelling along the frontage. There was a neat hedge going round a well-kept garden. Some white pants hung on a washing line.

The front door of the cottage half opened and Chris's head appeared. His face was flaked with eczema. Nigel went to step inside. Chris tried to pull the door open further but it stuck against the piles of letters and newspapers behind it. Nigel had to help with a push of his shoulder. The door opened in a judder and he squeezed inside. The house smelled of old rubbish and bad food.

The living room was stacked with oak furniture. Wardrobes and dressers lined the walls. A couple of old guitars leaned against a chest of drawers. Bin bags full of old woollen carpets were piled in one corner. And in the middle of the floor stood a huge dining table with two church pews at either side of it.

Nigel sat on one side of the table with Chris at the other. They could have been Norman knights or an old rich couple stuck in a draughty mansion. A pile of letters sat on the table between them. There was also a half-eaten box of chocolates.

'Hungry?' asked Chris as he pointed to them.

'I've just had my lunch,' said Nigel with a shake of his head.

'I can't eat them,' said Chris. 'They give me a sore tummy.'

'How old are these?' asked Nigel, picking up the box.

'I got them for Christmas.'

'But it's May. What's the sell-by date?'

'I don't know,' said Chris as he shrugged his shoulders.

'They should be chucked out,' said Nigel, putting them back down. He picked up the pile of letters. 'What have we got today?' he asked as he sorted through the envelopes. He worked through them till he had two piles. 'Right, these can go in the bin,' he said, pointing to the larger one.

Chris picked them up and took them into the kitchen.

He came back through and sat down. Nigel opened one of the letters. 'You need to fill in a Housing Benefit renewal,' he said.

'Is that hard?'

'No,' said Nigel, straightening the paper on the table. 'Have you got a pen?' he asked and Chris reached under a pile of paper and brought one out.

'It might seem like chaos but it's organised,' he said.

Nigel didn't see how it could be. He opened the form out and turned it towards
Chris. It took them ten minutes to complete. Chris signed it and Nigel checked through it. 'Looks good,' he said.

He passed it back to Chris, who put it in an envelope, licked it and sealed it. Nigel picked up another letter. 'You need to pay the electric twenty-three pounds forty-two,' he said.

'How can I do that?'

'Post office.'

'Will you take me down to the town?'

'Sure.'

Chris stood up and stretched. He had a half smile on his face and gazed upwards. He looked like a cherub. He seemed totally harmless. Nigel liked him because he was his least troublesome patient. He was easy to be with. A good combination that made the afternoon appear as if he was spending it with a friend instead of working.

'Can I have a cigarette first?' asked Chris.

'Of course you can,' said Nigel. 'Shall we go in the garden?' he asked and they went out and sat in a couple of deckchairs.

Nigel glanced at the sky. It was mainly blue with

cumulus clouds moving to the east. When the sun came out it was warm enough to sit and relax and felt like summer was almost here.

Chris had a long garden that backed onto the woods. The grass was short except for tufts around the washing line posts. He brought out some bread and scattered it at the bottom of the garden. Then he came back to the deckchairs. By the time he lit his cigarette a few sparrows had landed and were attacking the food. They flew in and out of the bread zone in a jumble of cheeps and wings.

'You've got a nice place here,' said Nigel.

'I like it,' said Chris, looking around. 'Peaceful it is.'

'Did you get help with the grass?'

'One of the neighbour's boys did it.'

'That's good.'

'It makes the place look a lot better when it's cut regularly,' said Chris. 'Worth a fiver every couple of weeks. And it gives the boy some extra pocket money.'

'Parents know, do they?'

'Yeah. Can't be too careful in this day and age.'

'Sad but true. The days of innocent chats with other people's children are over.'

They sat back like two old men grieving the passing of a golden era.

Chris smoked the last of his cigarette.

'Ready?' asked Nigel and they walked to the car.

The post office was inside a grocery store that had a Victorian mailbox on the front wall. A bell rang as they pushed inside. To get to the queue they had to walk a gauntlet of stationery. Cards for all occasions. Birthdays, funerals, weddings. There were some of the arty cards that you can use for any purpose. Maybe an Impressionistic rendition of a flower on the front. Just the sort of thing Sarah sent to her friends to congratulate them on a new job or the birth of a child. Nearer the counter there was a selection of elastic bands and paper glue.

An old man was being served as they approached. He pulled out a few papers and the clerk asked how she could help. He replied very quietly and the clerk repeated herself. This is going to take a while, thought Nigel. He would have left Chris and gone to look at the cards but he knew that wasn't a good idea. Especially as he could feel Chris draw closer to him the further they got from his home. He was like a sick child who needed the contact of his mum.

And Nigel was a professional mother. He realised people were needy for a reason, usually a terrible upbringing, filled with abandonment and brutality. His job was to nurture patients until they gained enough skills to do things for themselves. This could take months and years of accompanying them before they had the confidence to walk into a shop on their own. Sometimes they never managed and their lives alternated between detention in institutions and restricted freedom in the community.

The counter clerk shouted next and interrupted Nigel's thoughts. He went forward and then subtly let Chris go ahead so he would have to ask for what he wanted. Chris turned to Nigel and shrugged. Nigel urged him on. Chris faced the clerk. 'Could I pay my electric bill?' he asked.

'Let me see it,' she asked and Chris passed it through. She looked at it and stamped it. 'Twenty-three pounds, forty-two pence,' she said and Chris gave her twenty-five. She counted out his change.

Chris gave Nigel a sheepish grin as he turned away from the counter. They went outside and Chris dropped the letter to the Housing into the mailbox. They walked back to the car. Just as they got to it and Nigel had his hand on the door handle he had an idea. 'Shall we have a cup of tea?' he asked.

Chris seemed to shrink inside his clothes. He shook his head as if to say no but said: 'Yeah OK.'

'Are you sure?'

'Course I am.'

Nigel thought about what to do. He knew Chris didn't really want to go to the cafe. He wanted to go straight home after the experience of the post office. Retreat like a snail back into its shell after an experience with the salt of life. But at the same time doing both might be good for him as long as nothing bad happens. He'll realise he can relax more in public and maybe even get to know some of the locals. A positive risk worth taking, Nigel concluded before dragging the half-willing Chris to the cafe.

The inside of the windows were steamed up and the place smelled of stewed tea. Nigel thought the best place for Chris was a corner seat. Get the man sat down where he can feel something solid at his back and slowly assimilate his surroundings. He pointed. 'Grab that table,' he said. 'I'll get the drinks.'

Nigel watched the blinking Chris take his seat as he ordered two teas from the fat lady behind the counter.

'Sugar?' she asked as she poured the teas from a giant teapot.

‘No thanks,’ he said as he looked at it. ‘Just milk.’ He paid and backed away with the drinks.

‘You don’t take sugar, do you?’ he asked as he placed the mugs on the table. Chris shook his head as he picked one up. He blew some steam off the top and had a slurp.

‘Nice,’ he said and put it back down. ‘You don’t mind if I smoke, do you?’

‘No, you go ahead,’ said Nigel. Chris pulled out a fag and put it in his mouth. He scraped a match and lifted it shakily. He managed to light up and have a few puffs. He seemed a lot more secure after he did so. Nigel pointed to the packet.

‘Do you mind?’

‘I didn’t know you smoked.’

‘Now and then,’ said Nigel. ‘I try to keep it at a minimum. But I have the odd binge. This is my second today.’

‘You should watch though,’ said Chris with a serious expression. ‘Before you know it you’ll be a twenty-a-day man like myself.’

‘No. I’ve got willpower.’

‘You don’t look too sure,’ said Chris with a grin.

‘You’re probably right,’ said Nigel as he flicked at his cigarette. ‘They say nicotine is more addictive than heroin.’

‘I’ve tried to stop loads of times but I can’t manage it,’ said Chris.

‘I know I’m better off not doing it,’ said Nigel. He had a swig on his tea. ‘This is all right, eh?’ he asked and Chris smiled like he was at home relaxed.

‘Yeah. I’m glad we came in. I just get worried when

I'm facing places like this. I'd rather go home than come here. But I'm glad we did.'

'You've done pretty well today.'

'It's nothing really,' said Chris.

★

I left Probation and took a breath through my nostrils. It was a nice day for a walk by the side of the cathedral. A big saggy wall made from flint and powdery cement curved over the path. It looked like it was about to fall down but the thing had been there for eight hundred years so it would be there for a while yet. It was menacing though, walking beside it and it looming over you as if it was about to crumble and collapse on top of you.

I came across an arched gate and instead of walking into the city I decided to take a wander into the cathedral grounds for a sit down and a look to see what was going on. A man with a uniform on stayed in a sentry box as I passed. He was old and on the minimum wage so there was no chance he was going to do anything to stop trouble. He was an empty sign I could blow out like birthday candles. If he went down in one go I could stand over his broken old body and make a wish.

I spotted a bench and sat down. One arm along the top of it and the other on my leg. Every inch the cool bloke taking time out from a busy day to admire the architecture. And lovely it is. A huge structure towering over everything for miles. It's awesome to a modern mind that's seen the world. The skyscrapers of New York and Tokyo and Hong Kong. The wastes of the Antarctic and the peaks of the Himalayas. I've seen all these amazing sights on the telly, yet I can sit on a bench and glance at this eight-hundred-year-old pile and it takes the breath from my throat.

They built Norwich Cathedral with limestone brought from France. On canal boats all the way up the river. A construction project rivalling Canary Wharf or the Channel Tunnel, without men in hard hats driving dumper trucks or a health and safety officer. Just sweat and bread and a bit of Latin chat from some fat monk. Block after block manhandled off the boat and up the hill to the site. A big chance of crushed fingers and toes and a lifetime of begging for alms.

Imagine the magnificence of the cathedral in the minds of the medieval Norfolk peasants. This country is flat and featureless. They'd have seen nothing but sky and clouds and no buildings higher than two storeys.

They walked for miles from their work in the fields, along paths and bridleways and through woods and marshes, to worship the god named Jehovah.

As I was thinking of the Almighty, a clerk from the solicitors walked past the bench. She had a white shirt on and little breasts that wanted to poke right through the material. A tight black skirt and calves bunched up from the effort of holding her feet at odd angles inside her pointy shoes.

Clip-clop she went like a skinny colt.

My balls jumped at the thought of her tight little body. I whistled in a low tone as she passed and she looked at me with contempt. I got off the bench and started walking behind her. At the same pace, six feet behind, my dick twitching against the inside of my jeans as if he was entering her struggling body.

She glanced back and I heard her clip-clop miss a beat as her heel caught something on the path and her leg twisted. She recovered her step and increased the pace. I walked quicker too. Still six feet behind.

I could taste the sweat on the bones of her neck. I could feel the cold shiver travelling up her spine as she realised who was behind her. I'm fucking mental. I can do anything I want and they'll put me in hospital till I'm better.

I increased my pace and drew nearer to her as she approached the door to the solicitor's. She was on the verge of running. I could smell the impulse and it made me cooler. I drew level with her as she reached the door.

Excuse me.

She turned with a jump and I got between her and the door. She had lost her contempt and all I could see was confusion and fear.

Yes?

Could you tell me the way to the library?

She relaxed and smiled like she was grateful I didn't drag her into an alleyway and rape her. She pointed at the archway.

You go through there and take a left. Follow the road for about three hundred yards and it's on your right.

OK thanks.

I stepped out of her way and she went into the office. I stood and watched her through the glass. She turned to look back before she pushed through an internal door and I winked at her.

*

Legionnaire Galileo reached behind his back to try and itch the sore spots. The sun was intense. He couldn't wait to go off duty and get a few beers. He reached for his canteen and had a swig. It was bitter. It left a man almost as thirsty as when he started.

He glanced towards the technician's station and saw a bottle of spring water. It only had a couple of centimetres missing from the top. He looked left and right, leaned his rifle against the fence and climbed up to the passageway into the station.

He got there without incident. He lifted the bottle and drank half of it in a long swig. Then he walked back, keeping his eyes open for superiors. He was shinning down the scaffold when he felt something pointing into his back.

You're nicked Galileo, said Gaston.

Leaving your rifle can get you shot, said Betts.

Galileo turned to Gaston.

But I was thirsty, sergeant.

Gaston reached for his whistle and gave it a blow. Within thirty seconds an officer appeared.

What's going on here?

This man abandoned his position and his rifle, sir.

The officer looked at his watch.

Tie him to his post.

Gaston and Betts pushed Galileo against the scaffold and bound his hands behind a pole.

You can't leave me here, he said.
Gaston turned round as they walked away.

You made your bed, so lie in it.

The siren sounded. Thirty seconds later the earth rumbled as the bomb was detonated.

Galileo staggered with the movement. He had to spread his legs to stay upright. The corrugated sheets on top of the technician's shelter rattled up and down.

Please God, let me live, said Galileo

A nun appeared before him. She looked up into his face and smiled.

My name is Chastity.
She held her hands in front of her chest like she was praying. She bowed like a karate champion. Then she reached out as if she wanted to dance or she was going to help him step down from a carriage.

Let us pray, she said.

Please God, he said. Tears ran down his cheek. Please help me.

The earth rumbled again. A corner of the structure holding up the roof gave way and it flopped to the ground.

Galileo prayed.

Please God, let me be free.
The nun stepped behind him and unfastened the rope.
Come, she said.

*

Charlie scratched her nose.

When's Jerry Springer coming on?

Clive pointed at a newspaper.

Have a look.

His wife picked it up and drew her finger along the listings.

Six o'clock.

Charlie glanced at the old alarm clock on the mantelpiece. It said quarter past five. She pushed herself from the chair.

I might as well see if I can get another punter.

Clive glanced at her legs.

All right then doll.

He nodded to his wife.

Let her out.

The door closed behind her and she walked down the stairs. She didn't feel so bad now she'd had a shower and a couple of bags. When she got to the bottom she pushed the doors and walked out into the sun. The rays didn't hit her like slaps from her mum. They caressed her and she could feel the vitamins soak into her skin. She smiled and swung her handbag as she walked, her boots flapping against her calves.

She'd not even got to the beat when a car drew up beside her. The window rolled down and a voice called out.

Excuse me.

She bent to look inside.

Hello.

The old man couldn't keep his eyes off her tits. She smiled.

What you after then darling?
Saliva shone at the edge of his lips.
A blow-job.
Forty quid all right?
He nodded and she got in the car.

*

I went through the large glass doors of the library, past the coffee shop and up the stairs to a reading area. What to study, I thought as I came to the shelves. I was too tired to bother with psychology or philosophy, so I found myself in the section of zoology. I ran my fingers along the spines till I found this old volume on tropical wasps.

I put the book on a desk and opened it up at random. It smelled of damp and I could even get a whiff of tobacco. Like it belonged to some doctor type who'd sit reading it while having a few blasts on his pipe.

Back in the days when places like this were for reading.

I read a few lines about the life cycle of a wasp they had a Latin name for but nothing in English. I turned the page and there it was, in a line drawing. It could have been an alien creature, red armour, black head, and powerful legs and wings. It had these huge jaws that could crush the life out of anything of a similar size. And the stinger looked like a weapon of mass destruction. I kept reading and found out it wasn't a weapon in the conventional sense. It was actually an egg-laying device.

I was totally engrossed when the library started to

get noisy. I had a look around. The place was filling up with school kids. Spots and bags and mobile phones and giggles. Fucking annoying. I wanted to have a bit of a read, but this stuff was difficult and it was easy to get distracted.

We should have the libraries of the old days. Where you came in and sat down and shut the fuck up. If there was any fidgeting an old lady with a moustache came up and told you to be quiet.

A boy sat next to me with a slump that jarred the table. He sniffed and swallowed. I could feel the catarrh going down my throat. It was like his head was attached to my body and I had become a digester of his snot.

As we sat together the connection between us got more solid. Every time he smacked his lips I could feel his saliva in my mouth. He burped and I felt it rattle in my belly.

He flicked through a motorbike magazine and I could see myself revving the shit out of one, flying round corners, pulling wheelies and being chased by the police.

It was like I was a slave to his bodily functions and his ideas.

I rubbed my ears and my face and tried to get back to the book. I got through some more words before the idiot pulled out his phone. He started texting and the keys beeped and my anger rose. I turned to him.

Mate.

He turned to me with a sneer.

What?

I looked deep into his eyes.

Fuck off with that phone.

He fumbled with his bag and went to join some other youths. I watched them talk and look at me. I stared at them and they disappeared behind some shelves.

I got back to my book.

I couldn't concentrate though. My mind was attacked by images of those boys. I would keep them all night till their bodies were crippled. I would shred their heads until they twitched every time they heard a door slam. When I was finished, I would drop the catatonic products on their mothers' doorsteps and ring the bell and walk away.

I put the book on the table and shook my head, but the violence would not leave me. I wiped the sweat from my brow and walked to the toilet. When I got there I swallowed two blue Valium and sat in a cubicle.

★

As the old man drove back to the city, Charlie put a chewing gum in her mouth to kill the taste of rubber. He was a nice old fellow. Hadn't forced his cock to the back of her throat or taken too long to come. He'd offered her a handkerchief afterwards to wipe her mouth.

There you go my dear. Can I drop you off anywhere?

Just near where you found me please.

He drove the car without hurry.

Do you have much more work this afternoon?

She wanted to tell him to mind his own business but he was just trying to be chivalrous. She touched him on the leg.

Too much.
She could see his old lips tighten with sorrow for her life.

As he got to the corner, she pointed.

This will do here, she said.
He stopped the car.

Thanks, he said. I'll look out for you again.

She reached across and kissed him on the cheek.

That would be nice, she said.

She climbed out of the car and shut the door. As he drove away she spat her chewing gum into the gutter. She pulled a fag out and lit it up. She tapped her foot on the kerb and jutted a knee towards the road.

★

Nigel noticed the girl on the corner. She had on a denim jacket and short denim skirt with frayed edges. And black cowboy boots that made her legs appear bandy. She was the one he'd seen before. Gary's girl.

He couldn't keep his eyes off her as he turned into Finkelgate. He almost collided with a car that was part of a row parked on the side of the road. He drove along the line of them until he saw a gap. He stopped just beyond it and reversed in against the kerb.

He got out and was just turning the key in the lock when he noticed her on the pavement. He gazed across the roof into her blue-green eyes. He gulped.

'You looking?' she asked with a smile.

'What?' he asked and continued to stare at her.

'You looking for business?'

Nigel glanced at the street and the eyes of his neighbours behind the curtains. 'No sorry love,' he said with a shake of his head. 'I'm married.'

Her eyes drilled right through him before she lifted her chin and sucked her teeth like a Jamaican. 'Suit yourself,' she said and swung her bag onto her shoulder before turning and ambling down the street. He stared at the boyish hips and the skinny legs.

She walked for twenty paces and turned to look at him as she walked. He was still by his car, frozen. 'See you later,' she said and turned again. She kept moving, swaying her hips as if she was a model on the catwalk or a lioness on heat.

★

After a few minutes the drugs moved along my nervous system and I left the cubicle and stood over a washbasin. I gave my face a swill of cold water. I blew my nose into a paper towel. I dried my hands. I left the toilet and made my way to the coffee shop.

I ordered a large Americano and went to sit by the window. I relaxed into a red leather easy chair and watched people come into the library. In the crowd I spotted Ralph. I thought of looking away and pretending I hadn't noticed him but he waved and I waved back. He pushed through the crowd and into the cafe. He sat in the seat opposite me and I got a wave of his aroma.

All right Gaz?

Not so bad. How you doing?

He nodded.

Good. I'm sorry about earlier, he said.

That's all right mate, I said. What you doing up here?

I've come in to use the net.

Can you access child pornography here?

He looked around.

No, he said with a frown. Then he laughed.

I leaned back in my chair and imagined him turning into a fat white maggot. His eyes rounded as he noticed his feet turning into claws and his legs becoming a see-through digestive tube.

Help me Gaz, he said with his hand outstretched. The whiteness bulged up into his stomach. I looked at my fingers and they wriggled like worms.

We're all changing mate. What can I do?

He screamed as the transformation crawled up his chest.

Nobody listens to me.

I relaxed and the worms morphed back into fingers. One of them pointed at the window.

See that?

Ralph turned.

The wasp? he asked.

I nodded as it buzzed up and down the window.

I've just been reading about one like it in the library. It flies around hunting for maggots. Big juicy ones with soft skin and loads of spare tyres.

Ralph nodded and I went on.

And the sly cunt only lays eggs in them.

Ralph wriggled.

Yuk, he said.

I had a look at the exit.

Anyway I better let you go, I said.

He got up and gave me another waft of his aroma.

What are you doing later? he asked.

I don't know, I said.

Could you get me some gear?

Have you got money?

A giro came in this morning.

I smiled without showing too many of my teeth.

Come round tonight, I said.

All right then. I'll see you about seven?

Make it half past.

He nodded and made his way out of the cafe and onto the forecourt. He crossed the watery marble leaving a wake of body odour that must have slapped against the faces of other library users. Then he climbed the stairs to the computers. The further away he got, the more normal he looked.

I reached for my coffee and took a sip.

Tuesday, 11th May 2004
Afternoon

Charlie stared down the security guard as she strolled into the supermarket. She headed straight for the drinks aisle and picked out a bottle of cider. She put it under her arm and went to kitchenware for some tin foil. Then she headed for the exit. As she stood in the less-than-ten-items queue she saw Gary's social worker paying for his shopping at an adjacent till.

She watched him closely. His clothes were vaguely stylish, but not too fashion conscious. He smiled at the checkout girl as he put his things carefully in the bags.

Charlie pushed her stuff through the till. She kept glancing towards the man. He seemed to dawdle. She slowed so she could wait for him. He stood straight with his bags and walked towards her. She could see he was nervous so she tried not to look too saucy.

She stepped out in front of him just as he came level with her. He stopped and their eyes met.

Hello, she said, giving him the smile of a shy woman.

Hello.

Come here often? she asked with wiggling eyebrows. They both laughed and she noted his teeth were a bit twisted and he had a scar on his upper lip.

More often than I want to, he said. What about you?

Once in a while.

She started for the exit. He walked in step with her.

So what did you get? she asked, looking at him.

Just the usual weekly shop. Nothing special.

The electric doors swished open as they went into the car park. She walked ahead and glanced over her shoulder.

See you later then.

See you.

She kept moving and didn't look back even though she wanted to. Along the path at the side of the cafe her heels clicked until she passed the barriers and came to the main road. Just as she turned to go along the pavement, his car drew up at her side.

Do you need a lift?

She looked at his innocent face and climbed in beside him.

I live down Oak Street if it's not too far away.

No that's easy enough.

She noticed he was leaning away from her. She felt like touching him just to see him twitch. She could put her hand on his thigh as she asked him a question. See how he reacted to that. But she decided against touching him.

Do you often pick up prostitutes? she asked.

He squirmed at the question. Then he smiled.

Only when they appear to be hungry.

So you think I'm skinny?

He squirmed again.

I'm sure a lot of men find you very attractive.

That's not what I asked.

You've lost some weight since the last time I saw you.

When was that then?

He stopped for a set of red lights and turned to face her.

It was in the winter, I bumped into you and Gary on the High Street.

You've got a good memory.

I have to in my job, he said.

He smiled and put out his hand.

I'm Nigel, he said.

Charlie, she said, shaking it.

Pleased to meet you.

She pointed ahead.

The lights have changed.

He looked and grabbed the gear stick. A car horn peeped behind them.

All right, he said and started to drive.

She watched his wedding ring move around his finger as he changed gears and gripped the steering wheel. They seemed like soft hands, with a hint of hair at the edges. She didn't say anything as the car weaved in and out of traffic and got closer to her home. He braked at the roundabout and turned to her.

What end of Oak Street do you live?

You do a left and it's about two hundred yards on the right.

As he drove he glanced round.

Where?

Just there in that parking bay, she said, pointing to a small block of flats. She picked her bag from the floor as they pulled in. She folded it into her lap and looked at him.

Do you know anything about DVD players? she asked.

You connect them to the telly and they show you films, he shrugged.

I've just bought one and I can't work out how to get it going.

They're usually fairly easy, he said with a frown.

She put on her best smile.

Could you check it out for me?

He seemed to make the decision with a jump.

OK. We can't have you spending your life without entertainment.

*

As he climbed the stairs behind her, Nigel watched a vein in the back of her knee stretch and crumple with her steps. He looked at a small mole just above the red line caused by the wear of her boots on her calf. He was surprised by the smell of freshly washed clothes and a hint of deodorant.

Three flights they ascended until she stopped at a door. She unlocked it and pushed her way in. He followed and was overwhelmed by the pink femininity of the hallway. She kicked her shoes off at the side of the door. He copied her and felt the sponginess of the carpet through his socks. He bounced behind her into the living room. There was a giant television in there and the open box of the DVD player lying next to it.

Nigel walked over and got down on his knees. He picked up the directions and started to study them.

'Can I make you a cup of tea?' she asked.

'Yes please,' he said, without looking up.

He read through the first three pages of the manual then placed it on the floor and picked up the player.

'You've put the receiver wire the wrong way round,' he shouted.

She came through to the living room and put the drinks on the table. She sat down beside them and looked at him. 'I'm not very good with electronics,' she said.

Nigel pulled the cable out and put it in the correct hole. Then he plugged the player in and placed it under the telly. He stood up and inspected the screen. A flashing image came on saying the signal was being formatted. Then a DVD sign floated across.

'What, is that it?' she asked.

'Yes,' he said with a nod.

'Oh, well done,' she said as she stood up. 'You've got to let me repay you.'

'It was nothing really,' he said.

'Not to me, it wasn't,' she said. She glanced at her watch. 'Are you hungry?' she asked. 'You could at least let me feed you.'

'OK,' he said as he thought about a microwave meal at home. 'That'll be nice.'

She walked towards the kitchen and he followed her. He leaned against the doorjamb with his hands in his back pockets. He watched her get packets from the fridge and cookware from the cupboards. 'Is there anything I can do?' he asked.

She frowned and looked about. Then she faced him and smiled. 'Do you want to make a salad?'

'Yeah,' he said and she handed him a packet of tomatoes and a chopping board.

'The black-handled one is the sharpest,' she said, pointing at a knife block. 'So be careful of your fingers.'

He pulled it out and sliced open the packet. It went through the tomatoes easily. He halved a number of them and slid them to the side of the block with the knife.

He watched her shake sausages round the pan, and not flinch at their spits.

'Do you want your bread toasted? she asked.

'Sounds good to me,' he said, poking at the tomatoes on the block. He looked at her. 'Do you have an apple for the salad?'

She took one from a bowl on top of the fridge and passed it to him. He touched her finger as he grasped the apple and almost dropped it on the floor. He got the knife and tried to peel it in one go, round and round, one long peel dangling from his hand. She watched him, hand on hip.

'Wow, that's impressive,' she said. 'I've never seen one so long.'

The flirty compliment caused him to cut into the peel. It dropped to the floor and lay there like a dead man's guts. She bent at the knee and scooped it up. She held it up in her hand and looked at him.

'That was a good effort,' she said as she dropped it into the bin.

She got back to the frying pan. She gave it another shake across the hob and the sausages spit and hissed some more. They were starting to look brown. 'These won't be long,' she said.

She rustled in her shopping bag. 'Do you want some cider?' she asked, showing him the bottle.

'Yes please.'

'Glasses are up there,' she said, pointing at a cupboard.

Nigel got them and put them side-by-side next to the salad. He poured the drinks and retired to the side of the kitchen to watch her finish cooking. She put two plates on the counter and buttered the toast. Then she sliced the sausages and arranged them on top.

His mouth watered as the smell of the food filled his nostrils. She forked the salad onto their plates. Then she picked them up and walked out of the kitchen. He got the glasses and the bottle and followed her into the living room. 'Sit yourself down,' she said as she put the plates on the coffee table.

She picked up her glass. 'Cheers, Nigel,' she said, clicking it against his.

He picked up his sandwich and munched in. The tastiness made him groan with pleasure. She laughed. 'You sound like one of my customers,' she said, holding the back of her hand to her mouth. Nigel managed to swallow his food without choking.

'I've always made a noise when I eat.'

'It's a sign of a passionate nature,' she said, licking grease off her finger. He was pleased by this assumption and smiled at the floor. He stuffed the sandwich back into his mouth and had another slow chew.

Charlie lifted her feet up to sit on them. Her toe stuck out at the side of her leg and gently touched against his thigh. It sent an electric shock through his body.

It was so powerful he was sure she must be aware of it too. He looked to the side and caught her profile as she ate. A crumb of toast rested on the side of her lip. She turned to glance at him and smiled.

'Good huh?'

He could do nothing but nod.

She reached for her glass and wiped her hand across her lips before taking a drink. Nigel imagined the crumb falling, tumbling down her clothes and bouncing off her legs onto the floor where it rolls and falls between a gap in the boards. But it hadn't. He noticed it was still stuck to the back of her hand.

'So what are you doing this evening?' she asked.

'I've got to take the shopping back,' he said, putting his plate on the table and wiping his mouth. 'I might go for a pint later.'

'What, with your wife?'

'No,' he said, picking up his glass. 'She's away for a couple of days.'

'Oh yeah?' she said with a lifted eyebrow.

'She's doing training for work,' he said, trying not to appear too flustered.

'What does she do?'

'She's a teacher,' he said. 'English.'

'I always liked that at school.'

'Yeah, me too.'

'My teachers were shit though,' she said, taking a swig. 'Made me out to be an idiot.'

'I had some like that. One told me I would end up driving a van.'

'Were you upset?' she asked.

'No.' He laughed. 'I thought he was giving me a compliment. I couldn't sleep for days thinking about it.'

'That's funny,' she giggled.

'It wasn't till a week later that I told my mum and she said no son of hers was going to be a delivery boy. She phoned the school up and had a word with the headmaster.'

'Wish my mum had done that.'

'Why didn't she?' asked Nigel, putting his hands together and resting them on his lap.

'She was drunk all the time,' she said, leaning back into the couch. 'All she cared about was her boyfriend and his pay packet. I had to take care of myself most of the time. So I didn't have a lot of time for homework and shit like that.'

'Did the school not notice you were having a hard time at home?'

'No. They just gave me detention for misbehaving. I spent most of the time behind the bike sheds.'

He looked at her and she laughed. 'Smoking, you dirty man,' she said.

'I wasn't thinking anything else,' he said.

'Course you weren't,' she said as she picked up the plates. As she walked out of the living room she turned to him. 'Anyway, I'm going to go back.'

'What, to school?'

'No,' she said like he was stupid. 'I'm going to give the City College a go.'

When she left the room Nigel noticed the application on the table. He picked it up and had a look. Access to Arts and Humanities. Charlie walked back in and sat on the arm of the couch.

'I'm sorry,' said Nigel, holding it up, 'I can be a bit of a nosy bugger at times.'

'I need to finish it before the end of the week,' she said with a frown. 'But it's difficult.'

'What do you want to study?' he asked.

'I was thinking of going into Criminology.'

'That's interesting,' he said as he scanned through the form. He noticed she hadn't filled in the Previous Jobs section. He pointed at the empty box. 'What sort of employment have you had?'

'Working girl?' she said with a shrug. 'Or I could leave it empty.'

He shook his head. 'That's not a good idea. You want them to think you've been productive.' He scratched his ear. 'Well, let's see. When did you leave school?'

'1996.'

'OK, we write that until 2000 you were a fruit-picker in the country, and since then you've been a part-time cleaner.'

'Who for?'

'Me,' he said and gave her a smile. 'Then I could be your referee.'

'But you don't even know me,' she said as her eyes narrowed. 'Why would you do that?'

'You're Gary's girlfriend, so it would be like helping him,' said Nigel. 'And he's told me you're really clever.'

'What, really?'

'Yeah,' he said with a nod. 'And anyway, I love it when people get into education.'

She stood up and stretched. 'I better get ready if I'm going back to work,' she said.

'Can I do the washing up for you?' he asked.

'I like you, Nigel,' she said, bending down to give him a kiss on the cheek. 'You're really sweet,' she added as she walked out of the room.

He fetched the glasses and the cider through and turned the taps on. He squirted some squeezy liquid in and filled the bowl. He was loading the dishes in when she walked into the kitchen. She had a towel stretched across her breasts. He couldn't help noticing it barely covered her genitals. Her hair was tied up and she was even more beautiful than earlier. She frowned as she looked into his eyes. She had a mobile in her hand.

'If you're going to be my reference,' she said, 'we should swap numbers.'

*

Clive pulled the door back onto the chain.

There's a drought, he said.

Since when?

This morning. Have you not heard about the busts?

I noticed his rosy cheeks and dry eyes and lack of snuffles.

You don't seem too ill.

I just took the last of it.

I stared down hard on him.

You always keep a bit back for emergencies.

Well one happened today.

Who's got some then?

You'll have to go to Yarmouth.

Where are you going to score?

I'm not leaving the house till tomorrow.

I watched his face and the wrinkles round his eyes.

Are you fucking me about?

Honest to fuck Gaz.

If I find out you are.

Clive looked scared, but he wasn't going to tell me if he had anything.

Me and Ralph could get you some in Yarmouth.

Don't worry about it. I'll get some in the morning.

I knew then he had gear in the house and felt like kicking the door in. He's lucky I didn't have a habit or I would have.

Give me a loan of your car, I said.

It's broke down.

You're fucking lying.

We can go down and see if it will start.

I turned to Ralph.

Right come on. We'll need to try plan B.

We went down the stairs with a bit less enthusiasm than when we came up. When we got to the front I picked up a half brick that someone used to prop open the door. I bounced it up and down in my hand as we walked onto the street. I turned to Ralph.

What one of those motors is Clive's? I asked.

Don't smash his window Gaz. Somebody will phone the coppers.

Big fucking deal.

Ralph pointed at a silver Mondeo. I decided not to throw the brick through the windscreen. Ralph was right. It would draw attention. So I tapped the side window. Not too much of a crash. Just enough to shatter the glass so I could elbow the rest out. Then I stood next to the window and got my dick out.

I was pissing on the driver's seat when I heard a whistle. I looked up the road and it was Charlie.

That's exposure. A fifty-pound fine, she said.

I shook my dick off and put it away.

If they saw the size of this thing it would be a hundred.

More like a tenner.

She walked over and gave me a kiss on the cheek.

All right babe? Is Clive in?

He's in all right but he's not got anything.

She looked gutted.

Bollocks.

That's what I thought.

She pulled her hand through her hair.

He was my last hope. I've been phoning all round the city. What am I going to do?

He told us to go to Yarmouth.

We could get a cab, said Ralph.

I shook my head at him.

That'll cost a fortune.

She rummaged in her handbag.

I've got a punter with a motor.

Give him a ring.

She got her mobile out.

I've no credit though.

We piled up to the Queens Road and the phone box

on the corner. She went in and put the handset in her neck as she punched out the number. She looked round at me and winked. I lifted my eyebrows to her and she got back to the call.

We listened to her talk. Her voice was all honey. It would have got my car keys, but not his because before long she was shouting.

If you want to see me again you best get round here now.

A pause.

I don't care. Just get round here.

Another pause.

OK, we'll see what happens the next time you need a favour.

She slammed the phone down and pushed outside.

The dirty fucker says his mum's not well.

I spat on the pavement.

I don't know anybody with a motor.

I nodded to Ralph.

Do you?

Just that guy Chris from the support group.

Have you got his number?

He felt in his back pocket and flashed a crumpled piece of paper.

Well get in there, I said, pointing to the phone box.

Ralph pulled open the door and dialled. His voice had a pleading whine that makes you want to kick the shit out of him. It seems to work on you by breaking you down. After a while you get that sick of it, you give him what he wants just to get rid of him.

He pushed out of the box with a big smile on his face.

Ten minutes.

I gave him a punch on the shoulder.

Nice one Ralph. I knew we could rely on you.

Charlie pointed to the pub.

Shall we have a drink while we wait?

I winked at her.

What, are you buying?

Yeah OK, cheeky.

*

Nigel was watching coloured images move around the television screen when his mobile rang. He grappled with his pocket before he managed to pull it out. He pressed the answer button.

'Hello?' he said, turning the telly off.

'Nigel, it's me,' someone whispered.

'Who?'

'Your wife.'

'Sorry love, I didn't recognise the number.'

'There's no signal here so I've sneaked into the office to use their phone.'

'That's my girl,' he said, nodding like she could see him. 'How are you doing?'

'My feet are sore. They've had us walking all round the moors.'

'What's the scenery like?'

'Wonderful. You can see for miles. And the heather, it's absolutely gorgeous.'

'What's the weather like?'

'It's cold and they reckon it might get frosty during the night. I wish you were here to keep me warm.'

'I wish I was there too,' he said as he looked round the empty living room. 'So what are the people like?'

'They all go about pointing at the ground in front of them with sticks.'

'Do they have beards and Icelandic jumpers on?' he asked and she giggled.

'Don't make me laugh, somebody might hear.'

'Send in the socks and sandals,' he said in a parody of an aristocrat.

'Don't, Nigel, I'm needing a pee,' she said in a whisper. 'What are you doing this evening?

'I'm going for a couple of drinks,' he said, touching his ear, 'with Wendy from work.'

'Try not to get too drunk. I don't want to come home to a burnt-out wreck.'

'I won't.'

'OK, I have to go. We're having a lecture on Educating with Enthusiasm.'

'Is that after Training with Trepidation?'

'More like Alliterating with Awkwardness,' she answered. He heard a bell in the background then she said: 'Listen, I really need to go. Love you.'

'Love you too, honey.'

The phone beeped as she rung off and he put it back in his pocket. He looked at his watch and stood up. He checked for his wallet and his keys. He pulled open the front door and stepped out onto the pavement.

He half expected to bump into Charlie as he walked up the street. There was a girl standing on the corner.

She had a black mini on but it wasn't her. He could tell by the thickness of her legs and felt relieved and disappointed as he walked towards her. She stood back as if to present herself properly. He had a quick glance but she was nowhere near as attractive as Charlie.

As he strolled from Finkelgate into the main road he heard the pop of chewing gum in the woman's mouth. It made him flinch. He kept going, and played with his keys as he walked. He thought about how vulnerable the streetwalkers were.

It was like they were a target for abuse. They were attacked by men who extorted money from them and called it protection. They were harassed by the police and the courts and forced to look for business in dark industrial estates where they would not offend the eye of decent society. And when they'd struggled through this lot, they were picked up and molested by sexual deviants, and left naked under bushes with their hands tied behind their backs, nothing left of their lives but images of their parents crying on national television.

⋆

Legionnaire Galileo let the woman Chastity lead him into the jungle. The sounds of animals and insects replaced the tremors of the earth. They walked amongst the footprints of sacred cows and bare feet. The path got damp and Galileo felt his feet sink further into the ground.

They came to a river, wide and shallow. Chastity

pointed to a hut on stilts at the other side. There was white smoke coming from the roof and a beached canoe tied to a tree.

You go there.

He smiled and put his arms out, imitating carrying her. She looked sad and gestured like a mother to her child.

No. You go alone.

She put her hands together in a prayer and bowed to him. He bowed back and watched her walk along the path, her sandals flipping against her feet.

Galileo looked at the edge of the river and the footprints that disappeared into it. The water browned as it licked the path. He pushed his boot into the mud and stepped out into the stream. It was cold. He swished across. It didn't get deeper than his knees. He looked left and right, but could only see unchanging greenery, hanging over the banks, trailing in the water.

As he reached the opposite shore an old man waved. He wore a lumberjack shirt and a pair of jeans. A hand-rolled cigarette smoked from his crumpled face.

Galileo stepped from the river and shook the old man's hand. He noticed the five-pointed star tattooed on his forehead. The old man smiled and showed his gums. His eyes were blue.

You come with me.

He climbed the ladders to his hut. Galileo followed. Inside it was smelly but comfortable. Bright coloured cloths hung from the walls. The old man sat cross-legged on one of the cushions that lay on the floor. He gestured to another. Galileo sat down.

The old man pulled a box of matches from his pocket and passed them to Galileo.

You light me, he said as he picked up a pipe.

Galileo took out a match. He scratched it alight and held the flame over the bowl.

The old man sucked until the opium was burning.

You smoke, he said.

Galileo inhaled until he felt like coughing. He held it in his chest for a few seconds before blowing it out. The old man nodded his approval.

He refilled the pipe three times then closed his eyes and started to chant. Galileo closed his and imitated the noises. He felt his body travel to a soft bed and a thousand-year sleep. Noiseless insects brought him messages written in fountain pen. He read them and instantly forgot what they said. A pile of paper grew by the bedside until he decided to burn them. He was holding a light against one of the sheets when he opened his eyes and was again in the hut sitting across from the crinkled old man.

The old man was asleep, but he smiled at Galileo.

You must go now.

Someone outside shouted.

Galileo, you are a Legionnaire and a deserter. Come back and meet your punishment like a man.

He looked out of the glassless window and Gaston and Betts stood at the other side of the river. They snapped truncheons into the palms of their hands. They stepped into the river and started to cross.

Galileo got to his feet.

Where shall I go?

The old man pointed to the trap door.

Where your head takes you.

The old man produced a candle and a box of matches.

You will need these. Don't get wet.

Galileo put the items in his breast pocket. He then dropped through the trap door and onto the earth below the hut. He looked around and spotted a path into the jungle. He jogged through the undergrowth towards it.

When he passed some trees he realised it was the entrance to a cave. He ran inside. After a few steps he came to a dead end and a hanging ladder. He stepped onto it and climbed. It took a few minutes to reach the top. He clambered out of the tunnel and onto a flat surface. He stood up and tried to survey the area, but all he could see was darkness. He spoke.

Hello, is there anybody there?

There was no echo.

The darkness was like a blanket thrown over a prisoner.

*

Charlie was about to tell me something when Ralph came back into the pub.

Come on then, he's here.

We stood up. I grabbed my pint and swallowed the last of it. She left a couple of inches in the bottom of her Breezer, so I swallowed that as well. She turned to me.

You were thirsty, she said.

You know me. Waste not, want not.

We pushed through the pub and out the door. At the side of the road was a tiny car with Itchy Chris in the driving seat. He looked like a child molester.

Ralph climbed in, then Charlie. I clicked the front seat into place and squeezed in. My knees rubbed against the dashboard, and I just managed to get the seatbelt over my body.

When we were settled, Chris turned to me.

Where are we going?

Yarmouth.

As we drove away, I put my hand out.

Good to see you mate.

He managed to shake without swerving.

And you.

I watched his face twitch as he concentrated on the road.

Keeping all right? I said.

His eyes flicked to me and back to the road.

Not bad.

We drove through some tree-lined streets and onto a dual carriageway. I pointed at a pouch of tobacco on the dashboard.

All right if I have a fag?

Chris nodded. I rolled one and put it in my mouth.

Do you want one?

Yes please.

I held the pouch over my shoulder.

Ralph, make the boy a fag.

He took the tobacco and I tapped Chris on the leg.

Why have a dog and bark yourself?

He laughed. Then he looked serious.

What are we going to Yarmouth for?

There was silence in the motor. Then I answered.

We're going to buy a bit of hash.

Charlie laughed. So did Ralph. Chris didn't. He just leaned further onto the steering wheel.

I had a puff on my fag, but it was almost out so I had to re-light it.

Do you want some yourself?

What, drugs? asked Chris, looking at me.

Yeah. Have a smoke with the lads.

Charlie coughed loudly.

And the lady, I said.

No. I've never done drugs before.

But hash isn't drugs really. It's fucking harmless. Have you not seen the news recently? The police don't even prosecute people for having it. This time next year they'll be selling it in Boots.

He's right mate, said Ralph with a laugh.

I patted Chris on the leg.

Don't let them pressure you. If you don't want to take any, that's fine by me. It's good of you to run us out there. We'll give you some petrol money. Won't we Ralph?

Sure thing, said Ralph.

Give the boy a fiver then.

Ralph tutted but stretched out so he could get at his cash. I took the money and passed it to Chris.

There you go mate.

He smiled and put it in his shirt pocket.

Thanks.

We drove in silence for a while. I watched Chris nod away to the conversations he was having in his head. I felt like giving him a clip round the ear.

I turned to Charlie.

How much are you after?

A gram.

We should chip in and get an amount.

That sounds like a good idea, she said.

What do you think Ralph? I asked.

Suits me, he said. But who's going in to get it?

Me, I said.

I could feel her fidget in the chair behind me.

We could go in together, she said.

OK love, I said.

What about me? asked Ralph.

You better wait in the motor with Itchy, I mean Chris.

But I'm paying for the gear.

Just shut up Ralph before you make me angry.

OK. I was only saying.

We drove in silence for a while. Taking the odd puff on our fags and staring out the window. It was a long straight road with telegraph poles down the side.

This is just like America, said Chris.

What, have you been? asked Ralph.

Chris shook his head.

I'm going to go next year.

No you're not.

Chris nodded like one of them dogs people have on the back of their cars.

I am. My mum and dad are taking me.

No they're not, said Ralph.

I could see Chris tighten his grip on the steering wheel.

Ralph, pack it in, I said.

But the only time he'll see America is on the telly.

Fucking shut up.

The silence in the motor was a bit icy for a while but Ralph broke it by getting out his fags. The road started to slope and by the time we reached the top and came across the lights of Yarmouth we were all pals again. We passed the bridge and went into the town. Two streets in and Charlie told Chris to hang a left. She guided him in and out of some terraces before we came to a rough-looking street.

Stop here, said Charlie.

I got out of the car and pulled the seat forward. Charlie leaned forward, one hand on the doorframe and the other on the seat. I reached in and grabbed her hand. I pulled and she popped out like the plunger from a syringe. As she brushed her clothes down I leaned into the car.

Ten minutes lads, I said.

Ralph leaned forward in his seat.

Can't I come?

I looked about the street.

And leave him here on his own? Are you kidding?

Ralph slumped back into his seat and I slammed the door.

We walked through an alleyway and rung the bell of a house that couldn't be seen from the car. A dog barked from inside and a guy shouted at it to shut the fuck up. The letterbox opened and the guy called out.

Who is it?

Charlie got down on her heels and looked in the opening.

It's me.

What do you want?

A sixteenth.

OK. Give me the money.

I got down and looked in the letterbox.

All right mate?

Who the fuck are you?

I'm a mate of Clive's.

He's sweet, said Charlie.

The guy smiled.

How you doing mate? I'd shake your hand but I can't get it through this hole in the door.

Well let us in then.

The guy's lips tightened over his teeth. He shook his head.

Sorry mate I can't.

Go on, we need to have a smoke.

No chance, I've got my wife and kids in here.

I passed Charlie Ralph's forty quid and she wrapped it up with her own.

Give him the money then love.

She handed it to the guy and the letterbox closed with a slam. We stood up and stretched our legs. Some woman in an overlooking flat shut her curtains. She checked us out though while she was doing it.

The letterbox opened.

Here you go. Be lucky.

Charlie grabbed the package, her face pinched up with greed. She was like the sort of rat I'd press with my feet until the goods fell out of its paws and a drop of blood ran from its mouth.

She stood up and went to walk back to the car. I blocked her way and put my hand out.

I'll take the gear.

She looked at the ground.

No. I want to hold it.

I stood close enough to see the nerves twitch beneath her skin.

Hand it over.

She shook her head. I grabbed the hand that had the drugs.

Fucking give me it.

Don't do this Gaz, she said with a tear in her eye.

I calmed my voice.

We've been here before. Give.

She looked down and let her hand go. I took the parcel and started walking.

Right come on.

She caught up as we walked to the car. I smiled at her and put my hand on her shoulder.

Don't worry love. We'll get you sorted in a minute.

She grimaced at me.

We got to the car and piled in. I leaned into the back.

I told you we wouldn't be long.

Good deal?

Fucking right. Just wait till you see it.

I turned to Chris.

Everything all right then old son?

He smiled and started the car. I patted him on the leg.

We need to stop at a pub for a quick drink before we drive home.

I rubbed my hands together.

You know how it is kid, when you've been on a mission, I said.

Thirsty work it is, said Ralph.

Chris nodded like he knew and focused on the road. He was like a little boy the bigger lads have took truanting. He drove round the corner and we came to a boozer with a huge car park and a neon sign that said Due East. Chris reversed into a spot in a dark corner. We all got out and I put my arm round his shoulder.

I need to talk to Charlie about something so I'll see you two inside.

He nodded.

Is it all right if we sit in the motor? I asked.

He nodded again and gave me the keys. Ralph frowned and hung about a bit as Chris walked towards the pub.

Fuck sake Ralph, I'll only be a minute.

He started dragging his feet towards the pub.

I opened the car up and me and Charlie got in. She took a folded piece of foil from her handbag. While she was sorting that I got the heroin out. It was wrapped in the corner of a plastic bag twisted into a little bubble, sealed at the knot with a lighter. I had to nibble at it with my teeth. It opened like a daisy with white creased plastic petals and a centre of brown powder.

Not bad, I said, holding the drugs out on my palm. She grabbed my fingers and pulled my hand towards her for a closer look.

Yeah.

She held out a piece of foil.

Put some on there.

I stuck the keys in the powder and shovelled some out.

Bit more, she said.

I gave her extra and wrapped the parcel back together.

Her movements became less jerky as she got a few lines into her body. I got a smell of the smoke and it made my mouth water.

Give me a blast, I said with my hand out.

She passed it to me.

We smoked until she was well and I was stoned. Then we walked towards the pub. I held her hand as we crossed the car park.

You know I wasn't being nasty taking the gear?

She nodded and I felt her squeeze my fingers.

I pulled her round to look at me.

You've got no control. Sometimes I need to take charge for your own good.

She nodded again.

I'll always take care of you sweetheart, I told her.

We walked through the doors of the pub. Chris and Ralph were at a corner table.

You go and sit yourself with them, I said to Charlie.

I went to the bar.

Two halves of lager mate.

The guy served them and I took them over. Charlie gave me a lovely smile when I handed her a drink.

Cheers, she said, and we banged our glasses together.

I nodded to Ralph.

I'm off to the shit-house, I said.

I pushed my way into the bleach-smelling coldness and stood by the hand dryer. Ralph came in after a couple of minutes. I handed him the foil and left the toilet as I heard the snick of a cubicle door. When I came out Charlie was talking away to Chris.

He was beaming. She had the trick of making every man feel he is the most important person in the room. I pulled a stool out and sat at the table. Charlie turned to me.

Chris was just telling me about the support group you go to.

I tried to look interested.

Oh yeah.

Chris held his drink and twirled it round.

We make friendships and get someone to talk to, he said to Charlie, picking up the talk they had while I was in the jacks.

She put her hand on his arm.

You're such a sweetie.

Chris picked at his jeans. I signalled to Charlie that he was a wanker, but she gave me a frown and a shake of her head.

So who runs the support group darling? she said to Chris.

He looked up with half a blush on his face.

Our social worker.

And what's he like?

Prick, I coughed and she gave me another frown.

Chris glanced from me to her before answering.

He's all right. He helps me a lot with my problems.

Is he nice? said Charlie, like she was talking to a mongoloid.

Chris nodded.

He's a tosser, I said.

Chris came across as shocked.

He thinks he's better than us, I said, and had a swig of my lager.

Ralph walked out of the toilets. He looked relaxed. He stood by the table and picked up his drink. He swallowed it.

Shall we get off home then?

Charlie put her fags in her handbag. Chris tucked his tobacco into his shirt pocket. I stood up and stretched. We drank up and left the bar.

We drove to the edge of Yarmouth and I spotted a newsagent's.

Stop there mate.

Chris pulled up. I turned in my seat.

Anybody want anything?

Ralph reached in his pocket.

I'll have a Mars Bar.

I raised my hand up.

No. It's all right. I'll get these. Charlie?

I'll have one too.

Chris?

He scratched the back of his neck.

Yeah.

I went into the shop and bought the sweets and twenty Bensons. When I got back in the car I threw the chocolate to them all and passed the fags to Chris.

There you go mate. Thanks for running us out here tonight.

He looked pleased. When we finished the chocolate, Ralph called out.

Give us a fag then Chris.

I opened the pack for him and passed them out. We puffed like lords as the car sped towards the city.

Ralph was pretty cheerful because he had a belly full of smack. He said we should all come back to his. I turned to Chris.

Does that sound OK to you?

He nodded.

Better give the boy directions, I said to Ralph.

When we got there me and Charlie cuddled up on the couch and Chris sat on the floor. Ralph stayed standing.

Do you all want a cup of tea? he asked.

We nodded. He looked at Chris.

What do you take?

Two sugars and milk, said Chris.

Yeah me too, said Charlie.

I put my hand up.

No sugar in mine cheers.

I got the heroin out and put it on the coffee table. I turned to Chris.

Go and see if he needs a hand with the tea.

When it was just me and Charlie in the room I split the drugs up and gave her more than was hers. She looked at me like I'd just told her I love her.

Thanks babe, she said.

I shouted through to the kitchen.

Bring some foil.

Ralph appeared with a roll. He told Chris to finish the drinks.

By the time Chris came into the living room holding a tray with mugs on it, us three were chuffing away and nodding to each other.

Good gear.

He put the tea in front of us and sat on the bed beside Ralph. I looked up from my hit.

Don't be forcing any of that cannabis on the boy.

Ralph blew out some smoke.

Of course not.

I looked at Chris.

Don't let them make you.

Chris sat on the edge of the bed like a nervous girl waiting for her first date.

Not unless you want some, I said.

He nodded so I got up off the couch and sat next to him on the bed. I put my arm round his shoulder.

Are you sure?

Yeah.

No pressure.

I put my tube between his lips.

When I burn the gear you suck in like it was a fag.

He nodded again. I stroked the lighter under the foil and the heroin melted and ran. It didn't look like a dragon but it smelt like one. Chris breathed up the smoke. I pulled the lighter away.

Now hold it in.

I gave him another couple of lines and he lay out on the bed.

I feel really good, he kept saying.

I sat back on the couch next to Charlie. I nodded at Chris.

I think the boy likes it.

*

Nigel looked up from the table as Wendy put another drink in front of him. Some of it swilled over the top and made a puddle.

'You seem a bit preoccupied,' she said.

'Yeah, sorry,' he said. 'I've got a lot going on.'

She arranged her glass, her mobile and her tobacco on the table. 'So tell me about it,' she said.

'I'm having problems at home,' he said, picking at a bar mat.

'Are you arguing?'

'It's not that,' he said with a shrug of his shoulders. 'It's more like a coldness, like she doesn't really care about me, us.'

'Poor Nigel,' she said, reaching across the table and putting her hand over his.

'It's like we do everything that pushes us apart,' he said, 'but not a lot of the stuff that brings us together.'

'Maybe you need to do some reconnection things.'

'Like what?'

'Go to the cinema, or a walk in the country.'

'Yeah. Sounds good.'

'How's your love life?' she asked.

'It's OK,' he said, then hesitated and sighed and went on. 'Well, it's kind of fading away.'

'Why?'

'I don't know,' he shrugged. 'Just don't feel like it, I guess.'

'How are you coping with that?'

'It's weird. We used to have a great sex life, but for the past couple of years – ' He had a sip of beer. 'It makes me feel like an old man.'

'Maybe that's what it is, you're getting older and your drives are receding,' she said with her hands outstretched. 'Perfectly natural.'

'But,' he said and glanced round the bar, 'sometimes I see good-looking women on the street,' he paused, 'or at work, and the urge is almost overpowering.'

'I'll need to watch myself, if that's how you feel.'

'Not with you, Wendy,' he said and she seemed hurt. 'I mean, you're pretty and that, but I don't see you that way.'

'That's good. I'll need to let John know you think I'm attractive.'

'But getting back to my point about the whole lust thing,' he said, 'yeah?'

She nodded for him to go on.

'How can it not be like that with Sarah?' he asked.

'Because you've moved past that. You could have it with someone new, but if you stayed with them long enough, you'd eventually come back to where you are now.'

'I know all that, it's just that – ' He couldn't find what he wanted to say so he had a drink instead.

'Why don't you try and talk to her about it?'

'She laughs at me and says I'm being predictable and

going through a mid-life crisis. Tells me if it's that bad I should buy a motorbike, or maybe start a stamp collection.'

'What does she think about your love life?'

'She thinks it's perfectly all right. Once or twice a week and she's happy.'

'That's a lot. We do it even less.'

'She called me a cliché.'

'Twice a week. I should be so lucky.'

'I mean, for fuck sake. Imagine me on a motorbike? I'd get crippled within a month.'

He had a long drink of his beer and stood up. 'Fancy a short to finish off the night?' he asked and she nodded.

'Make it a double,' she said.

Nigel fought his way through the crowd and ordered the drinks. He had an extra one at the bar before he came back to the table with two large whiskies.

'Cheers,' she said.

They were just banging their glasses together when a bent-over man came into the pub.

'Taxi for Wendy.'

'That's me,' she said and swallowed the drink in one gulp. 'I'll be right out.'

The old man left the bar and they started to get their stuff together.

'We should do this more often,' said Nigel.

'Yeah,' she said with a smile. 'It was a good evening.'

Nigel downed his drink and put his phone in his pocket. He stood up and his seat fell over onto the floor. He straightened it back up and they moved to the door. 'Goodnight,' he said to the barman with a wave.

'See you later, old mate. Take it easy on the way home.'

They left the pub and Wendy climbed into her waiting cab. 'Are you sure I can't drop you?' she asked.

'No, I only live round the corner.'

'OK. See you at work,' she said and waved. The car moved away in a cloud of diesel smoke. He felt it on his chest as he crossed the road.

He didn't see Charlie on the walk home. The streets were empty. Nigel got to his house and went into the kitchen. He made two slices of cheese on toast and a cup of tea. Then he put a chocolate biscuit on the plate and walked back through to the living room. He sat on the couch and put the telly on.

*

I got Chris to drop me off at home. Charlie piled out of the car with me and put her arm in mine.

What are you doing? I said to her.

She looked hurt.

I'm coming in for a while.

Not tonight baby, I've got things to do.

Like what?

I touched my nose.

I've got a bit of business to sort out.

Her eyes stared into mine.

Don't give me that shit. I want my big man tonight.

I told you I've got something to do.

Are you fucking somebody else?

I noticed Ralph and Chris watching us so I put my hand on her shoulder.

Don't question me, I said as I squeezed it.
She flinched with the pain.

You're a cunt, she said through gritted teeth.
I pushed her away from me.

Fuck off and go to your work.
I turned to walk up the path.

Call yourself a man? she said.
I kept walking.

That's it, you run away, she called.
I stopped and turned round. I could see the fear in her eyes, but she was still defiant.

I don't know why I'm with you, she said.

Get in the fucking motor before I start hurting people.

Come on Charlie, we need to get off, shouted Ralph.

Listen to the boy, he's talking sense, I said and walked up the path.

As I pushed into the hallway I heard the car drive down the street. I climbed the stairs and let myself into the flat. When the door was shut I turned all the locks. I dropped the keys on the couch and took my jacket off. I stripped my top half and walked into the bathroom.

I gazed into my eyes, at my rippling skin and the pinpoint pupils. I took the rest of my clothes off and played around with my soft dick. I smelled my fingers. Sweat and a bit of fish. I wiped a smear onto the reflection.

You dirty animal, said Galileo.
I smiled at him.

Yeah your mother, I said.

No your fucking mother, he snarled.
He growled again, like a tiger.

Go in the dead room, he said.

I don't like it in there.

Finish my story, he said.

I don't want to.

I know that kid.

I wanted to cry. He seemed to sense it.

There there, take it easy.

I snuffled and looked down at my feet.

Gary, he called.

I looked back up.

What?

Pull yourself together, you fucking wimp.

I rubbed my snotty nose with the back of my hand.

Get in that room and finish the story, he said.

I nodded.

OK, I'll try.

Don't fucking try. Just do it.

I went to the kitchen drawer and took out a fresh marker. I pulled the lid off and had a sniff of the nib.

I walked into the dead room and turned the light on. One wall was already half filled with writing. Some of it was fancy style and some of it plain.

I gripped the handle of the stepladder and climbed up it. I started a new paragraph by the ceiling.

★

Galileo came to in the dark place. He could smell a vague hint of patchouli, like a vision from a film about

Woodstock. He tried to speak but only a croak escaped his lips.

Who's there?

Chastity, said a soft voice.

He lifted his hand to her face and found her fingers.

Where am I? he asked.

Exactly where you're meant to be.

But I can't see anything.

She kissed his fingers.

Don't worry, you will.

When?

She put his hand across his chest and whispered.

Patience my dear.

He looked to where he thought she was.

Why is it so dark? he asked.

Only you can bring the light.

Where from?

She kneaded his shoulder.

The world you are living in.

But people hurt me there.

I know they do.

He fidgeted on the cold floor.

I want to stay here. Safe.

She laid by his side and put one leg over him. She whispered in his ear.

You can stay here forever.

Galileo felt so good he wanted to cry.

I'm glad.

But if you do there will never be light.

I don't care.

You will my dear, you will.

He fell asleep with her warmth oozing into him.

He was shivering when he woke up.

Chastity, he called.

There was no answer or even an echo. He called again, louder. She wasn't there. He wanted to lie there but he was cold and uncomfortable. He rolled onto his side and tried to snuggle down. The hard floor grated against his hips so before long he had to roll to the other side. Then he settled onto his back.

Fuck sake, where is she?

He sat up and rubbed his eyes. There was nothing to see. No draughts. No noises. Nothing.

He patted around the concrete and eventually touched something. The candle and matches. He sat up and lit it. The first thing he noticed was a piece of paper. He picked it up. There was writing on it.

You need to go back and find some light. I cannot live in the dark. Chastity.

He lifted the candle, and with his back stooped he looked around.

The hole he'd just climbed out of had a ladder coming up and bending round like one on the roof of a factory. His Foreign Legion lanyard was tied to it. He stepped away. He kept the candle down so he could see the floor. Five steps from the ladder stood another one. He examined it and it seemed exactly the same. He decided to climb down it.

★

Charlie knew the guy was trouble as soon as he rolled the window down and winked at her. He was handsome and cocky and fat in the face.

How much?

Thirty for oral, thirty for sex and fifty for both.

What about anal?

She shook her head.

I don't do that.

He looked at her legs.

Course you do. How much?

She glanced at the blue lights that shone under his car.

A hundred.

Get in.

The wheels screeched as they accelerated down the street, and again as they flew round the corner. Her heart started to beat faster so she pulled a fag out of her bag. She lit it and he turned to her.

Put that fucking out.

He pressed a button and the window went down. She had a last puff and threw it outside.

They drove in silence until they reached the ring road. She pointed to a sign for the industrial estate.

There's a good place in there.

I'd rather drive to the countryside.

No, this is really private.

He looked at her with narrow eyes.

Are you sure?

She nodded as they passed a furniture warehouse.

Just keep driving to the end and turn left.

The estate became more desolate as they drove. They

passed a caterpillar-tracked digger. There was a shed next to it. A light shone in the window and a security van was parked on the pavement.

I thought you said this place was deserted?

We're nearly there.

By the time they got to the end of the road there was nothing but empty hulks. Charlie pointed to a green unit with peeling paint and a For Lease sign half falling off.

Pull in there and go round the back, she said.

The guy drove in and stopped. He reached into his wallet and pulled out some money. She went to grab it but he held on.

Without a condom.

She shook her head.

No, fuck that. Are you trying to give me the virus or something?

I'll give you another fifty.

No.

The guy put the money back in his wallet. Charlie felt sweat run down her back.

What are you doing?

I'll drop you back.

But what about my money?

For what?

My time.

The guy looked at her and clenched his fist.

Shut the fuck up.

She tried the door but it was locked.

Let me out.

The guy laughed.

Do you want the hundred?

She nodded and let the handle go. He got the money out and gave her it. She tucked it inside her bra.

She put her hand on his crotch and rubbed it.

You're a big boy.

He half smiled and half growled at her. She flashed her eyes at him as she unbuttoned his jeans and took his dick out. She made a sound a horny woman would make and his eyes glazed over. She slipped a rubber on. He pulled the lever on her seat and it reclined. She got some lube out of her bag and pushed a fingerload up her bum. He grabbed her shoulder.

Turn round.

She climbed onto the seat and looked out the back window. She lifted her skirt and pulled her pants down. He climbed on behind her. She reached back and grabbed his cock and nestled it against her bum.

He brushed her hand away and forced into her.

Do you like that? he said as he banged her.

It didn't take him long to come and flop back into the driver seat. She pulled her pants back up and sat down just as he was throwing the condom out of the window. He smiled at her.

Sore?

She gave him a pained look. He smiled again and started the car. He put some music on. Loud techno style.

She sensed the atmosphere change as they drove back to the beat. By the time they got there, the guy was tapping the steering wheel with his fingers and breathing through his nose. He stopped at Finkelgate and turned to her.

Give me my money back.

Sorry darling, no refunds.

He looked at her with eyes that could be the last thing a woman ever saw.

Give me it.

She knew the door would be locked but she tried it anyway. It didn't open.

He grabbed her by the hair above her ear. It hurt. She dug her nails into the back of the hand but he laughed and started shaking her head. He slapped her face a few times.

Give me my fucking money.

He tore her shirt open and wrestled the notes out of her bra. Then he let her head go with such a jerk it hit the door pillar.

The locks clicked.

Get out, he said.

You can't take the money back.

He showed her a twisted smile.

I just did.

But I need it. I worked for it.

He raised his fist.

If you don't get out I'll punch your face in. Then you won't do any more business.

You'll be sorry for this, she said as she opened the door and leaned to get out. He pushed her and she stumbled on the pavement before falling to her knees. She sat down and heard the car screech down the road.

You cunt, I'll get you for this, she said, tears dripping from her nose onto the pavement.

★

The banging letterbox woke Nigel up. He rubbed his eyes and saw the half eaten toast on his lap. He put it on the plate with the other slice and the biscuit. He clicked the telly off as he rose from the couch.

'Hang on,' he shouted and walked to the front door. 'Who is it?' he asked as he pulled it open.

'Charlie,' she whispered.

'What are you doing here?' he asked.

He stood aside. 'Come in,' he said and she crossed the threshold and stopped in the middle of the living room.

'Are you all right?' he asked. She shook her head. He noticed the tears on her cheeks and the dirt on her legs.

'Sit down and I'll get you a hot drink,' he said, putting his hand on her shoulders and manoeuvring her towards the couch. She sat like an automaton and he picked the dishes up from the coffee table. He had another glance at the dirt on her knees and thighs. Her skinny arms held her handbag close to her stomach.

He made some tea and sat next to her. 'What's the matter?' he asked with his gentle voice. She raised her head and looked at him. She smiled like a little girl with a twisted ankle, to her father or her teacher. Then she went to say something and just shook her head. Tears glistened in her eyes, but didn't spill onto her cheeks.

'Come here,' he said, lifting his arm. She leaned into his body and he put his hand on her shoulder. He stroked and patted and thought of things to say to comfort her, but he couldn't come up with anything that wasn't stupid or inane, so he decided to say nothing.

She groaned and he gave her shoulder another pat.

'You're all right,' he said. She snuffled a couple of

times, then straightened herself up and reached for her tea.

'Thanks for this,' she said, back in control. 'I don't usually visit unannounced.'

'It's a bit late for a social call,' he said as he glanced at his watch. Then he looked at her. 'And how do you know where I live?' he asked with a shrug.

'I saw you go in after I spoke to you earlier,' she said with a coy smile. 'Not that I'm a stalker or anything.'

He hoped she wasn't as he watched her search in her bag. She pulled a pouch of tobacco out of it. 'Mind if I smoke?' she asked.

'Go right ahead.'

She fumbled with the papers, so he took them from her. 'Let me do that for you,' he said. She leaned back into the couch while he rolled her a cigarette.

'I've had a bad night,' she said.

'What happened?'

'Some idiot robbed me.'

'Was he violent?' he asked and passed her the roll-up.

'Thanks,' she said, taking it. 'They always are.' She lit it and took a puff. 'Look at me, I'm filthy. I need a wash.'

'You can use the shower, if you want,' he said as he made himself a fag.

'Thanks, but – '

'What?'

'Won't your wife mind you having me round here?'

'She doesn't need to know, does she?'

'OK. If you're sure,' she said with a smile.

'I'll get you a towel,' he said, standing up.

WEDNESDAY, 12TH MAY 2004

I was in the kitchen making some breakfast. I was in a hurry so I could catch the last episode of World at War. It was going to be about the Holocaust and the punishment the Germans got for fucking up the Jews.

My door banged like the police were out there with a warrant. I put my stuff down gently and sneaked into the living room. When I pushed my eye to the spy hole I spotted Charlie standing outside. She was hunched over a fag and looking up and down the corridor like she was waiting for somebody to shoot her.

I opened up and she came in.

How you doing? I asked.

I'm not well.

She didn't look it. I hoped she didn't spew on my carpet.

Go and score some gear then.

Clive still hasn't got anything.

What do you want me to do about it? I asked.

Give me some of what you got last night.

That's Ralph's stuff.

So what?

I can't just give his gear away.

She tutted.

Fuck sake Gaz, how can you put him before me?

What, after last night?

I was upset because I wanted to be with you, she said.

She looked me up and down and had a puff on her fag.

Let me have some baby and I'll give you a blow-job.

The adverts were finishing and the guy from the History Channel announced the World at War. I tried to look round her at the telly.

I don't want my dick sucked.

She frowned like she didn't know what to do.

Sit down, I told her and went into the kitchen.

I got on my hands and knees. I poked under the fridge with a fork till it hooked Ralph's gear and I could drag it out. I went back into the living room.

Here.

I reached for her chin and lifted it so she could see my eyes.

Just remember how good I am to you.

She nodded, but her eyes were on the drugs.

Thanks Gaz.

I sat down and waited for the Nazis to get what was coming to them.

Right shut up. I want to watch the telly.

*

Charlie smoked another line and relaxed into the chair. She watched him spoon cereal into his mouth. He turned to her.

What's up? he said, chewing. A dribble of milk ran down his chin.

Nothing.

He drew the back of his hand across his lips and turned back to the telly. He tried to shout and spluttered bits of food onto the carpet.

Dirty cunts.

She eyed the telly and a pile of skinny bodies on the back of a cart.

That's terrible.

It's worse than that. How anybody could treat them poor bastards like that, he said before pushing the spoon back in his mouth.

He looked at her.

Six million of the fuckers.

Can we watch something else?

His eyes blazed at her.

What do you want to watch? Some fucking soap? Or idiots telling everybody about their affairs and how their husbands beat them up?

I was only asking. No need to get offended.

He pointed at the telly.

This is history. This shit really happened and there is people going about saying it didn't.

Charlie fidgeted but couldn't break eye contact. She nodded, mute, and he went on.

They want us all to watch senseless shit and just eat

our food and take our medications. They don't want us to remember what's really happened in our world.

Who's they?

He pointed upwards.

Them cunts. The government and that.

Well I like watching soaps. It takes my mind off things.

He tapped the cereal bowl with his spoon.

That's exactly what I'm saying.

She was about to reply when the door was knocked. Gaz put his finger to his lips. He flicked the sound on the telly down and put the bowl on the table. He went to the door and looked through the spy hole.

Who is it?

Gary, it's Nigel.

Charlie felt her ears tingle. Gaz turned to her and waved her into the bedroom. She stood in the hallway and heard the chains and locks and the door opening.

I cancelled the appointment, said Gaz to the visitor.

I know you did. I was just worried so I thought I'd check to see you were OK.

I'm fine really. Just not up for a visit.

Are you sure? I could come in for a little while.

The house is a mess, said Gaz.

He laughed before adding more information.

Not fit to be seen.

OK. As long as you're well. I'll come back next week at the same time.

I'll write it on my appointment card.

The door closed. Charlie walked into the living room just as Gaz was putting the chain back up.

He sounds familiar, she said. Like a punter of mine. His eyes widened.

Oh yeah? What's his name?

I can't tell you. Client confidentiality.

Shut up you stupid cow.

She laughed and walked to the window. Just as she got there she saw Nigel get into his car. She turned back to Gaz.

No it isn't him.

Pity, that. We could blackmail the cunt. He's got a wife, and a career.

They don't earn much though, said Charlie.

More than me or you.

She laughed.

Well maybe you.

Gaz scratched his chin.

He's always giving me hassle. I wouldn't mind having something on him.

Everybody's got secrets.

Not that cunt. He's as dry as an old nun.

Music started on the telly. Gaz shook his head.

And he's made me miss the end of my programme. Fucking wanker.

Charlie sat down and picked up the remote.

Can we watch Oprah?

He put his hand out.

Give me that.

She handed it over and he flicked the channels till Oprah came on. Then he looked at her with his angry eyes.

Straight after this you better get out and get some cash.

She nodded and watched a fat woman talking about her dad coming into her room at night. Oprah reached for a hanky in a box and passed one to her.

Thank you, said the woman.

You're welcome, said Oprah.

Gaz shook his head and tutted.

Fucking muppets.

Charlie looked at him and smiled.

Thanks for letting me watch this.

His eyes softened like they loved her.

Do you want a cup of tea babe? he asked.

Oh yes please. Two sugars and milk.

All right. Roll me a fag while I'm in there.

*

Galileo descended into uncertainty. It didn't take long to reach a floor. He lit the candle and saw he was in a small living room. The wallpaper was woodchip painted a beige colour. There was a seventies vintage television in the corner. The other corner had an easy chair with a standard lamp next to it. He reached for the lamp and switched it on.

There was a door in one of the walls. He tried it but it wouldn't open. He went to the telly and turned it on. An episode of Coronation Street came on. He switched the channels but every one had the same programme. He looked round the room. The carpet was filthy with crumbs and dog hair and a couple of old burnt matches. There were cobwebs in the corners and a packet of cigarettes on the arm of the chair.

He sat and watched the telly. He'd smoked four fags and watched the same episode twice before he started to get bored. He glanced in the corner and spotted an extension cable.

He plugged it in behind the telly. Then he started back for the ladder, uncoiling it as he climbed. When he got to the top he tied it to the top rung and fetched the lamp. He connected it up. He reached under the shade and flicked the switch.

It came on and he noticed Chastity standing with her hands in front of her stomach.

Hello Galileo.

*

Charlie sat on a stool next to the window, and waited for Gaz to get the drinks. It was nice and warm. She glanced through the newspaper, turning pages, not really reading. Something outside caught her eye and she looked up. A girl on the corner was leaning on the door of a silver hatchback.

Gaz, she called.

He turned round from the bar, a fiver in his outstretched hand.

Yeah? he said with a frown.

She pointed out the window.

There's the guy that robbed me.

He crushed the money into his pocket and walked out of the pub. She ran after him, her heels clicking on the pavement. He dodged between vehicles and stood in the middle of a line of traffic. She caught up with him just as he stepped to the other side.

She watched his shoulders swing as he reached the car. He nudged the girl out of the way and his hands went inside.

By the time Charlie got there, Gaz had pulled the guy half out of the window and was slamming his head against the door.

Not so tough now, are you?

He gave the guy a couple of slaps on the face.

It's not a woman you're struggling with here. Is it?

Charlie reached in and took the keys out of the ignition.

Is this the cunt? asked Gaz.

Charlie nodded and pointed at the guy.

Where's my fucking money?

The guy just looked, open-mouthed. Gaz shook him.

She's asking you a question.

I've not got any money.

The other girl started.

How were you going to pay me then?

Charlie spoke to the girl.

This cunt robbed me last night.

The other girl leaned over and spat in his face.

Fucking slag.

Gaz opened the car door and dragged the guy out onto the pavement. The women pounced on him and Charlie ripped his wallet out of his back pocket. She put it inside her jacket.

Gaz gave him a couple of kicks. The other girl gave him some as well. Charlie dangled his keys in front of him.

Are these yours?

The guy reached for them and Charlie threw them into the bushes at the side of the road.

You fucking slut, he said.

What did you say? she screamed at him and he flinched.

Gaz leaned over the guy.

Fucking nonce.

He turned to the women.

Come on. Let's get out of here before the old bill turn up.

The three of them crossed the road. Charlie pulled the wallet from her jacket and gave the other girl a twenty.

There you go. Sorry to spoil your turn.

The girl tucked the money away.

Don't worry about it. You probably saved me from getting robbed.

They stood on the pavement and watched the guy stumble out of the bushes before getting back in his car. He drove away. He wasn't wheel-spinning.

The other girl started walking back across the road.

All right. Be lucky, she said.

Gaz waved.

Cheers doll. And you.

He stuck his hand out to Charlie.

Give me that wallet.

She gave him it.

*

Nigel pulled his mobile out and checked for a message. There was none. He pressed a button and the microwave hummed. He watched a plastic box turn on the plate. He poured himself a glass of elderflower cordial and put it on the coffee table. When the oven stopped he opened the door and pulled out the floppy package. It was hot and steamy. He left it on the worktop to cool while he got a bag of salad out of the fridge. By the time he'd arranged the salad on his plate the food was cool enough to open and serve.

He sat on the couch and put the telly on. The Six O'Clock News filled the screen. He watched famine and death and crime-ridden inner cities. Then he rested back into the couch and burped. His eyelids became heavy.

*

I pushed the card in. The machine asked for the pin number so I entered it. Then I did a balance enquiry. The guy had five hundred and fifty-three pounds forty-six pence in his account. Did I want any other service?

Fucking right I do, give me the money.

How much did I want? said the machine.

Two hundred and fifty, I said and Charlie nodded. The machine returned the card and started counting the money. We waited for a few seconds and a sheaf of notes appeared at the slot. I grabbed them and we walked.

I can't believe that stupid cunt had his pin number in the wallet.

Charlie had a sour look into the distance.

Serves him right for being a scumbag, she said.

Fucking right it does. He's paid for what he had now.

Charlie nodded and pulled her jacket round herself.

So how much have we got now? she asked.

Four hundred.

More than enough for a fun couple of days.

We seemed to be walking back towards the beat.

Do you want to go back to work? I asked.

Charlie shook her head.

Fuck that. I've had enough cocks up me for one day.

What do you want to do then?

She looked at me with eyes of smoke.

Clive's?

Oh yes, I said like a football commentator.

As soon as the dealer clocked the amount of cash his eyes lit up and he was bowing like a servant. I could imagine his fork-like tongue flicking between the cheeks of my bum.

Master, I clean your hole. Ten dollar, I lick you long time.

If I kicked him he'd scuttle along the carpet, eyes blinking and tail twitching, up the side of the sofa and along the top of the backrest. There he'd sit, watching the surroundings, just out of reach of a punch, and he'd still try and sell stuff.

You want opium?

Is it good?

Best best. Most strong.

With an image of Clive as a lizard, I sat on his greasy couch. His tongue came out again and I expected him to hiss. But he didn't, he ordered his wife to make us tea.

And bring through some biscuits. Nice ones.
He shook his head at us.

If you don't tell her she brings in the stale ones.
Then he smiled like Fagin.

What are you after?

So the drought's over then?

Sure is. Some gear just arrived from East London. Top stuff from the Pakistanis.
Charlie pulled herself forward against my knee.

Have you got any white?
Clive smiled and we caught a glimpse of the mouth his wife kisses. No wonder she seems so disgusted all the time.

Is that what you want?
Charlie sucked in some saliva and nodded.

I'll have a teenth, she said and looked at me.

You have what you fancy doll. I'll just have some of the brown.

OK, she said and turned to Clive.

Give us a sixteenth of each.
He seemed a bit shy for a second.

A hundred and thirty.
I peeled the money off my wad.

He went out of the room and appeared with two clingfilm-wrapped packets. He went to give them to me but I nodded towards Charlie. He handed them to her. She opened the brown one and we had a smoke. I felt mellow really quickly so I knew the gear was good.

Charlie nodded to Clive and spoke in a husky voice.

Sweet, she said and Clive smiled.

You should try the white.

Have you got a pipe?

Clive shouted and his wife brought one in. Charlie pulled out a packet of fags and we all lit one up. Clive pushed an old saucer towards her. She lit three fags and put them in it. We flicked our ash in there till we had a small pile. Then Charlie reached for the pipe.

I watched my girl in action. She put a small heap of ash on the gauze of the pipe. Then she broke off some rock and put it on top. She sparked her lighter and sucked in the smoke. Her face looked like she was in communication with God or she was a porno star sliding onto a massive cock. She sat like a Buddhist for a few seconds. Then she looked at me and smiled.

All right handsome? Do you want some pipe? she said with one eyebrow raised and a crooked smile on her lips. I nodded so she made another and handed it to me.

I sucked as she burned the lighter above the drugs. I felt it crackle in my ears. It was like an orgasm, only better.

Fucking lovely, I said and Charlie and Clive nodded at me and each other. I gazed at my girl.

You're beautiful, I said. She smiled and sunbeams flowed from her eyes. I wanted to touch her and lick the sweat from her skin. Stroke her softly and nibble her neck.

That was good.

Charlie reached for the pipe and had another. I had some more brown. Clive left the room and I heard him speak to his wife. Charlie passed me the pipe and I had another smoke. As I finished I looked at her and she was watching me with her mouth half open like she wanted to strip me off. I winked.

It's all right this stuff.

Too nice, she said as she reached for the pipe.

We smoked the teenth of crack in under an hour. I didn't have that much. It was mainly her. As soon as she finished the last rock she called for Clive. He walked into the living room rubbing his hands together.

What can I do for you?

Charlie picked at her face.

Give me an eight ball of white.

She didn't look so beautiful now. More like a mental patient who'd just woke from a nightmare.

I spoke to Clive.

She's had enough.

He ignored me.

What do you want love? he asked Charlie.

I stood up and took him by the arm.

A word.

We went into the other room. His wife lay on the bed reading a magazine. I grabbed him by the scruff of his shirt and whispered in his ear.

Don't try to make me look like a cunt.

I put my hand to the back of my trousers, but lucky for him the knife was at home.

He shook his head, his eyes filled with fear. He gulped like the lizard he is.

I wasn't, honest mate.

You fucking were. Cunts like you will do anything for money. I said she's not having any more so leave it.

And I looked at him and thought, lucky man. The blade would have slid out of my waistband with a ching, and a whish through the air. The point to his neck, pressing the skin, and then a nick off his ear to show him I wasn't messing around.

I pushed him against the wall and went back into the living room. Charlie looked past me to Clive.

So?

I've not got any left.

She gave me an angry look. I shrugged.

What do you want me to do? He's got none left.

I'll go and get some elsewhere.

Clive tutted.

See, you can't stop her. Now she's taking her business to somebody else.

I pointed at her.

You've had enough.

I turned to Clive.

And as for you, watch it or I'll take everything.

He backed away from me.

Listen to him Charlie. You've had enough.

I gestured behind me with my thumb.

Do you hear that?

She seemed sulky but nodded.

OK. I've had enough.

I picked up the foil.

Here, have some gear. That'll calm you down.

She snatched it from me and sucked the drugs into her chest as if they were the last breath of air on earth.

By the time she'd smoked an amount of gear that would have killed me and Ralph put together, she looked a bit calmer. I nodded.

Better now?

She looked sad, but relaxed.

Yeah. I just get the fever with white.

I noticed.

She glanced around for her bag.

Shall we get out of here?

Hang on.

I shouted.

Clive.

He appeared at the living room door.

What?

Do me another teenth of brown.

He went and got it. I opened it up and took enough to replace what was Ralph's from earlier. Then I wrapped up the rest and gave it to Charlie.

Cheers babe, she said.

I slid Ralph's down my sock and stood up.

Off then?

Charlie reached her hand to me. I pulled her upright. We stood for a second, looking into each other's eyes. I felt her breath on my cheek. Considering how she'd spent the day, it smelt quite sweet. I let her hand go and we left the room.

Clive met us in the hallway. He opened the front door and we walked out. On the way down the stairs she wrapped her hand round my fingers.

We left the building and she turned to me with a smile.

Do you want to come round mine? she asked.

I looked at her fragile little body and I wanted to say yes, but I shook my head.

Sorry love, but I need to give Ralph his gear back.

She frowned.

I thought you loved me?

I put my hand on her shoulder and squeezed it gently.

I'll see you in the morning, I told her.

You can be a right cunt, she said.

I felt my anger rise at that statement. But I stayed cool.

We can do something nice then.

I pulled her face next to mine.

Give me a kiss.

Our lips touched.

Shall I see you tomorrow? she asked.

Of course you will, I said.

When we got out on Queens Road a taxi was passing. She put her hand out and it slowed and stopped. She ran up to it, calling over her shoulder.

I'll come round about twelve.

★

Nigel had a shower and went to his bedroom to get dressed. He tried on three T-shirts before going back to the one with The Ramones on it. A pair of faded jeans and his trainers and he was ready.

He ran down the stairs and popped back into the bathroom to squirt some deodorant under his arms. As he walked through the living room he had another quick glance in the mirror.

'Not so bad,' he said and winked. Then he turned off the light and stepped outside.

When he got to her flat he paused to get his breath and arrange his hair and his clothes. He rang the bell.

'Who is it?' she called.

'Nigel,' he said and the locks clicked and she opened the door. She looked fantastic.

'Hello,' she said. 'Come in.'

'Thanks for texting,' he said as he stepped over the threshold. 'Otherwise I'd have spent the evening slobbed in front of the telly.'

'I've got something for you,' she said as she led him into the kitchen. He thought of a present, a love token. She brought two bottles of beer from the fridge and opened them. She handed one to him. 'Well, cheers,' she said and had a swig.

'Cheers.'

'Come through,' she said, walking into the living room. He followed and they settled down on the couch.

'You must have been tired at work today,' she said. Then she grinned, 'Especially after me keeping you up last night.'

'Yeah,' he nodded, 'I was a bit.' He felt the condensation on the beer bottle as he picked at the label. He didn't know what to say next.

They looked at each other and beamed, then looked away.

'Is it good being a social worker?' she asked and her head tilted to one side. 'It must be really interesting.'

He rubbed his forehead as he thought about his job. 'It's pretty stressful,' he said and she nodded. 'There's too much work,' he counted on his fingers, 'not enough time and inadequate resources.'

'Sounds difficult.'

'Yeah, sometimes I have to make tough choices.'

'Like whether someone goes into a loony bin or not?' she asked with a smile.

'Yeah, that kind of thing,' he said.

'So why do it?' she asked and had a swig of beer. 'If it's so hard.'

'I find it really satisfying.'

'How so?'

'Some people have emotional and mental problems that make them unable to take care of themselves. My job is to help them learn the skills to cope with life.'

'It makes you sound like Robin Hood or something,' she said. Then she looked into his eyes. 'Does it make you feel good, helping people?'

'Yeah,' he said. He glanced round the room and pulled his hand through his hair. 'One morning I went to see a patient who hadn't been outside for weeks. I didn't enjoy visiting him because he was emotionally draining. Depressives can be like that. Spend an hour in their company and you can feel yourself sucked into the pit with them. Anyway, it was like he wasn't making any progress and all I was doing was allowing him to sit at home and smoke fags and eat too much.'

'Was he fat?'

'No.'

'So how was it bad helping him eat and smoke?'

'He was naturally self-obsessed and he didn't like himself, so the more time he had on his hands, the worse he got. Me doing all his shopping enabled him to sit at home and contemplate his existence.'

'I never thought about it like that,' she said, 'but it's

true enough. Sometimes when I'm stuck indoors all weekend, I get kind of down.'

'But anyway, that morning I went to see the guy and he smiled as soon as I arrived. "Will you come to the shop with me?" he asked, "I need to get some milk." I was dumbstruck. I didn't know what to say.'

'So did you do it?'

'Yeah, we took a walk up to the Co-op, and I stood by and watched him while he picked the milk off the shelf and paid for it. Then we went back to his and he made me a cup of tea.'

'Your eyes sparkle when you talk about it,' she said, sitting on the edge of the couch.

'It doesn't sound like much,' he said, 'but it was the start of the man's recovery.' Nigel took a swig of beer and looked at her. 'You'd know what I meant if you ever did the work yourself.'

'I wish I could,' she said, flicking her cigarette against the ashtray.

'You'd be good at it,' he said. 'You're intelligent, and you've got a gift for making people feel at ease.'

Her face screwed up into a massive frown. 'I'd like to,' she said. 'But they wouldn't take somebody like me.'

He turned to face her. 'That's just where you're wrong,' he said. 'Overcoming personal problems is seen as a qualification for social care.'

'So what are you overcoming?' she asked.

'Nothing really,' he said and scratched at his ear. 'I was just brought up to believe it was my duty to help those less fortunate than myself.'

'You sound like some sort of happy clapper,' she snorted.

He felt the start of a blush working its way up his neck. 'My mother made me realise I was privileged,' he said. 'That's all.' He concentrated on the smoke rising from his cigarette then he had a puff on it and crushed it into the ashtray.

She reached across and put her hand on his forearm. 'I'm sorry,' she said. 'I didn't mean to offend you or anything.'

He coughed and tried to look at her, but couldn't. 'That's OK,' he said to his knees.

There was a few seconds of silence that she interrupted. 'I like your top,' she said.

'I got it from Camden Lock.'

'One of my step-dads used to listen to The Ramones.'

'I've never really been into them.' he said. 'I just thought it was a cool T-shirt.'

'He saw them at Essex University. Always going on about it. "Forty minutes it lasted," he used to say, "but best gig I ever saw." Me and mum would look at each other and roll our eyes.'

Charlie gazed at the window with a half-formed smile on her lips. Then she sighed and clapped her hands together. 'I've finished my college application,' she said.

'Do you want me to check it over?' he asked.

'Yes please,' she said and went over to the windowsill and fetched it.

He quickly read through it. Her Personal Statement was interesting and he noticed she'd put him down for an employer and a reference.

'This is good,' he said. 'It should get you an interview.'

'Do you think?' she asked as she sat on the arm of the couch. 'I meant to post it this morning, but it's just as well now you're here to read it for me.'

'You should send it fairly soon because I phoned the admissions tutor at City College,' he said. He hesitated before going on. 'He's a friend of mine and I told him to expect your application. He asked a couple of questions about you.'

He became aware she was shaking her head. 'What's the matter?' he asked.

'I don't want them knowing about my history.'

'I didn't say anything about that,' he reassured her. 'I just told him you were clever and talented and he would do well to consider you.'

'What did he say?'

'That if you were as brilliant as I was making out, he couldn't see any problems with you being accepted onto the course.'

'You're setting me up as an intellectual,' she laughed before the smile fell from her mouth. 'I hope I can live up to it.'

'I'm sure you can,' he said.

'It's a big step,' she whispered.

'Of course it is, but we can get you prepared so that you hit the ground running.'

'How?' she frowned.

'For a start, you could aim to read a quality paper every day.'

'What,' she asked, 'like the Guardian or something?'

'Yeah.'

'That's what Gary does.'

'And try listening to Radio Four.'

'That too,' she said, looking at her nails. 'He's always quoting some statistic he heard on it.'

'I'll get some books in the next few weeks,' he said and touched her on the forearm. 'We'll give you a good head start.'

She slid onto the couch beside him. She kissed him on the cheek. 'You're fantastic, Nigel,' she said. Then she kissed him on the lips and pulled him against her.

'Do you want to watch a movie?' she whispered to him.

'What have you got?' he asked.

'Oh Brother, Where Art Thou.'

'That's a brilliant film,' he said. 'It's based on – '

She pushed away from him and looked into his eyes. 'The Odyssey,' she finished.

'You knew?' he said with a frown.

'Yeah,' she said as she sat upright. 'Someone bought me a copy once.'

'Have you read it?' he asked and she nodded and stood up.

'I certainly have,' she said and danced round the coffee table with her hands in the air and her hips swinging. She sang a musical accompaniment sounding like a twangy Hawaiian-style guitar.

'You need to watch me,' she said, wiggling her eyebrows and laughing, 'I'm a bit of a Siren.'

*

Ralph sat down. I pulled the parcel from my pocket and threw it at him. He peeled it open and smiled.

There's loads here.

Well I had an earner today.

He got up and went into the kitchen. He rummaged around in there for a while and appeared with a roll of foil and a happy look on his face.

Do you want some tea?

No thanks.

He had a smoke and we passed the gear between us for a while.

I looked round his dump of a flat.

Shall we go out? I said.

Where?

We could get Chris to take us for a run in his motor.

I can't be bothered with him.

Why not? He could be useful to us.

So?

I felt like getting up and giving him a clip on the head.

Just give him a phone.

I've not got any credit.

Stop being fucking awkward, I said and got mine out.

I passed it to him and he rang the number.

Chris, how you doing?

It's Ralph. What you up to?

Come over, me and Gaz have got a surprise for you.

He listened for a minute.

OK. See you in a bit.

He hung up.

He'll be right over.

Did he seem pleased to get asked?

He did actually.

I thought he might be.

I looked around.

Tidy this place up a bit before he gets here.

He frowned like I'd insulted him.

Why what's up with it? he asked.

It's a fucking shit-hole. Are you trying to frighten the guy off before we even get started?

He stood up and picked some of the cups off the floor. He took them into the kitchen. I heard bottles clunk together in a rustling bag. I heard the taps go on and the sound of dishes in the sink. He was in there for ten minutes before he put the bag outside the front door.

His cat walked out of the bedroom. It stretched and licked its lips. Its eyes flicked from the door to the kitchen to me. I put my hand to the floor and rubbed my fingers together. It came over and I stroked its neck.

Puss, puss, puss.

It rubbed its face into my hand.

Good girl.

Ralph walked into the living room and the cat disappeared back in the bedroom.

Go on, fuck off, he shouted, and flicked water in its direction.

He smiled at me.

Well done, that's the way to treat them, I said.

The door knocked. I looked at him.

Get it then.

Ralph answered it and brought in a twitchy Chris.

All right Gaz?

I stood up and put my hand out.

Good to see you, I said.

We shook and I pointed to the couch.

Sit down mate. Do you want a tea or something?

He nodded.

What do you take? asked Ralph.

Two sugars and milk.

Ralph looked at me.

What about you Gaz?

I'm all right for now. Give me a bit of hash.

He got it from under his sideboard and I skinned up a joint.

Do you want a blast?

Chris nodded so I passed it to him. He sucked it in like a professional.

You're a natural.

He smiled like an old hippy.

It's good, he said.

Ralph came through with the tea.

Listen to him Ralph. It's good he says. Tell him Chris.

His eyelids lifted and he smiled at Ralph.

It's good.

Ralph sat next to him and nudged him.

That's the boy, he said.

Ralph looked at me and frowned. I put my hand out for the foil.

Give me a smoke of gear.

I had a couple of lines and passed it back. Then Chris reached for it.

You stick with the hash, I said.

Chris looked gutted.

Just a little one, he said.

No. We're going out in a minute. You can have some later.

I sat and watched them drink their tea. Chris seemed to go into a bit of a trance. He was burbling on about some friend of his that had committed suicide.

I walked into the room and he was hanging there. Blue tongue sticking out of his mouth.

We'll need to watch, giving him so much, I said to Ralph.

Before we know it he'll be at the door every day wanting more, said Ralph.

Just hanging there, said Chris.

So what do you want to do? I asked Ralph.

We could go for a run into the country.

What, with him like that?

We could take him to Charlie's.

No we're not going round there tonight.

Ralph laughed.

Had a lover's tiff, have we?

Do you want a slap? I asked, pointing my finger in his face.

His tongue was blue, said Chris.

Ralph nudged him.

Shut up mate.

Then he looked at me.

What about a game of snooker?

That sounds about right.

I couldn't even speak to his mum, said Chris.

Ralph turned to him.

What was that mate?

I couldn't speak to his mum at the funeral.

Ralph looked at me with a cruel smile.

Why not?

I felt ashamed that I hadn't saved him.

Ralph shouted in his ear.

So why didn't you?

Chris blinked out of his nightmare.

What? What?

Leave the boy alone, I said to Ralph.

All right mate? I said to Chris.

I feel a bit sick, he said.

He stood up and gazed at something in the distance.

Just hanging there, he said.

Fuck sake, said Ralph.

Shut it, I said.

Chris was a bit pale in the face. He walked to the wall and stared at it for a minute. Then he lay down on the floor with his face tucked against the skirting board.

Me and Ralph had a couple of lines then Ralph got up and fetched his baseball bat from the bedroom. He put his finger to his lips when I looked at him. I shook my head at him. He bent down to Chris and pushed the bat between the cheeks of his arse. Chris jerked and whimpered.

Ralph laughed and leaned the bat against the mantelpiece as he sat down.

There was no need for that, I said.

Just hanging there, whimpered Chris.

Listen to the cunt, said Ralph.

We sat in silence for a minute.

Don't Ralph, I shouted and Chris twitched.

We laughed like drains. Every time I caught Ralph's eye, the two of us snorted so hard it was coming out of my nose.

I wiped my eyes.

Poor cunt, I said to Ralph. Get him a glass of water.

Ralph went into the kitchen. While he was in there I went over to Chris and shook him by the shoulder.

No, he said, trying to burrow himself into the wall.

Chris get up, I shouted and he stood.

Ralph appeared with a glass.

Have a drink mate, it'll make you feel better.

He came over to the couch and had a swig.

Give me that gear, I said to Ralph.

He passed me the foil.

Come here, I said to Chris.

He leaned over and I ran a couple of lines.

This will sort you out.

He sucked them in.

But not too much, I said. We don't want you getting sick at the snooker club.

I don't feel like playing snooker.

Come on. You'll be all right. Me and Ralph will look after you.

But I can't drive like this.

Give me the keys.

He handed them over.

We piled out of the flat with Chris between us. I opened the passenger door.

You better get in the back, Ralph said to Chris.
He fell in there and stretched out on the seat.
I'm feeling sick, he said a couple of times.

*

The credits rolled and she turned the television off. She stretched.
I'm shattered, she said. It's time I went to my bed.
Nigel lifted himself from the couch.
Yeah me too.
She looked at the clock.
Two nights in a row I've kept you up late.
He laughed.
You're a bad influence.
Would you like a cup of tea before you go?
Yes please, he said.
Charlie went into the kitchen and made it. While she was in there she had a smoke. She came back through and handed him a drink. Then she sat beside him. She had a taste of hers.
Lovely.
She put her cup on the table and turned to him.
You haven't even tried it on with me.
He spluttered his tea.
I wouldn't want to take advantage.
She kissed him on the cheek and brought her hand up to his neck. She kissed him closer and closer to his mouth, till their lips touched.
She felt it build inside him. His face pressed against

her. He breathed in her ear, and his hands reached round her shoulders and pulled her against him.

She let him, till his fingers reached under her shirt.

Then she pulled her face away.

Easy cowboy, she said.

She could see the rejection smart in his eyes.

I thought – he said.

We shouldn't go too fast, she said.

He didn't say anything, couldn't look at her. She grabbed his chin and pulled his face towards her.

I don't see you as a punter, she said. You make me feel special.

He smiled and snuggled into her neck. She looked at the ceiling and patted his back.

I should get some sleep, she said. I've got work tomorrow.

Why do you do it? he whispered.

She sat up and pushed him away.

Why does anybody work? I need the money.

Can you not get an ordinary job?

She lit up a cigarette.

What's it to you anyway?

He looked hurt.

I care about you.

You've only just met me.

He touched her wrist.

But there's something about you.

She blew smoke out.

What? My cunt?

He pointed at her heart.

No, here. You're a lovely person.

I'm not. I'm horrible.

Don't say that.

She crushed her fag into the ashtray.

But it's true. I'm dirty and horrible.

He tried to cuddle up to her.

You're beautiful.

She pulled away from him.

I'm a junky and a whore. What's lower than that?

Is that why you do it? For drugs?

She didn't speak. Just nodded.

But why? he said.

Because I need them.

No you don't. Nobody needs heroin.

She brushed the hair back from her face.

What would you know? When have you ever woken up with withdrawals ripping your stomach apart?

He looked away from her.

You haven't, have you? she asked.

I don't understand how anybody can let that happen.

Let it happen? My uncle fucked me when I was nine years old. Did I let that happen?

He didn't say anything.

When I told my mum she said I was a liar. I started misbehaving at school and they sent me to a home. By the time I was fourteen I was hooked on smack and working the streets. Did I let that happen?

He still didn't say anything.

And what were you doing? Getting kisses from your mum and going to university and laughing at girls like me and calling us whores and junkies.

I've never spoken about women like that.

Well you're unusual.
He edged closer to her.
I can help you.
She pulled away again.
How the fuck can you?
Get you into rehab.
I've been in six already and they haven't worked.
Maybe you weren't ready. Maybe this is your time.
She shook her head.
But the council said there was no more funding for me.
He puffed up his chest.
I could get that for you.
And what am I going to do in the meantime?
We could get you on a methadone programme or something.
He was close to her side now. He put his arms round her.
Let me help you.

*

Galileo surveyed his new territory of light, a circle centred on a wooden lamp with a frilly amber shade. He could see that the ground he stood on sloped upwards as it moved away from him. It was filled with holes that sprouted curving ladders and shadows of rungs and uprights, all pointing away from the radiance in the middle.

And then there was light, he said as he looked at the reaches and the blackness beyond.

Chastity smiled and held out the half-burnt candle.

You should keep this safe.

But we have the lamp.

She gestured towards the dark.

Light is at a premium here. You can never have enough.

But we're safe up here, aren't we?

Only when it is dark.

So why bother lighting everything?

Do you want to live in the dark?

He looked at the floor.

No.

She pulled some wood from behind herself.

I have presents.

He went closer.

What are they?

When he touched them he realised they were two folding chairs and a table. He popped them out and they sat down. Chastity took a packet of cards from the folds of her habit.

Shall we play?

Galileo was good at cards so he nodded.

Gin rummy.

Chastity dealt seven cards each and an extra one for herself. They were halfway through their game when Galileo heard a crash.

What the fuck was that?

Chastity didn't look up from her cards.

Ignore them. They are trying to scare you into putting out the light.

Galileo tried to focus on his hand but the thought of Gaston sneaking up behind him interrupted his concentration. He looked round when the hair on the back of his neck became cold and tickly.

I thought I felt a draught there.

Chastity smiled above her cards.

Forget about them, but be prepared when they come.

What shall I do then?

She put her cards down.

Gin.

Galileo tutted as he counted his score.

Thirty-two.

He swept up the cards.

My deal.

Make my hand a good one.

He dealt the cards. Chastity picked hers up and fanned them neatly.

Are you not curious?

About what?

The life at the edge of the light.

He stared at his cards.

Let's finish the game.

They played for the rest of the hand. Galileo counted his cards onto the table. He was going to win. He dropped the last one.

Gin, he said.

He felt another draught on the back of his neck. He looked behind. There was no one there.

He turned back to the game and Chastity was gone.

Where are you?

All that was left of her was the echo of her voice in his head.

The life at the edge of the light.

He looked at the dark outside his circle and imagined them sitting there. Watching him.

*

When we got to the snooker club we had to help Chris out of the car. He could just about manage to walk on his own, but staggered a bit as we climbed the stairs to the desk. I thought they might not let us in, but the woman just smiled.

He's had one over the eight.

Yeah. He won't be any trouble.

Just prop him up in a corner and make sure he isn't sick on my carpet.

OK love.

We dropped him at the table and Ralph went back for the balls and the cues. There were two lads playing a couple of rows over. One was wearing a tracksuit and a baseball cap. The other had a hoodie on. They were in their early twenties and had Reeboks on their feet. They seemed pretty good at snooker though and were getting reasonable breaks. Baseball Cap gestured his cue at Chris.

I'll have a pint of what he's had.

I laughed.

Yeah. He's put a few away tonight.

The two of them came over. The one in the hoodie bent to look closer at Chris.

He's proper fucked. Skunk was it?

I shook my head.

Just a bit of hash.

A couple of lines of whiz would sort him out.

Have you got any? I asked.

He laughed and picked at his nose with his thumb.

What do you think gives us the energy to play snooker all night?

Sell me a tenner's worth.

Hoodie walked towards the toilets.

Follow me.

We went in there and he got a bank bag out of his pocket. It was full of paper wraps.

Just the one? he asked.

That'll do.

We done the deal and I left him having a piss. When I got out I nodded to his pal. He winked and lined his cue over a couple of balls.

Ralph had finished arranging the table by the time I got back.

Where were you?

I pointed at Chris.

Just getting some speed for sleepy arse there.

Nice one. I'll have a bit of that.

Come on then. We better get him in there, I said.

I gave Chris a couple of slaps on the face and he woke up. We picked him up and he stumbled between us into the toilets. I passed the speed to Ralph and he set some up on the edge of the sink. Then he rolled a tenner up and had a line. I had one myself and we stood looking at each other rubbing our noses.

Not bad, I said.

Yeah it tastes pretty good.

Then we went into the cubicle and picked Chris back

up. We dragged him over to the sink and pushed the tenner up his nostril but he wouldn't sniff it up. I let go of Chris. His head banged on the tiles.

What the fuck are we going to do? I asked Ralph.

We stood over him laid on the floor. Ralph left the toilet and came back with a glass. He filled it with water from the tap and handed it to me.

He leaned over Chris and pulled his head back by the nose. He poured what was left of the sulphate into the open mouth.

That's too much, I said.

Ralph put his hand out.

Just give me the water.

I passed it to him and he poured some of that in too.

Chris looked like he was surfacing from a swimming pool. He swallowed the water and started coughing. We gave him a few slaps on the back.

He'll be all right in a minute, said Ralph.

We dragged him back into the cubicle and propped him up on the toilet. We made sure his head was jammed in the corner so he wouldn't choke himself. Then we got back to our game of snooker.

Ralph got a ball down and walked up and down the table like he was Jimmy White. He leaned over the edge and put his hand on the felt, with his middle finger flicking up and down. He lined the shot up and clicked the cue. But the black missed by loads.

Unlucky, I said.

I bent over and slid an easy red into a corner pocket. It left me with a straight blue into a middle pocket. Ralph tapped his cue on the floor.

Good shot, he said.

I popped the blue in and was leaning into another cushy red when Hoodie came over. He had a stupid smile on his face.

Is your mate all right?

I stood up from the table.

Yeah. He's just waiting to come up on the billy.

I think he's already there. He's doing exercises in the shit-house.

Ralph slammed his cue into the corner.

He's a fucking liability. I told you not to bother with him.

We went in there and Chris was doing press-ups on the floor. I bent down and tapped him on the back.

Get up.

He stood up blinking, with his eyes looking everywhere and chewing on his lips.

This is a good toilet, functional, yet with decorative aspects. The white of the cisterns contrasts with the blue of the ceiling. Do you see that? he asked.

What's up with this guy? asked Ralph.

We'll give him a smoke and that'll calm him down.

A couple of lines of heroin and he was fit to be seen in public. We walked back into the snooker hall. The two guys were racking up another frame. The one in the baseball cap flicked his cue at Chris.

All right is he?

He's sound.

We went to our table and Chris picked up a cue.

Whose go is it?

Ralph snatched it from him.

Fucking mine. Sit down.

I stepped in front of Ralph.

You're wrong. It's my go.

I leaned across the table at the red I should have got earlier. It went in and left me with a good shot on the pink. That went down too and I had a thirteen break. Two more balls and I was up to twenty. Hoodie and Baseball Cap came over from their table to watch as I sank another red.

Twenty-one, said Ralph. He seemed pleased for me. I lined up a black.

Go on Gaz, you can do it, said Chris.

Shut the fuck up, said Ralph.

I cracked the white and the balls connected and sent the black to the far corner pocket. It looked like it was going in. It went all the way into the jaws of the pocket, where it banged against the edge and stopped with a rattle.

Good break, said Hoodie on the way back to his table.

Cheers, I said and sat down.

Ralph went to take a shot. Chris leaned over the seat.

You're a good player, he said to me.

Thursday, 13th May 2004

The train jerked into movement and I watched the brick-work slide by. Then the city was exposed and we went past shops and factories and over the river. We picked up speed and before long we were flying through the countryside.

Charlie laughed and opened her magazine towards me.

Check this out.

I pulled the page to see a picture of a tiny dog with a pink jumper on and a hat with a tassel.

Brilliant, I said.

And listen to this. Chi-chi will only eat chicken breast steamed with rosemary, garlic and a pinch of salt. That's cute eh?

Very, I said and turned my eyes to the window. Half the world's starving and that dog gets gourmet food. She grabbed my hand.

Come on, lighten up.

I pointed at the photograph.

But look at it.

She put it on the table.

Babe, we both know the world's fucked up, but if you have it on your mind twenty-four-seven you end up totally depressed. Sometimes you need to relax and laugh at how ridiculous it is.

I opened my mouth to reply when the trolley appeared down the aisle.

Tea or coffee? asked the fat woman pushing it.

I'll have a Coke, said Charlie.

She asked if I wanted one but I didn't. She paid for hers and popped the ring-pull. It foamed over and ran down the side and left a little puddle on the table.

I'm such a slob, she said and had a swig. I gazed at her fingers as they curled round her drink. They were gorgeous slim things with just a hint of a tan. You wouldn't believe they had touched thousands of cocks. She had a silver ring on and clicked it against the can as she read her magazine. It was like she was tapping along to music people in the pictures were dancing to.

As she glanced through, she tutted every once in a while.

State of her the flash bitch, she said about someone I couldn't see.

I looked up and she was eyeing me through the vee at the top of the pages.

What is it you see in me? she asked.

The question took me by surprise.

Where did that come from? I asked.

She shrugged.

Just curious, she said.

It wasn't the sort of thing I could just answer, with a snap of my fingers. I had to think.

Well? she asked.

You're beautiful, I said.

She tutted.

Apart from that.

You're a caring sort of bird. You're a good laugh. And you don't judge a guy because he's made a few mistakes in his life.

Her eyes narrowed as she stared at me.

So it's not just the money? she asked.

No, is it fuck. I'd still go out with you if you had nothing. And anyway, you spend most of that cash on gear. It's not as if I see much of it.

Does it not bother you what I do for a living?

I haven't really thought about it.

She sucked her teeth.

Not even once? she asked.

Well maybe, I said. But you've got to do what you've got to do.

She reached across the table and gripped my wrist.

I'm sick of it babe, she said.

I thought she was going to start crying.

So don't do it, was all I could think of saying.

She looked at the table and dragged her fingers through the spillage of Coke.

But I need the money.

I watched the spiral she made.

Yeah. It's a hard one. What can I say?

Do you think I should go into a rehab?

The countryside flicked past like a short life.

Why not?

It's tough though, all that therapy.

Better than selling your arse.

*

Nigel looked across the kitchen table. 'You're quiet today,' he said, putting his mug down. Chris nodded but didn't reply.

'Are you not feeling very well?' asked Nigel.

'Just had a rough night,' said Chris and rubbed his forehead with the heel of his hand. 'I went out with Ralph.'

'Where did you go?'

'We played a bit of snooker.'

'Doesn't seem like such a bad night to me.'

'I feel rough today though,' he said. As he spoke, Nigel noticed sticky bits at the sides of his lips.

'Were you drinking?' he asked.

'No,' said Chris, looking around the room.

'Are you sure?' asked Nigel, trying not to frown. 'Because you shouldn't drink while you're taking medication. You could have an accident or something.'

'I wasn't drinking,' said Chris. 'I wasn't.'

'So what's the matter?' asked Nigel.

He softened his voice and reached across the table to touch his patient on the forearm. 'Come on mate, you can tell me.'

'I took some drugs,' said Chris through chewed lips.

'What kind?'

'I don't know, I was sleepy one minute and wide awake the next.'

'Where did you get them?'

'They gave me them.'

'Who's they?' asked Nigel as calmly as he could.

'Ralph and his mate Gary.'

'They gave you drugs?' said Nigel, leaning forward in his seat.

'You can't tell anyone.'

'I should phone the police.'

'But you can't.'

'Why not?'

'Because I asked you not to,' said Chris through tears. 'Please don't.'

'But if I think people are taking advantage of you,' said Nigel as he folded his arms across his chest.

Chris reached under his chair and pulled out a knife. 'If you phone the police,' he said as he poked it at his wrist, 'I'll kill myself and it'll be your fault.'

'OK,' said Nigel, moving his hands towards the floor. 'Calm down.'

Chris's face was red and tears streaked his cheeks. 'I know just where to cut,' he said and pushed the knife against the skin of his wrist.

'Take it easy,' said Nigel, slowly. 'I won't call the police.'

'Promise?' asked Chris. Nigel nodded and he put the knife on the table.

'Tell me,' said Nigel as he crossed his legs, 'about the drugs.'

'It started last week when Ralph phoned and asked if I could give them a lift to Yarmouth.'

'Why there?'

'That's where they bought the stuff,' said Chris with a shrug.

'Ralph and Gary?'

'Yeah,' said Chris with a nod of his head. 'And they had this nice woman with them.'

'Who was she?'

'I think she was Gary's girlfriend.'

★

The sun shone as Charlie walked to the pier. The wind brought the smell of salt and crabs and diesel, and teased her hair from her ears. She had her arm hooked in the elbow of her big man. She felt happy and free.

He pointed at a red-brick tower with windows all around.

Imagine living there.

Yeah. Waking up to that view every morning.

And all the people like ants, going in and out of the shops with ice creams and beach balls.

She studied his face, the skin slightly red with the sea air, and a glisten of tears at the edge of his eyes.

You're a bit of a poet, she said.

He frowned at her.

What are you trying to say?

I was making a compliment.

He looked at her for a moment before walking on.

Shall we get to the pier?

She spotted a cafe with steamed-up windows.

Can I buy you a tea, handsome? she asked.

Yeah OK.

A bell pinged as they went in the door. The woman behind the counter pointed to a table by the window.

Sit yourselves down and I'll be right over.

Before long they were tucking into a scone and a

cuppa each. Charlie looked at him and the piece of cream on the corner of his lip. She reached her finger out and wiped it from his face. Then she put the finger in her mouth and sucked it.

Mmm. You're tasty, she said in a saucy voice.

He laughed and looked round at the other customers.

Fucking tart.

She reached across the table and wrapped her fingers round his wrist.

Don't call me that.

He showed her his eyes, brown as the earth.

I'm only teasing, he said, tender as a big brother.

She took her hand from his arm and had a sip of tea.

It's nice out here eh?

Yeah. Prettier than the city, he said.

Do you think you could live here?

He rubbed an arc of steam from the window and looked out.

It would get boring after a week or two.

Yeah probably.

He hunched closer to her.

I mean look at these cunts, he whispered.

She turned her head to the side. The woman next to them had a set of earrings cutting into her large lobes. She had thick powder on her nose and bright pink lipstick. She smiled and showed them the pastry stuck to her teeth.

Charlie smiled at the old lady and turned back to Gaz.

It comes to us all, she said.

Doubt it. People like us die young, he said through a curled lip.

And beautiful?

He nodded and lifted his eyebrows.

Well I think so.

You're funny.

All part of the package, he said.

*

'Hello,' said Wendy.

'What?' Nigel snapped as he sat at his desk and pulled his folder out.

'No need to talk to me like that,' she said.

'Sorry,' he said. 'I'm not having a very good day.'

'Do you want to go outside for a fag?'

'No thanks.'

'Well, I'm going to have one,' she said as she got up from her chair. 'I'll see you later.'

'Bye,' he said as he flicked through his paperwork.

He started to do his timesheets but couldn't focus. He added the numbers up wrong. He scribbled over the bad figures and re-started. But it still wasn't right. He threw the pencil onto the desk and sat up straight. He took a deep breath and pulled his fingers through his hair.

He went to the filing cabinets and pulled open the H–K drawer. It came out smoothly and he fingered over files: Jackson David, Jeffries Phillip, Jobson Malcolm and Johnson Fred.

'There you are,' he said and pulled out Johnson Gary.

He walked back to his desk with the heavy file under

his arm. Then he settled in his chair and read it with more concentration that he ever had before.

*

Galileo descended the ladders till he came to a tunnel. It was a long one, painted green. There was a conduit cable along the top connected to electrical light fittings. Fluorescent tubes flickered and buzzed. The sound of elevator music filled the emptiness. He took a deep breath and started to walk.

He came to a door in the wall. It had his name written on it. He tried the handle but it wouldn't open. He kept walking, when somebody called behind him.

Galileo.

He turned and two men in nurses' uniforms approached.

Yes? he said.

The largest put out his hand.

Give me the candle.

Galileo realised who they were and tried to run. But they were too quick for him and he was forced to the floor with his arms squeezed painfully up his back.

He struggled.

Let me go, he shouted.

Betts banged Galileo's head against the floor.

Where did you get the candle?

Galileo tried to spit but his face was scraped onto the ground. He fought to get them off but they were too strong. He knew it was useless when he felt cold metal on his wrists, then the click of handcuffs.

They picked him up by his pinioned arms and dragged him down the corridor.

The front of his feet scraped along the concrete floor. He screamed and he was punched on the back of the head. Another nurse joined the tormentors. He kicked Galileo as he followed.

They brought him into a carpeted room. One of the nurses grabbed his head and lifted it so he could see a desk and a man sitting behind it. He had white hair and wore glasses. He looked at Galileo.

What have you done now?

He had a candle, said one of the nurses.

The old man frowned and turned to Galileo.

Is this true?

Galileo brought up a mouthful of bloody snot and tried to spit it on the doctor. But it didn't even reach the desk. A nurse punched him on the ear.

You dirty fucking –

The doctor held up his hand.

Enough. We'll have no more of that.

He spoke gently to Galileo.

Where did you get the candle?

Galileo shook his head.

I didn't have a candle.

You're fucking lying, said Betts.

The doctor silenced the nurse with a shake of his head. He scratched the side of his head with his finger as he looked at Galileo.

What am I going to do with you?

Then he turned to Gaston.

Give him twenty milligrams of Haldeen and put him in Room K.

They dragged him out to the corridor. The nurses laughed as soon as they were out of earshot of the doctor.

Plenty good enough for you.

Galileo lifted his head as they stopped by the dispensary. The pharmacist was on the telephone.

Yes doctor.

He nodded and put the receiver down. He winked at Galileo and unlocked a white cabinet. He picked a package up by its corner and dangled it in front of Gaston. It was a paper-and-polythene wrapped syringe.

Careful with this. They use it to euthanise animals.

Gaston snatched it and tore it open with his teeth.

This fucker is an animal.

He straddled Galileo and shot the drugs into his left buttock. Galileo screamed.

I'll get you for this you cunt.

Gaston patted his bum.

Yeah, yeah, yeah.

They picked him back up by his arms and dragged him to Room K. Gaston unlocked the door and they pushed him inside. They sat on top of him and undid the manacles. Then Betts called.

One, two, three, go.

And as one they jumped up, left the cell and slammed the door behind them.

Galileo tried to shout as they left but nothing came out except dribble. He rested his cheek against the floor and watched the spy hole spin round like water going down a drain.

Some time later, he was woken with kicks and torchlight in his eyes.

Come on you lazy bastard. Time for your swill.
He didn't respond. Just sat up and grabbed the bowl of mush. He was so hungry.

Day after day the same procedure. He was roused with kicks and a light slashing through the dust before stabbing his eyes. His body got used to the treatment though and he started to wake before they entered. But he was still too tired from the drugs to do anything but grunt with the blows, and plan for the future when he was stronger.

One morning he came round long before they appeared. He stretched and loosened up his body. When he heard the rubber shoes squeak down the corridor he lay back down and pretended to sleep. The keys grated into the lock and the door opened.

Before Betts could swing his boot, Galileo jumped up and gave him a hard punch on the balls. Betts crumpled and Galileo grabbed the breakfast bowl. He slammed it into Gaston's face and kept banging until he dropped to the floor, hands cradling his crushed nose. Galileo picked the torch up and pushed it into his waistband. He closed the door and locked both nurses in the room.

Two lefts and a right, he said to himself as he walked into the corridor. He walked fast, like a nurse on an emergency call. He heard the slamming of a door in the distance and thought it might be the trapped nurses. But in here no one pays any attention to banging or screaming. Might as well fire a gun in Belfast, or let an atomic bomb off in the South Pacific.

Galileo soon recognised where he was and ran faster. As he moved the lights flickered in the tunnel and went out. He turned on the torch and kept running. Behind him he could hear a door being opened. Someone shouted.

Galileo's escaped.

A siren sounded and he heard dogs yelping.

Get him, someone called.

The dogs barked louder as they were released. They sounded like Dobermanns. Galileo pushed his legs harder as he rounded a corner and heard their nails scrabble on concrete. A cold shiver ran up his neck and an image of hounds getting a fox flashed in his head. They panted behind him and snarled at each other in their race to get him.

The end of the tunnel was in sight. Galileo bent forward and sprinted. He reached the ladder and jumped and caught hold of a rung just as the dogs hit the bottom of the wall.

He climbed a few steps till he was safe. Then he stopped and looked down and into the mouths of the animals. Teeth and tongues and saliva, hungry for meat.

He tucked the torch back into his waistband and wiped the sweat from his brow. He started the long climb, his footsteps clanging in the dark.

When he got to the top, he pulled himself into the stillness of the lamp and the card table and the empty seats. He felt for the torch and pointed it at the floor before turning it on. He raised the beam till it pierced the darkness at the edge of the light. He swept it round slowly, afraid of what he might see.

But there was nothing except more sets of ladders protruding from holes in the floor. Every set looked exactly the same as the one he just climbed. Looping out of the hole and bolted to the floor.

As far as the torch could arc there were these evenly spaced holes with ladders descending into them. He pointed the torch upwards but there was nothing there. Well nothing except an enfolding darkness.

Chastity was right. To make sense of this place he'd need more light.

*

Nigel sat by his desk and picked up the phone. He punched the number in and heard it ring at the other side.

'Probation,' it answered.

'Margaret, it's Nigel.'

'Hello, what can I do for you?'

'It's about Gary Johnson.'

'What's he done now?' she asked with a groan.

'He's getting out of hand.'

'In what way?'

'I had an appointment with another patient today who told me that Gary,' Nigel said and coughed and cleared his throat, 'supplied him with Class A drugs and drove his mobility car whilst being under the influence.'

'And how do we know this other patient is telling the truth?'

'I've never had any reason to doubt him in the past.'

'OK, Nigel, what do you want to do about it?'

'I'm phoning you for some suggestions.'

'Do you think we need to look at his fitness for living in the community?'

'That would be something to consider.'

There was a silence before she spoke. 'In that case we should arrange a meeting of his care team,' she said. 'I'll leave you to get in touch with Doctor Frederick.'

Nigel put the phone back on its cradle. He looked at the ceiling. He felt a bead of sweat loosen itself from his hairline. He reached for the box of tissues on the table and wiped his forehead. He crumpled the paper and threw it in the bin. He arranged some pencils on his desk.

He stood up and grabbed Gary's file. He marched to the filing cabinets, dropped the folder in its place and slammed the drawer shut.

*

Me and Charlie sat in deckchairs. She had her jeans rolled halfway up her leg. Her toes dug into the sand as she spoke to me.

So are you going for a swim or not?

I lifted my head from a beach ball I was blowing up.

I might do. Are you?

I've not got a costume with me.

I shook my head.

Well that wasn't very clever.

Have you got yours?

I pulled a pair of shorts out of my jacket pocket.

Of course I have.

What about a towel?

You don't need one in this weather. The sun gets you dry.

You'll end up with pneumonia.

I flicked some sand at her.

Shut up.

She stood up and brushed it off.

I'm off to the toilet, she said.

Yeah OK. See you in a minute.

She grabbed her handbag and threw it over her shoulder. She walked off up the beach, bum swinging as she went. She'd walked about twenty feet when she turned round.

Do you want a drink? she asked.

*

Charlie got the gear out of her handbag and had a smoke. She glanced about the cubicle. Leanne is a slag, George has a tiny prick, and Kylie were written on the walls and door. She looked down at her feet on the wet floor.

I have to stop this, she whispered.

She took a bit of toilet paper and gave her nose a blow. She dropped the paper in the pan with the scrunched up tin foil and flushed it all away. Then she went back out into the sun. She bought two cans of orange and flip-flopped to the beach.

Gaz sat up straight as she approached. He reached his hand out. She passed him a tin.

Thanks baby, he said.

She sat down next to him and opened hers.

Any time.

They drank and he burped. It was loud and seemed to echo.

Spoken like a true gentleman, she said.

I like to think so.

She burped on the back of her hand.

Done like a lady, he said.

They swallowed the rest of their drinks. Then she stood up. She stuck her hand out for his can. He passed her it.

Cheers doll, he said.

She took the empties to the bin at the side of the promenade and dropped them in. When she walked back Gaz had his tobacco on his lap.

Do you want a fag? he asked.

She nodded and he rolled one and lit it. She thought he was going to pass her the packet, but he passed her the one he'd already made.

Thank you kind sir, she said.

My pleasure, he said as he rolled himself one.

She had a long drag and blew the smoke into the sea breeze.

It's beautiful here.

He looked up and down the beach.

Sure is.

I wish I could do things like this more often.

Why don't you?

It's the gear. If I'm not out of it, I'm running about trying to get money together.

You should pack it in then.

Yeah, I know.

They leaned against the groyne and didn't speak for a few minutes. The sea hissed as waves crashed against the beach. Two seagulls had a noisy fight over a chip. A naked toddler jumped and screamed to the music from a radio.

I've got this punter yeah? said Charlie.

Gaz screwed up his face and looked at her.

And?

Well he's a social worker.

Oh yeah?

She nodded.

He said he'd help me get funding so I can get into treatment.

Go for it then.

Do you think I should?

Fucking right I do. Get in there girl.

She put her hands on the ground and pushed herself upright. She kicked the ball along the sand.

Are we going to play with this? Or did you get it for an ornament?

He stood up and ran after it.

Come on then.

He knocked it towards her. She caught it and passed it back. He threw it towards the sea.

They splashed in and out of the shallow water, throwing the ball around and laughing. He kicked it and it went high into the air. She ran out of the water and caught it and looked towards him. He was running for her, smiling with his hands out. He caught her by the waist and they both rolled to the floor.

They lay there, out of breath. She reached up and brushed sand from his cheek. She looked into his eyes. He leaned forward and their lips touched.

*

'Nigel, I've got your wife on the line.'

'Put her on,' he said and the phone clicked.

'Have you forgotten about me?'

'No, what are you talking about?'

'I'm at the train station,' said Sarah. 'You're supposed to be picking me up.'

'Shit,' he said with a glance at his watch. 'I'll be there in five minutes.'

He put the phone down and picked up his coat. Wendy looked up from her work. 'You're in trouble,' she said and smiled like a devil.

Nigel couldn't think of anything to say back. He was too busy pushing things into his bag on his way out of the office. He ran down the stairs and into his car.

When he got to the station she was standing outside with her bag at her feet. She waggled her finger at him as he pulled up beside her. She picked up her bag and approached the car. He leaned across the seat and opened the door. She passed her bag in and he put it on the back seat. She climbed in.

'Sorry love,' he said and kissed her on the cheek. 'I was engrossed at work, I forgot all about you.'

'It's good to know where I stand.'

'Did you have a nice time?'

'Yeah, it was OK,' she said. 'Kind of tiring though.'

'Oh,' he said as he drove towards the traffic lights at the exit of the station, 'why was that?'

'All that fell-walking and a hard bunk,' she said. 'My bum's killing me. I can't wait to sleep in my own bed.'

'We'll soon have you home, love.'

It didn't take long to get there.

'I need the toilet,' she said as she got out of the car. 'Can you get my bag?'

He entered the house like a burglar. As he stepped into the living room he scanned it for evidence of Charlie's presence. He went into the kitchen looking for clues, trying to see his crime through the eyes of the detective. He didn't notice anything out of the ordinary.

Relieved, he went back into the front room just as he heard the toilet flush. Sarah came out and pushed her way into his arms.

'Hello,' she said as she rested her head against his chest. He reached for her hair and drew his fingers through it.

'It's so good to be home,' she said. 'I don't like roughing it.'

'Yeah, me neither.'

'Did you miss me?' she asked, tilting her face towards him.

'Yeah.'

'You don't sound too sure.'

'Of course I missed you,' he said as he looked into her eyes.

He held her at the end of his arms. 'You must feel all grimy after the trip. Why don't you get in the shower and I'll put your clothes in the wash.'

'I'll just have a sit down first,' she said, going into the living room.

'What about a cup of tea?' he asked as he walked into the kitchen.

'Yes please,' she called. 'Where's my bag?'

'There it is,' he said and pointed to the side of the couch.

The kettle clicked as it turned off so he went back into the kitchen to pour the tea. When he brought them through, she was sitting with her bag half open and there were clothes strewn around it.

'I got you something,' she said with a sparkle. He put the tea on the coffee table. She patted the cushion beside her. 'Shut your eyes and put your hands out.'

He looked and it was a small pink piece of card. Shaped like a love heart, with a picture of two people kissing and written across the bottom was, Forever yours.

'It's a bookmark,' she said. He continued to gaze at it.

'Don't you like it?' she asked.

'Yeah, it's just – ' he stalled and pulled her close. 'I don't deserve you.'

'Yes, you do,' she said with a kiss. 'We love each other, don't we?'

*

I went to the kiosk to get us a cone each. When I returned she was sitting on the sand with a smile on her face.

What are you laughing at? I asked.

Nothing.

Her tongue snaked out of her mouth and dragged along the ice cream.

Lovely, she said.

So when can this social worker get you into a treatment centre?

She shrugged.

I don't know.

Are you sure he isn't full of shit?

Her lips tightened.

No chance.

Oh yeah, why's that?

She bit her bottom lip.

I think I might have something on him.

What?

She tapped the side of her nose.

Aha.

I ignored her and rubbed my hands across my jeans. Then I leaned down and unfolded the turn-ups I'd made to go in the water.

What's your social worker's name? she said as she scooped up some sand and let it flow between her fingers. I slapped her on the arm and laughed.

You are kidding me.

No.

I looked at the cunning in her eyes. I couldn't help smiling at the cheek of her.

You sly fucking bitch.

*

Nigel sat on the couch with a can of beer on the arm and the remote control on his leg. He flicked through the channels. Nothing came on that he found interesting enough to watch. He heard the stairs and looked over. Sarah came down with a towel wrapped round her chest and a bottle of shampoo in her hand.

'I'm just going for a shower.'

'Yeah OK,' he said, turning back to the screen.

'Are you all right?'

'Fine.'

He didn't take his eye from the telly and heard the bathroom door close and the lock click. The boiler rattled into life when the shower was turned on. He heard the toilet seat being banged down.

A programme about motorcycles came on Discovery. It was interesting. Two middle-aged Americans were making a chopper from an old Triumph.

We have three weeks before Daytona and the bike is only half done. Will Fred and Ted manage to roar through the opening ceremony with a British flag fluttering on the handlebars?

Nigel had a mouthful of beer and watched the silver-haired hippies wield spanners and talk mechanics.

The toilet door opened. He heard her bare feet on the kitchen floor and the creak of the stairs. Then he heard her above, the squeak of the wardrobe door, drawers from the chest, and the bedsprings as she sat down.

*

The sun was on the wane and it felt cold by the sea, so they walked into the town. He put his hand on her shoulder and she pushed into his side.

Shall we walk through the lanes? she asked.

He nodded and they changed direction. They stopped outside a shop selling tourist tat. He reached up for another beach ball and rubbed the plastic between his fingers.

Cheap shit.

She gestured with her palm upwards.

You're obsessed with balls.

Spheres actually.

Why?

He looked left and right then coughed.

I'm going to make a model of the human psyche.

What? she asked.

He told her again and tapped the side of his head.

But why? she asked.

The shrinks and that yeah?

She nodded and he went on.

They've got it all wrong, he said.

She frowned at him.

And how's that?

It's obvious. They've been trying to fix people all these years and they can't manage it.

So?

It's because they're starting from a faulty model. Mine is more like the real thing.

How do you know?

He tapped his nose this time.

When I've been in and out of puzzle factories, I've talked to no end of nutters. They've told me things they wouldn't dream of telling shrinks or nurses. And I've came to realise that our heads are a mess of the mixed up bits of our lives, and at the centre of us all, yeah?

She nodded.

He thumped the top of his head with his knuckles. It made a hollow sound.

There is a big empty space, he said.

He stared at her and the clunk echoed round her head.

What, you mean like a vacuum or something? she asked.

He thumped his head again and it made the same sound.

Exactly what I'm on about, he said.

So what's it there for? she asked.

His eyes fell to the floor.

To be honest, I'm not exactly sure.

Then he looked at her.

All I know is that it gives me an idea of everything that's possible.

His eyes narrowed.

Do you know when sometimes, for a split second, you think you know the answer to life? Then it all crashes down and you realise you don't? he asked.

Charlie nodded.

I think so, she said.

His hands mimed holding a sphere.

Well that's the moment your thoughts are echoed and amplified around the emptiness.

She didn't know what to say.
He shrugged.

Trouble with most people is they can't handle it, so they avoid facing up to it by trying to fill it up. It's like they're treating their most valuable possession as a fucking rubbish dump.

He pointed to a fat man waddling down the street.

I mean, look at that cunt, he's trying to fill it with doughnuts.

But maybe he gets hungry, she said.

Gaz screwed his face up with contempt.

Nah, he said. The hole inside is making him feel that. Hunger's just how it seems on the surface.

How do you know? she asked.

He tapped the side of his head again.

I just do right?

She laughed.

You're funny.

His forehead creased even more and he gripped the fringe of his hair.

But it isn't funny. It's fucking tragic.

She squeezed his hand and spoke gently.

I know it is.

He looked at her with a frown.

Some people fill it with drugs.

She turned to face him.

Yeah and some people fill it with TV programmes about Hitler.

The aroma of fried food drifted amongst them and broke the spell. He tugged at her hand.

I'm hungry, he said.

Don't you mean you feel empty? she asked.
She tapped him on the side of the head and laughed.

You want to fill up that big hole that lives inside you, she said.
He lifted his hand to her, but smiled.

That's it, fucking mock me.
She decided to let him off the hook.

Where's the chippy? she asked.
He pulled her towards the smell.

Just follow your nose, he said.

They walked for a while until they came to a huge window with Tony's written across it. Up three steps they climbed and they were swimming in fluorescent light. A Chinese woman stood behind the counter.

What you want?

Two bags of chips.
The woman shovelled them into paper cones. She passed them over and Gaz held them while Charlie paid.

I'll get the next ones, he said as they walked out of the shop and into the evening.

*

Nigel swigged from his can and watched the re-built Triumph wow the crowds at Daytona. A busty girl in a lime-green bikini gave old Fred a kiss on the cheek. He turned to the camera and winked. He climbed back on the Triumph and kicked it into life. The girl climbed on the pillion.

'See you next week,' said Fred.

He let the clutch out and the Triumph roared down the boulevard. The girl looked back and waved and the credits rolled.

Sarah brought his food. He put the plate on his knees and waited for her to sit. They ate while adverts flashed half-price leather sofas and the latest high-speed computers in front of them.

'What did you do while I was away?'

'Work, sleep, eat.'

'Did you miss me?'

'Yeah,' he said as he forked food into his mouth.

'I missed you too.'

'What's for pudding?'

'Ice cream.'

'Nice.'

*

It was a tight squeeze in the pub. Charlie could see a couple of the boys eye her up but they looked to the floor when they thought Gaz might see them. She moved closer to him and grabbed his elbow as they got to the bar.

What can I get you? asked the barman.

Gaz gestured to an old lady.

I think she's next.

The old lady turned to him.

God bless you son, she said.

Then she nodded at the barman.

A port and lemon please.

I'll get that, said Gaz.

The old lady faced him.

Oh thank you, thank you.

No problem, he said and turned back to the bar.

A pint of Stella.

He looked at Charlie.

And what do you want babe?

The same.

The barman poured the drinks and they took them to a seat in the corner.

That was really nice, said Charlie.

You've got to take care of the old.

She gazed into his eyes.

I think I love you Gaz.

*

An advertisement for a cheap-rate consolidation loan finished. The ITV symbol twisted round the television screen. The baritone voice of the announcer said 'It looks like Carver's got himself some trouble in this week's episode of The Bill.'

The theme tune started and Nigel groaned. 'I'm not watching this shit,' he said and clicked the remote until a man with long hair painted the hallway of a house.

'Oh come on,' said Sarah as she tried to grab the control. 'Let me see it.'

'No,' he said, gripping it harder. 'It's rubbish. You know I can't stand police shows.'

'But I've been away for a few days. Give me a break.'

'No, you give me a break.'

'What's up with you?'

'Nothing. I just don't want to be subjected to that shit.'

'But I watch it every week.'

'No, you don't,' he said and crossed his arms.

'You've been really strange since I got back,' she said. 'What the hell is wrong?'

'Oh, fuck off,' he said, standing up.

'Don't talk to me like that.'

'I'm going for a pint,' he said as he lifted his coat from its hook. 'Don't bother waiting up.' He slammed the door. He pulled his mobile out of his pocket as he walked down the street.

★

It was dark by the time we got back to Charlie's. We sat on the couch and had a can of lager and a couple of smokes of smack. I leaned my feet on the coffee table and lay back. Charlie brushed her hand under my shirt and rubbed my belly.

Gaz? she said.

Yes babe.

Can I ask you something?

Go ahead.

Why are you mental?

I rubbed my temples and tried to concentrate.

It's a long story.

She leaned back on the arm of the couch.

We've got all night, she said.

I pointed to my head.

Remember what I was saying earlier about the hole?

She nodded and I went on.

Well society uses that by selling us stuff to fill it up.

She frowned.

So?

I prodded my thumb at the ceiling.

They're using our human weaknesses to line their own pockets. Instead of trying to bung us up with junk, they should be helping people see that the only way to feel full is to admit the emptiness inside us.

I banged my heart with my fist.

We'd all make better choices if we weren't caught up in the need to fill it.

She looked at me and her forehead was screwed up in concentration.

But how would we?

I stretched my hands out to describe it.

If we thought about it as a space to sit and think, somewhere we can take time to look at our lives. That would be a start.

She shrugged her shoulders.

But what if you can't find it?

Everybody can.

She snorted and shook her head.

Tell that to the woman with three kids and no money, she said. Where's the space in her life to sit down and think?

I rested in the corner of the couch.

Any time she gets a free minute she probably smokes

a fag or has a drink. If she didn't do that she could try and consider her options.

What, like walk out on them? What would that make her?

I put my arms out.

Free, I said.

But she wouldn't be. They'd still be in her head, crying for milk.

I had a swig of my beer and smacked my lips.

Decisions are what we have to live by, I said.

So she should take responsibility for her choices?

Fucking right she should.

What, like slave away to provide food for kids she's already made a choice to have?

I nodded like a wise statesman.

Yup.

So the only choice she's really got is whether to have a fried egg or a sausage with her chips?

I struggled till I was upright.

OK Charlie, it's not as simple as I'm making out.

Nothing is, love, she said.

I watched the reflection of the living room in the window.

The point I'm trying to make is, when I told a doctor about the hole, they locked me up and pumped me full of drugs.

I stopped for another swig of my beer.

And the ones they give you make you want to sit about all day eating and watching telly. Exactly the things I'm trying to fight against. They're fucking with my basic human right to self-determination.

Friday, 14th May 2004

Nigel lifted his head off the pillow and looked at Sarah. She scowled at him and turned her face to the other side of the bed. He lay back down with his hand on his forehead.

'I feel rough,' he said as he got up. He stretched his arms. 'Was I drunk when I came home?' he asked.

'Can't you remember?'

'No.'

'I think that answers your question.'

'Do you want some breakfast?' he asked.

'I'll get my own.'

He went down to the kitchen. After some food he felt a bit better. He climbed back up the stairs to get dressed.

'Are you angry with me?' he asked her back.

'What do you think?'

'Listen love, I'm sorry,' he said and sat on the bed. He put his hand on her hip. 'I've had a lot of pressure at work and I'm taking it out on you.'

'I won't be spoken to like that.'

He rubbed his hand into the groove of her waist. 'I know, I was out of order,' he said. 'Can you forgive me?'

he asked and she reached behind and pushed his hand away.

'Just go, Nigel.'

'OK,' he said as he pulled his jumper over his head. 'I'll see you tonight,' he said, but she didn't answer.

On the drive to work he thought about his behaviour. He felt terrible about swearing at Sarah. He couldn't act like that in future. When he got home tonight he should cook for her and maybe get a video in. If he didn't start to hold himself together he was going to lose everything.

His phone buzzed and he pulled it out of his pocket. He tried to see the screen and negotiate the traffic at the same time. It was Charlie. He pressed the green button.

'Hello,' he said as he steered the car to the left. He looked in the mirror and indicated.

'Nigel,' said Charlie. 'What are you up to?' she asked as he managed to glide the car into a side street. He bumped up the pavement and turned the engine off.

'I'm now on my way to the office,' he said. 'What about you?'

'I'm just sitting at home.'

'I tried to call you yesterday,' he said, 'but you didn't answer.'

'I know, my battery was flat. I only just got the message.'

'I was worried about you,' he said as he watched a policeman talk to an old lady. The pensioner pointed up the street and the officer spoke into his radio.

'So what are you doing this afternoon?' asked Charlie.

‘I don’t know,’ he said as he reached over for his bag. He picked out his diary and opened it. ‘I’ve got a couple of appointments.’

‘That’s a shame because I was going to ask you round.’

‘I could cancel them.’

‘Come round about two o’clock,’ she said.

He started his car and turned the hazards off. As he manoeuvred back into the road he thought about Charlie. If he got her off the drugs soon, she’d be in a great position for starting college. Without the urge to score and find money he was sure she would do well. She was obviously intelligent, all she needed was to focus her mind on something productive and she could be a success.

As he mingled with the traffic he glanced at the dashboard clock. He needed to hurry if he was going to get to work and arrange things for the care meeting about Gary Johnson.

*

When I got back from Charlie’s I knew it was time to start on the model. I got a bag of wallpaper paste from under the sink and poured it into the basin. A potato masher was the ideal tool for mixing it up, and I found it in the cutlery drawer. I beat the mixture with wank strokes, up and down, up and down. With the same ache in my forearm and knowing I had to keep going till the paste was ready.

I lifted the basin through to the living room and put

it on the floor in front of the couch. Then I hunted round for newspapers. I found two under the bed and a free advertiser in the space between the chair and the wall. I tore them into strips and sat them next to the paste.

I went into the bedroom and got the paper lantern from the cupboard. As I walked back through I peeled the plastic off. I fluffed the light up as I sat on the couch. I squeezed the wire insert into it until it stretched round the frame and became a giant sphere. Then I placed it on the floor, between my ankles.

I dipped a strip of paper into the paste and stuck it on. Then another. One at a time I worked, slowly covering the globe. It was getting on the carpet and maybe I should have put something down to protect it.

But I didn't care because I knew it would soon be over. They were closing in on me. Dogs and death drew ever nearer.

It was important I left a record of my vision of the human mind. It would be something that would let the world know my life wasn't a complete waste.

Sometime in the future they would roll my model out in Cambridge University lectures. They would hail it as a new dawn in the history of psychology. Students all round the world would know of my existence. From me would radiate original knowledge, a giant leap forward, a platform to support advanced theories of consciousness and its interactions with life.

They would mention my name in the same breath as Darwin, Marx and Freud. My ideas would become the centre of new schools, new faculties, new departments, a shelf in the library and television programmes on Channel Four.

Gary Johnson lived in Norwich and reached his hypothesis in the first years of the new century. After a traumatic childhood, made worse by society's indifference to his plight and its insistence that he be medicated for all of his adult life, Johnson refused its poisons in the first years of the new millennium and within two weeks had constructed the model that changed the way we look at the psyche. One can only wonder at what he might have discovered if society had let him realise his full potential and he'd been given the privileges of the other members of his class when he was a little boy and his daddy was hitting him and drinking all the fucking money.

I felt my heart beat fast and a pulse in my throat.

Calm down, Galileo said in a whisper.

I breathed slow and easy and dipped a piece of newspaper into the paste. I smoothed it over the lantern with my palm.

The model grew before my eyes. A damp sphere of sticky paper. It was almost ready to progress to stage two. First it would have to set.

In case it stuck to the floor, I unfolded a sheet of newspaper and set the ball on top of it.

I stood up and caught my reflection in the mirror. I looked like an old photo of an artist. Paste on my hands and my face and all over my T-shirt.

I needed to go to Homebase. It was a bus journey away, or a trip in a car. Either way I couldn't go out looking like I was crazy. It would draw too much attention and they would have the excuse to lock me away. They would send me to Roehampton and a few years banging my head against a rubber wall.

I went into the bathroom for a wash and a shave. As I looked into my eyes they swam around and flicked and then looked back at me. It was as if they weren't mine. That they belonged to another me that lived somewhere behind the glass, a bad me that wanted to kill the people who fucked me about.

They're up to something, said Galileo.

Who?

He was angry now and he spat back.

Them.

I was confused.

Who are you talking about?

Betts and Gaston.

I tried not to look him in the eye.

Oh.

Yes, he said. They're planning it right now. While you waste time putting scented soap on your skin, they're thinking up strategies to get us.

★

Nigel went into the meeting room about ten minutes before the others were due to arrive. He turned on the kettle. Then he arranged some chairs round the table. He opened the stationery cupboard and dug out a couple of markers for the white-board.

Margaret was the first to arrive. 'Hello?' she said as

she put her head round the door. She put her hand out as she approached.

'How are you?' said Nigel, feeling the dampness of her palm.

'Busy,' she said with a frown. 'As usual.' She scratched her head and touched the back of a chair. 'Am I here?'

'Sit where you like.'

She pulled the chair out then changed her mind. 'So what have you been doing with yourself?' she asked as she sat on the one next to it.

'The Gary thing has been keeping me fairly busy,' said Nigel. He wiped the board clean and arranged some markers in the tray. 'You?'

'I'm trying to get that new women's project off the ground.'

'Oh yeah,' he said. 'How's that doing?'

'We've got some funding,' she said, 'from the Europeans.'

'That's a start,' he said.

'It's just planning permission now,' she said. 'Some of the neighbours are making waves, so we'll need to do a bit of PR.'

She was interrupted by a knock at the door.

'Come in,' called Nigel and Frederick strode into the room. He was wearing a tweed suit and carried a leather briefcase.

'Am I late?' he asked.

'John,' said Margaret, standing up with her hand out, 'how are you?'

The doctor's blue eyes flicked to Nigel and gave a crease of recognition, before settling on the probation officer. He took the hand and shook it.

'Sit yourself down,' said Nigel as he pulled out a chair. 'Do you want some tea?'

'Oh, yes please,' they both said at the same time. They looked at each other and laughed. Then they sat down.

As he made the drinks, Nigel listened to them talk about mental health policy changes.

'Regulation 47b will ensure we spend more time filing and less time with patients,' said Margaret.

'It will definitely increase my workload,' said the doctor. 'But on the other hand, it could mean a decrease in long-term detentions.'

Nigel put the cups on the table. He cleared his throat as he moved towards the board. They reached for their cups and turned to face him.

'I've asked you both here so we can discuss Gary Johnson,' he said as he picked up a marker. He popped its cap off and underlined the name on the board.

★

I finished my shave and went into the bedroom. I tried not to listen to him but maybe he had a point. Just because you're paranoid doesn't mean they're not out to get you. As I changed my clothes I could hear him.

Galileo will protect you.

No you won't, I said.

Do you think they will?

I thought of that as I sat on the bed. They wouldn't. I stood up quickly.

Just fuck off, I shouted to the room.

You need me. You can't face them on your own. They're too much for you.

I walked out of the bedroom and into the kitchen. I thought I would be better safe than sorry so I pulled my nine-inch blade from the drawer. I slid it into the back of my jeans.

Just in case, I said to the living room mirror.
He nodded back like I'd made a wise decision.

Don't go on the bus, he said.

Why not?

Too vulnerable.

I could ask Charlie to come with me.

She's no good to you son, you should forget her.

She's all right, I said.
He shook his head.

As long as she's a junky, she'll sell you down the river for the price of a bag.

How am I going to get to Homebase then?
Galileo smiled and touched his nose.

Phone that prick Chris, he'll take you.

*

Charlie opened the windows and lit a scented candle. She got the vacuum from the cupboard in the hall and gave the place a quick going over. She went into the kitchen and washed the breakfast dishes and wiped the worktops. Then she had a bath. By the time she got out, it was one-thirty.

She decided to look homely for this visit. She was subtle with the make-up. Not a lot of foundation. No eye shadow but a tiny bit of liner and mascara. She put on a white shirt and a pair of loose-fitting jeans. She opened her lipstick and had half twisted it out when she changed her mind and put it away.

Too tarty, she said with a shake of her head.

The intercom buzzed at two p.m. exactly.

Nice timing, she said to the clock.

She let the second hand crawl round for a minute before getting off the couch to answer. She pressed the button.

Who is it?

Nigel.

Come up.

She had a last look in the mirror when he knocked on the door. She opened it and he stepped inside. She reached her hand out and caught hold of his fingers.

Come through, she said and led him to the living room.

He sat down but she stayed standing.

Would you like a cold drink? she asked.

Yes please.

She went back into the kitchen and fetched two glasses of fizzy water.

Here you go.

He grasped his and had a sip.

Thanks, he said.

She sat beside him.

Good to see you, she said.

He turned to look at her.

And you.

She rested her hands on her lap.

I've been thinking about what you said about getting clean and that.

He seemed to come to life.

I'm glad, he said. This is no kind of life to be leading.

She let tears grow in her sad eyes.

Yeah but I can't do it on my own.

I've already told you I can get you into a rehab, he said.

You're not just saying that? she sniffed.

Of course not. I'll make some calls this afternoon.

She snuggled in against him and started crying.

I don't want to work the streets any more.

He stroked her hair.

You don't have to.

She whispered.

You're so nice. I've never met a man like you.

I'll do anything I can to help.

She waited for a few seconds.

I'm just scared about my rent.

We could apply for Housing Benefit.

She snuffled some more.

They don't accept that here.

She left it another few seconds then held him tighter and cried.

I don't want to end up homeless.

She felt him fidget before he coughed.

How much do you need? he asked.

She lifted her head to look at him.

About three hundred.

He frowned as if he was doing mental arithmetic.

OK. I'll see what I can do.

*

Homebase was busy. There was the usual selection of customers. The family types who are on the property ladder and climbing before the debts chasing them bite at their ankles. Men and women with linked arms and a child walking in front, best clothes on for a trip to the shops. I hate every one of the cunts. Fucking muppets they are, and suckers for cheap television.

The doors slid open as we approached.

Open sesame, said Chris.

I felt like giving him a slap on the ear but laughed as a payment for giving me a lift.

Well done mate, that was funny.

We walked into a crossroads of shelving. I looked up to the hanging signs and scratched my scalp.

What are we here for? asked Chris.

I headed down an aisle.

We're looking for tubing, I said.

What, like copper pipes?

Yeah but flexible.

I nodded towards a spotty youth in an orange uniform.

Ask that cunt.

Chris wandered over and I watched them have a chat.

Look at them, said Galileo.

Shut up, I said.

Like a pair of faggots setting up a date, he said.

Can you not have a rest for five minutes? I asked.

If I did that, you'd let the cunts capture us.

The assistant pointed and Chris came back.

We have to go to the plumbing section, he said.

Well lead on then son.

They had clear plastic hoses, grey ones for washing machines and blue ones for fresh water supplies, brown ones for sewerage and copper for the traditional kitchen.

I reeled off a few metres from each of the drums. A good selection I was building. It was piling up on the floor beside us.

I turned to Chris.

Go and fetch us a trolley.

By the time he brought it I had enough hoses to complete the model. I wound them up into hoops and tied them with string hanging from a dispenser. I passed the bundles to Chris and he stacked them on the cart.

Chris pushed the trolley like he was my wife with a pram. I stood by him, protective of our child. We got to the wire looms and I grabbed his arm.

Here we go.

I tugged and felt the different gauges till I found one that was the same sort of thickness as coat-hangers. I thought of running off a few metres but then decided to get the whole drum. I unhooked it from the mounting and placed it on the pile of hose.

The next display held a selection of pliers. I grabbed the most expensive pair and tried them on the wire. They clipped through it like scissors through a shoelace.

Perfect, I said and dropped them in amongst the rest of our shopping.

Expensive, said Chris.

Don't worry about that, I said and winked at him.

I told him to push the trolley towards the exit. I kept my eye on the security guard all the way. When we got closer I noticed he was just standing there with his arms folded over his chest, looking like a bouncer.

I picked up a top-quality tile-cutter from one of the displays. It was the type favoured by shoplifters because they can get a good price for them at Cash Converters. Homebase knew this, so they'd put an electronic alarm on them.

An old couple were heading for the exit with a trolley stacked with wallpaper and a big roll of lino. I sidled up next to them and dropped the tile-cutter in amongst their stuff.

When they went through the door the alarm went off and the security guard pounced on them. It was like they were the people who had been thieving from his children's piggy banks.

I pushed our trolley through the scene of the crime and out the door. As we went past I heard the old man trying to talk. He was well flustered and probably had visions of spending time in Pentonville.

I don't know how they got there.

We'll let the police sort that out sir.

There's no need to contact them, is there?

We always prosecute shoplifters sir.

But I didn't steal them.

OK sir. If you'll just come with me.

Me and Chris made it safely to the car and we loaded the stuff into the boot. I pushed the trolley away and it spun and came to a rest against the kerb. I climbed into the passenger seat. I banged the dashboard.

Good stuff mate. Job done.

First time I've ever committed a robbery.

I put my hand on his shoulder.

Is it? Well you must be a natural.

He smiled like a girl being told she was lovely.

We should get out of here, he said.

Yeah, good idea. See? You are a natural.

He started the car and we drove home. I got him to help me in with the pipes and we piled them on the living room floor.

*

After eight hours swinging a pick, Galileo stretched out his back and smacked his lips. He reached for the generator and turned it off. The room became dark and he made his way out of the cellar.

The foreman was standing at the site gate. He handed over a brown envelope. Galileo ripped it open and pulled out a wad of tenners. Dust and thirst kicked into his throat. He turned to Raphael.

Shall we go for a beer?

Sounds good to me.

They walked away without a glance at the half-demolished factory. They called into the newsagent's at the end of the street and bought a sausage roll each for their dinner.

When they got to the pub Galileo ordered two pints of lager. He licked his lips before putting them to the glass. He had a long draught.

That was worth the wait, he said and Raphael nodded.

A stripper came out of a side room. She was accompanied by whistles from the crowd of workmen. She squeezed between them and pulled her body onto the stage. When she was up there she played with her elasticated garments in time to the music. The men banged into each other and made grunting noises. Beer spilled with the jostling.

Galileo watched her peel her clothes off. She was hooking her thumbs into the waistband of her knickers when he felt a tug at his arm. He glanced over his shoulder, but found it hard to take his eyes from the pubic hair that showed above the teasing panties. The crowd of men shouted louder and pushed forward to get a better view.

The tugging on his arm got harder and harder till he turned with a snarl.

What the fuck, he said and realised it was Chastity. Her face creased as she spoke.

What are you doing?

I'm having a beer after work.

Why do you waste time here? she asked.

He felt the weight of the beer in his hand. The music was too loud and the men too rough. He put his unfinished glass on the table and walked out of the pub. Chastity followed him. When they were in the street she took him by the hand and looked deep into his eyes.

We need light up there.

He nodded.

OK, I'll get some from my work.

I'll see you later, she said as she walked away from him.

Where are you going? he asked.

Just get some light, she called over her shoulder.

Galileo leaned on the wall as he watched her habit disappear into the evening. He got a fag out and lit it. Then he straightened up and walked back to the demolition site.

It took him half an hour to drag the generator and the lamps from the cellar, and to coil up as much cable as he could find. He stacked everything onto a barrow and tied it with a bit of rope. He grunted as he lifted the load. He leaned forward and pushed it past piles of twisted metal and bricks.

At the far corner of the site was a concrete building. It had a missing door and broken windows. Galileo stopped the barrow next to it and threw the cable over his shoulder. He walked inside and clambered through a hole in an internal wall. It led to a tunnel.

When he pulled himself into the dome Chastity was waiting for him.

I knew you wouldn't disappoint me, she said.

They climbed back down and managed to bring the generator up between them. Another journey and they had all the equipment stacked neatly beside the table and chairs.

Galileo wiped the sweat from his forehead.

So what do we have to do now? he asked.

Set up these lamps, said Chastity.

He pointed to one of the holes.

What about Gaston and Betts?

You can't get away from them.

But you said the light attracts them.

It does, but the only alternative is darkness. Is that how you want to live?

He thought about it.

No, he said.

He uncoiled the lengths of cable and stretched them into a big circle with the lights between lengths.

Point the lamps outwards, said Chastity.

He walked round and did as he was told, then came back to the middle for the generator. He dragged it to the circle and connected it to the cables. He pulled on the string three times before it started in a chug of diesel fumes. He was expecting the noise to echo, but it didn't.

When it was revving steadily he pressed a big red button and the lights came on with a ping.

He gazed at what he saw with his mouth hanging open.

He was at the base of a gigantic saucer the size of a football stadium.

Chastity put her arm through his and dragged him over to the table.

Sit with me for a minute, she said.

He placed his bum on a chair and kept looking at the sight of the holes.

Awesome, he said.

There is more to see.

He focused on her.

Is there?

I want you to see it all.

How can I do that?

She pointed to a hole.

Go down there. And I'll tell you what to get.

*

Nigel pulled the money out of the machine. He crushed the receipt into his pocket as he walked across the pavement to his car. He shut the door and started to drive home. He was halfway there before he thought about the thick wad of notes in his wallet. He could feel it pushing from the car seat through his jeans and against his bum. It was obvious he had a lot of cash in there and it would be best if Sarah didn't see it. He thought about hiding it somewhere in the house, but he wouldn't be able to rest, he'd be too worried she might find it.

'Where did this come from?'

'I don't know.'

As he approached the St Stephen's roundabout, he looked in the mirror and indicated right. He drove back the way he'd come.

He pulled up at her door five minutes later and rang the bell. She seemed surprised to hear it was him on the intercom, but buzzed him into the building.

'To what do I owe this pleasure?' she asked with a smile.

'I've got the money for your rent,' he said in a half whisper.

She glanced past him into the corridor. 'Nosy neighbours might get the wrong idea,' she said as she pulled him inside. 'Do you want some tea or something?' she asked.

'No,' he said. 'I can't stop.'

'That's a shame,' she said.

'I've got some good news,' he said.

'What's that?' she asked.

'I spoke to my friend in Social Services,' he said with a nod. 'We can get you into rehab next week.'

'Oh Nigel, that's fantastic,' she said as she jumped the space between them and hugged him. 'How can I ever thank you?' she asked.

'You don't need to thank me,' he said. 'I just want to see you off the drugs and getting on with your life.'

'I will,' she said. 'I promise.'

'I want what's best for you,' he said. 'You do understand that, don't you?' he asked as he extracted his wallet.

'Yeah, I really trust you Nigel,' she said as she nodded. 'And your judgement.'

'I hope so,' he said, 'because if I give you this money, it might become difficult for me. I need to know I'm doing the right thing.'

'But you are, Nigel,' she said as she reached for his arm and held it. 'You really are.'

He held his wallet in front of him and moved it up and down as he spoke. 'I'm giving you this so you don't have to walk the street,' he said and she nodded again.

'And it wouldn't be good to spend it on drugs,' he added.

'I won't,' she said. 'I promise.'

'And there's something else,' he said. He hesitated before going on. 'I think it would be better if you stopped seeing Gary.'

He noticed she was shaking her head. 'I know you feel strongly about him,' he said. 'But he's not good for you, and I don't think you're good for him.'

'But I love him, Nigel.'

'Maybe you do,' he said, 'but you must have noticed he's getting unwell.'

'Yeah,' she sniffed. 'I am worried about him.'

'He's vulnerable at the moment,' he said. 'He's on the verge of being put in hospital.'

'Don't let them put him away,' she said. 'He couldn't handle another section.'

'Well, you've got to play a part in that, by leaving him to get on with his recovery. He's very sick at the moment.'

'But I can help him,' she said.

Nigel put his hand on her shoulder and looked in her eyes. 'The psychiatrist thinks illegal drugs are making him worse.'

'But I'm going to get clean.'

'You've got a long hard journey in front of you,' said Nigel. 'Have you thought how selfish it would be to drag Gary along with you?'

She bowed her head and he offered her the money. She took it and held it against her chest.

'You get on with your rehab,' he said as he put his

empty wallet back in his pocket, 'and I'll try and make sure Gary gets on with his.'

'You will take care of him, Nigel?' she asked.

He pulled her towards him and gave her a hug. 'Of course I will,' he said as he glanced over her shoulder at his watch. 'I better go.'

He held her at arm's length. 'I'll call round in the morning and see how you're getting on.'

'OK, catch you then,' she said in a barely audible whisper.

*

When Chris left I checked out the sphere. The paper had hardened and the circle was complete. I tapped it a few times around its surface but in some spots it seemed a bit hollow. Like it wouldn't be able to handle the weight of the pipes.

I hunted around the flat but I couldn't find any more newspapers. I went out the front door and there was a telephone directory leaning against the wall next to the neighbour's. I made sure there was nobody around and then I picked it up.

When I got back inside, I locked up and sat on the couch and tore the whole book into strips.

As I pasted them on the globe I realised the model was all the better for having the phone numbers of a million different people. It was like a symbol of the untold souls that are weaved into a single human brain. A picture of my head made from bits of everyone else's.

I spent a couple of hours applying the strips. By the time I was finished the skin was thick enough to handle the next stage of its fabrication. All I had to do was wait until it had dried.

It's looking good, said Galileo. I'm proud of you.

I felt a glow on my cheeks.

I just want the world to know what's going on.

And that's exactly where we are heading. As long as we work on it together, everything will be all right.

I know.

You should get some rest, he said.

I liked Galileo when he wasn't so angry. He made sense and it was good to know that he cared about me. I went into the bathroom and found my stash of Valium. I swallowed the whole packet and drank four cans of Stella. Then I climbed onto my bed and lay down. As I drifted off I heard Galileo sing an Italian song as he danced round the dome with Chastity.

*

Nigel stirred the pot of spaghetti sauce. He heard the front door close. He moved into the living room just as Sarah was taking off her coat.

'Let me help you with that,' he said as he took it from her and hung it up.

'Something smells good,' she said.

'I thought I'd cook tonight,' he said. 'Try and make up for my behaviour last night.'

She walked into the kitchen and turned to lean against

the counter. 'What do you want me to say?' she asked. 'Oh, that's sweet of you darling, I don't mind if you shout and swear at me as long as you make my dinner?'

'Listen, I'm trying to make peace,' he said. 'I was a bit outspoken last night, I admit that.' He paused and went on. 'I'm sorry, what else can I say?'

'OK, Nigel,' she said.

She saw the roses resting in the sink. 'And you've bought some flowers?' she asked.

'Yeah,' he nodded as he lifted the bunch up for her.

She held them to her face and sniffed them. 'Mm,' she sighed. 'These are beautiful.' She put them back down and walked towards him. 'Give me a cuddle then,' she said.

He held her tight. 'I love you,' he said.

Saturday, 15th May 2004

I poured myself a pint of water and sat on the couch. I rolled a fag and coughed my way through it. I turned the telly on and watched the news while I swigged from the glass.

My balls were itchy from the withdrawals. I put my hand in the fly of my shorts and gave them a scratch. My knee jumped up and down. I rolled another fag. I sat like this for an hour or so. Staring at the telly and sucking cigarettes. Sometimes I would blow smoke rings. My fingers had orange tips to them and my nails were bitten to the quick.

You're a fucking mess, said Galileo.

So what? I said.

You should be ashamed, going about like that.

What's it to you?

Do you want everybody to know you're going mental? he asked.

Why should I listen to you?

I'm the only thing between you and a locked ward, he shouted.

I growled at him.

You're only a projection of my own mind's fear of nothingness.

Where did you learn that talk? One of those group therapy sessions?

I put my fingers in my ears and chanted.

Not listening, not listening.

But I could still hear him so I pulled them back out.

So I'm a projection? he asked.

You certainly are, I said to the swirling patterns of the living room wallpaper.

How can you be sure?

I just am.

But maybe you're a figment of my imagination, he said.

I leaned forward and cradled my head in my hands.

No, I said in a long groan.

I puffed my cigarette till the head was glowing and held it to the back of my hand.

Can you feel that? I shouted.

Galileo headbutted the mirror. It rattled against the wall.

Can you feel that? he shouted.

Then he started to rant.

I'm a fucking projection? Me that's slaving through these tunnels and nut-houses and army camps. Trying my best to bring light to an ungrateful bastard who'd like nothing more than to take medication so he can forget everything. Life's too much, he whines and lays in bed like a fucking woman. You fucking wanker.

I realised it was pointless arguing with him so I puffed my fag and watched the smoke fade into nothingness.

My phone beeped. I picked it up and looked at the screen.

Charlie, I said out loud and Galileo shut up.

I pressed the answer button.

Hello, she said and I pictured her with the handset on her shoulder, in the kitchen making tea or some toast and marmalade.

Hiya, I said.

There was a silence that lasted for ages, but not even for a second. I held the phone tight against my ear.

The thing is Gaz, she said.

Here it comes, said Galileo.

I like you, she said, I mean I really like you.

But, said Galileo.

But, she said.

Yeah? I said.

I need to take some time away, she said.

I gulped.

Why?

I'm going to try and get clean.

Likely fucking story, said Galileo.

I coughed.

That's brilliant Charlie.

Thanks babe, I knew you'd understand.

I rubbed my itchy chin with the phone.

What? I said.

She spoke really quietly.

I can't see you for a while.

Oh.

There was more silence.

Gaz?

What?

Oh nothing. Take care of yourself.

The phone beep-beeped the end of the call.

I told you, said Galileo.

Shut the fuck up, I shouted.

*

Charlie hung up the phone and leered at Nigel.

Are you happy now?

Of course I'm not happy, but you know it's the right thing to do.

She went into the bedroom and started pulling clothes out of drawers. He followed her in.

What are you doing?

I'm going to work.

But you can't.

She looked him in the eye.

I need to get some money to score.

He grabbed her by the wrist.

Don't.

She tugged against his grip.

Let me go. Let me fucking go.

He released his fingers. She examined her wrists and showed him the red marks.

See what you've done to me, you fucking animal. You're just like the rest. Men, you're all pigs. Only happy when you're getting your own way.

He turned away from her and she saw his head shaking as he stood by the window.

You could do so much better than this, he said.

I don't care. I need some gear. And you're not going to stop me.

He turned back round to face her.

OK, OK. Just don't go back on the street.

She screamed at him.

Where am I going to get the fucking money then?

What about the three hundred I let you have last night?

I gave it to the landlord.

Are you sure?

So I'm a liar now as well as a whore and a junky?

I didn't say that.

She stepped to the side of her bedroom door.

If you don't think I'm telling the truth, you might as well fuck off, she said. I'm sick of you standing over me, making me do stuff, then not believing me when I do it.

Charlie calm down, I believe you.

She pushed home the advantage.

I still need some money to score, she said.

OK, I'll give you some.

What? Just like that? Do you want a fuck? Where do you want to put it? My fanny or my mouth or my arse? Yeah that's it you sick cunt, you want to fuck me up the arse.

I don't want anything.

She felt the anger leave her like a snap of fingers. She sat on the edge of the bed and picked up a T-shirt. She folded it on her lap.

I'm sorry Nigel. This life drives me crazy.

He sat beside her and put his arm on her shoulder.

I know.

She leaned against him.

You must think I'm pathetic.

No, of course I don't.

She whispered to his ear.

Thanks for helping me out.

He kissed her on the head.

I'd do anything for you.

I feel really sick.

He stood up.

OK, get dressed and we'll go and get you sorted.

Are you going to take me?

You don't think I'd let you go on your own, do you?

★

I got on with the model. I tapped it with the handle of a screwdriver. It sounded solid. I rolled it to rest in the corner of the living room.

I needed to make the attachments for the hoses.

I rifled through the living room cupboard until I found an old gas valve. I lifted it up for a proper look. It was a brass thing in a conical shape, going from a two-inch diameter down to a half-inch. From the side it looked like a small funnel.

I put it on the floor next to the couch. I wanted to make springs that were the same shape as the valve. I twisted the wire from Homebase onto it, round and round, like thread onto a spool. I started on the small end so that as the circumference got bigger the loops would tighten in on themselves. Round and round it went till I had a conical spring. I clipped the wire at an angle to make sure it had a sharp edge. I held the finished article up and examined it.

Not bad, said Galileo.

The next spring I made was even better. More uniform. Then I made one after the other until I had a pile of twenty. My hands were aching by this time so I went into the kitchen and made a cup of tea. I had a biscuit as well.

You need to get back to work, said Galileo.

I know, I'm just having a break.

He shouted at me.

While you're doing that, I've got people to kill, so get on with it.

*

Galileo descended the ladder until he came to a damp tunnel. It was squelchy on the floor and there were bits of root dangling from the ceiling. Not tall enough for a man to walk through or even crouch. He had to crawl like a dog. The cold and wet seeped through his trousers and into his knees. He was wearing the khaki green of the British Army. He took his hat off and saw it was a claret colour. Like a paratrooper.

He came to the end of the tunnel and climbed out into a wet trench. Raphael was lying along the top. He had camouflage netting draped over him and a pair of sights in his hand. He turned to Galileo and whispered, steam coming from his mouth.

All quiet.

Galileo blew hot air into his hands. He checked his watch. Half past three.

I'll make a brew in a little while.

Yeah, nice one. It's fucking cold this morning.

Galileo picked at the bits of Armagh soil stuck under his fingernails.

Don't know why we bother with this place. Should just hand it back and fuck off to Gibraltar. Least you get a tan there, and you can always get over to Morocco for a bit of hash.

Raphael continued to scan the countryside.

Never mind mate. We'll be out of here in the morning. We can have a beer later.

Galileo picked up his rifle and started to clean it.

And a hot dinner, he said as he pushed a rag into the barrel.

Raphael's feet twitched.

Shh! he whispered.

After a long five seconds he put his hand on Galileo's shoulder.

Couple of Patricks, two o'clock.

What they up to?

They're poking about in a hedge with a stick. Stupid cunts can't even read their own maps.

Galileo picked his rifle up and made sure a bullet was in the breech. Raphael was folding up the netting. He dropped it down to Galileo, who put it in the corner. He passed the night-sight and Galileo popped his head up and studied the outlaws. They were definitely searching for something, and were near enough to the dump to justify an arrest-and-interrogate.

Galileo climbed out of the trench.

Right, let's do it.

He crept towards the men, half hunched over. He held his rifle across his chest. He put his hand down and signalled Raphael to take the left flank. They planned to attack from right angles.

When he was twenty yards away from the men he stood up and showed his rifle.

Hands up, you're under arrest, he shouted at the top of his voice.

The men started. One of them reached into the lapel of his jacket. Galileo put three bullets into his chest.

The other man stood with his arms raised above his head. Raphael patted him down. He turned him round and secured his wrists with a cable-tie. Then he tripped him to the floor.

Lay fucking still.

Galileo kneeled and felt the pulse in the neck of the wounded man. It was feeble and he didn't expect the guy to survive until a pig arrived. He pulled out his radio.

Kelly Alpha One to base, Kelly Alpha One to base.

Reading you loud and clear, Kelly Alpha One.

Two captured, one wounded, two captured, one wounded.

We need your position.

The sky was starting to lighten and they could see

the tower at the top of the hill. Galileo took a small torch from his webbing and flashed a red light at the base. Twice long and once short. The radio crackled.

Got you. Secure position, reinforcements on way. Galileo turned the radio off and paid more attention to their immediate area. Raphael was standing over the trussed man.

Lights bucked in the distance with the sound of a Land-Rover. Before long there were two of them shining their headlights on the kill-zone. A flatbed truck drew up the rear. Squaddies jumped out and fanned into the fields. A couple of officers inspected the ammunition dump.

A nun appeared from the rear of the truck and approached Galileo and the fallen soldier. She kneeled at the wounded man and started speaking in Latin.

In nomine patris.

Galileo looked away to give the dying man some dignity but the nun grabbed his sleeve and turned him to face her.

It was Chastity.

Steal the flares from the truck and take them to the dome, she said.

Galileo looked at the soldiers milling around. He had a puff on his cigarette and dropped it into the damp grass. He walked to the lorry and climbed in the back.

Near the cab was a locked chest. It had a beware sign on it. He crawled up to it and lifted his rifle. He smashed the padlock with the butt. Three times he banged it before it snapped and the hasp hung by a couple of bent screws.

Inside was a yellow box with a handle. It was the shape of a briefcase. He lifted it out and jumped off the truck.

*

Nigel drove from the dealer's with Charlie nodding in the passenger seat. He stopped at a traffic light and she bounced forward against the seatbelt.

'Are you all right?' he asked.

'What?' she said, blinking as she gazed round the car. He lifted her by the chin. 'I said are you all right?'

'Yeah,' she said with a smile. 'I feel fine, baby.' Her eyes closed. 'So fine.'

The lights changed and he pressed the accelerator. The car moved forward and her head banged back against the seat.

'Fucking scumbag,' said Nigel as he thought about the drug dealer.

'What?' she asked.

Nigel tried to concentrate on the road but was battered by thoughts of the drugs business.

When he was at college he'd bought hash a couple of times. He'd sit with his friends and they'd listen to records and make some joints and pass them round. That was a thing that had fascinated him. People seemed to share their drugs. He'd liked it and used it as an excuse to smoke more. Like Marxist principles were involved. Modern society makes us individuals where we keep things to ourselves, but cannabis is about re-distribution, therefore it is an anti-capitalist act we should all get involved in. He'd grown out of this philosophy when he'd got married and started to pay taxes and a mortgage, but still retained romantic memories of teenage rebellion.

The drugs den Charlie took him to was very different. Nobody sat in a circle, passed joints or watched Animal House. The dealer had bad teeth and was horrible to his wife. He ran his business like an absolute monarchy, his word was law, and all the junkies bowed and sweated and hung on his every word.

There was no sharing. When someone bought drugs they either scurried away to a bedsit somewhere or retired to a corner where they had a lonely injection and fell into a stupor. The misfortunes of others were meat they could chew over while waiting their turn at the scales, or sucking the juice into syringes, or running the powder down foil.

Nigel shivered at the recollection. The smell of patchouli in his long-term memory was veneered with the acridity of sweat and dirty socks.

He braked as he pulled up outside her flat and her head bumped against the door.

'What?' she asked.

'Nothing, love, soon have you home.'

'You're a good man, Nigel,' she said and her eyes closed again.

He lifted her out of the car and propped her against it while he locked up. They staggered to the stairwell as if they were in a three-legged race, her limp body hanging onto his.

He climbed like a mountaineer until he was at the summit and could rest for air. He held her up with one arm and opened the door with the other. He pushed into the flat and through to the bedroom. He lay her on the bed and turned her into the recovery position.

He went into the bathroom and washed his hands. Then he stepped into the kitchen and made himself a cup of tea. He sat on the couch and pushed the remote. Football came on the telly. He smiled as a ball bounced against the back of the net.

When he had finished his tea he put the mug in the sink and went to see how she was.

She lay on the bed, curled up with her thumb in her mouth.

'Charlie, are you all right?' he asked, then bent over and shook her.

'Help me off with my shoes,' she groaned and rolled onto her back. She held her foot in the air and twirled it around. He slid it past her heels and felt the heat of her sole in his palms. He massaged it and she groaned some more.

'Oh, that's lovely,' she said and lifted the other foot. He repeated the procedure, her pleasurable noises making his penis twitch.

He reached to take off her jacket and she shrugged her shoulders to help him. He put his arms round her waist and loosened her shirt. She put her hands up as he pulled it over her head. Then she flopped back onto the bed. He grabbed her trousers and unbuttoned them. She lifted her waist as he dragged them down her legs.

He folded them onto a chair and turned his attention to her knickers.

He manoeuvred them off her hips and along her thighs. She kicked as they reached her ankles and he fondled them before he threw them into the laundry basket.

Then he rolled her under the duvet.

He stripped his own clothes off and climbed in there with her. He kissed her and she flopped against him. He put his hand between her legs and they fell open. He placed her hand on his erect penis. She grabbed it and pulled it towards herself.

He climbed on top of her and pushed himself against her.

'No,' she said as she moaned and wriggled away. 'I'm tired.'

'Ah, come on,' he said and he pushed again.

'No, I don't want to.'

'OK,' he said and climbed off her.

He reached for the side of the bed and picked up her handbag.

'Would you like another smoke?' he asked.

'Give me it,' she said, smacking her lips like she was sleeping and dreaming of a cool glass of water.

She sucked up a few lines. He watched her till her head fell forward. Then he took the foil and put it back in her bag.

He pulled her close to him and she moaned like a cat and rubbed her body up against him. He pushed her onto her back and wedged himself between her legs. He squeezed his penis against her. It was dry and he had to shove hard. It went in a bit at a time, until he had the whole lot in there.

She made contented sounds and he quickened till he came spurting inside her. He lay on top of her and felt lovely.

Her snores brought him out of his fantasy and he got off and lay by her side. He cuddled up to her. She put her hand on his hip and pulled him close.

'Lovely Nigel,' she said as she went back to sleep.

*

I left the springs by the couch and rolled the model over from the corner. I sat down with it between my legs and picked up the screwdriver. I felt the sharp tip, then I moved the sphere around till I found the right spot. The first letter of the forename of a Smith, John, was just the place, I thought.

Stick it in, said Galileo.

I put the point against the J and banged the handle with my other hand. It went through like a knife into a social worker's back. I pulled it out with a squeak and chose a spring from the pile at my feet.

I inserted it and wound it into the hole. A few turns I gave it till it was firmly attached. It stuck from the sphere like a nipple from a breast.

Suck it, said Galileo.

I bent over and nuzzled the end with my lips.

Mama, I said.

Good boy, said Galileo.

I inserted another spring, in the exact opposite side from the first. Like that one was in London and this one Auckland.

I picked up the globe and held it just above the carpet. I spun it slowly on its axis. Telephone numbers flashed in front of my face until Galileo called.

There.

I popped a hole with the screwdriver and wound in a spiral of wire. Then I fitted one after another till the whole thing was covered.

When it was finished I picked it up and carried it into the bedroom. I put it on the floor underneath the light fitting.

I stood up and looked at the writing on the walls as I thought what to do next. I needed somebody to help me mount it, so I sent a text to Ralph.

Get round here now.

*

Charlie woke with a need for a piss. She climbed out of bed. On her walk to the bathroom she felt something running down her leg. She unrolled some paper as she sat on the pan. She wiped the inside of her thighs.

After peeing, she stomped back to the bedroom.

You dirty bastard, she shouted as she pushed through the door.

Nigel lifted his head from the pillow.

What?

You came inside me.

He blinked at her and shook his head.

You asked me to.

Fuck off.

No, you did. You grabbed me round the hips and said come, I want to feel you come.

Her anger was diffused by doubt.

I never let punt, I mean men, come inside me.

He didn't say anything.

She pulled the duvet off him.

Get up.

He covered his cock.

What?

Get up you dirty cunt.

He stood up with her handbag and searched through it.

What do you think you're doing with that? she asked and grabbed the handle. Before she could stop him he'd pulled the parcel of smack out and held it in his fist.

I bought the drugs so I'm taking them, he said and tucked them into the pocket of his jeans.

Suit yourself, she said. I'll soon get some more.

He put his clothes on. Quickly he stretched his head through the neck of his T-shirt. Then his pants were flicked over his cock. He slowed as he pulled his jeans up his legs. He kept glancing at her, but she stood with her hands folded and tapped the floor with her foot.

He put his socks on like they were the last things he'd do before he was executed. Then he sighed. He looked down as he kicked his toes together.

Don't make me leave, he said.

She put her hand out.

Just give me the gear Nigel.

He sat up and grappled in his pocket. Then he dropped the parcel into her palm. She held it tight.

You need to go, she said.

But I gave you the drugs.

I don't feel safe with you in the house.

He stayed sitting.

I'm not leaving, he said.

I thought you were different and you could respect a woman. But you're just like the rest. If you were half decent you'd give me the time and space to have my own life. You'd trust me to come back to you.

He stood up.

OK, I'll go.

She walked down the hallway and stood over him as he put on his shoes. He reached to kiss her.

I'll phone you later, he said.

She pulled her face away from him.

Don't bother, she said.

As soon as he was outside she slammed the door and clicked the locks.

*

Galileo climbed back into the dome. He opened the yellow briefcase and took out two flare guns. He checked them to make sure they were loaded. He held them up. Chastity clapped from the table.

Fire them at the same time, she said.

He held one in each hand. He was like a spaghetti western gunslinger, elbows digging into his hips. The pistols pointed up and away at an angle. He leaned back so they would fire as straight up into the air as he could manage. He squeezed the triggers slowly till they reached the end of their springs and clicked.

With a huge bang the flares soared into the air. They scored two arcs of red into the darkness. Then they seemed to hesitate before they burst into light, and for the first time in his life Galileo saw what he was living in.

Wow, he said.

Chastity laughed.

Yeah wow, she said.

They were in a gigantic sphere, dotted with innumerable ladders coming out of holes, all set out in a pattern as regular as the dimples in a golf ball.

The flares dropped slowly. They swung on the end of parachutes, like pendulums ticking the seconds away. Eventually they hit the floor in the distance and went out.

For a couple of seconds Galileo could still see the sphere. It must have been imprinted on his eyes. As he watched it fade and disappear in the dark, he heard her heels approach. He was so awed by the site of where he was he didn't pay attention to her till she was standing by his side.

She put her arm through his.

What do you think?

Does every hole –

She finished his sentence.

Lead to a possibility?

It's hard to contemplate.

It's more than that. It's impossible.

He shook his head as he thought about the infinite choices that could be his life.

So where do I go next?

That's your decision.

He stood and listened to the beat of the generator.

It's too much.

She pulled him round so they faced each other.

You can handle it.

He looked deep into the green of her eyes.

Only if you help me.

She whispered.

I won't always be here.

The knowledge hit him like a freight train, ding-ding, ding-ding.

But I can't manage on my own, he said.

She touched his chin.

You'll be OK.

There was a bang from somewhere beneath them. The sound of metal screeching against metal.

What was that? asked Galileo.

The noise got louder and louder then stopped. The silence returned for a few seconds. Then it was broken by the hollow echo of ladders being climbed.

Chastity turned to him.

They're here, she said.

*

Ralph followed me into the bedroom. He pointed to the globe.

What the fuck is that?

I want you to help me fix it up there, I said and gestured to the light fitting.

I dragged the stepladder over and opened it out. I climbed halfway up and reached to him.

Right, hand me it.

He bent down and picked it up.

He's going to drop it, said Galileo.

Careful, I said.

OK, I've got it, said Ralph.

I grabbed a couple of the springs and lifted it towards the ceiling. When it was close to the light fitting I looked at Ralph.

Just hold it there.

He positioned himself under it and grunted with the effort.

It wasn't completely still but I managed to tuck the electric cable of the light fitting inside the sphere. I doubled it round the frame and clipped it into place. I pulled a roll of tape from my back pocket and twisted it round the joint. Six turns I gave it.

Right mate, let it go.

Ralph stepped away and it eased down.

The weight of it pulled the creases out of the cable, then stretched it with a creaking noise. For a second I thought it was going to snap, but it held.

I got off the stepladder and leaned it back against the wall.

Do you want a can of beer? I said.

Is the pope a child molester? he asked and headed for the living room.

I turned as I was closing the door on the death room. I could see the sphere hanging there. It was like a giant sea mine waiting for reckless shipping.

Sunday, 16th May 2004

I woke up to a text from Charlie. It said she loved me. I tried to call her but she didn't pick up the phone or reply to my message. I got a bit worried about her so I decided to go round and find out what was happening. When I got there I rang the bell. There wasn't an answer. I walked back into the street and had a look up at her windows. I could see her curtains were closed so I knew she was in.

She's ignoring you, said Galileo. Try the neighbours.

I pressed a few different buttons. Eventually some guy answered. He sounded sleepy.

Hello?

I've got a package for you.

Who's it from?

I don't know, I'm just the delivery boy.

But it's Sunday, he groaned.

Do you want the thing or shall I leave it out here?

The lock buzzed and I walked into the building. I sprinted up the stairs and passed a man popping his head out of a door.

Have you got my parcel? he asked.

I scowled at him and kept climbing.

When I got to Charlie's floor I banged on her letterbox. I sat on my haunches and opened it to see in. I got a whiff of her smell, like talcum and soap.

It's Gary, come on love, let me in, I called.

That's it, said Galileo, sweet-talk her.

Are you all right in there? I asked.

She came out of her bedroom and walked up the hall. She was holding a bit of toilet paper to her nose. Her hand reached up and the locks clicked. She opened the door, but didn't meet my eyes. She just turned round and walked back to her room.

By the time I had followed her in there, she was already underneath her quilt. She had it pulled over her head. Only her face showed and that was half covered in a hanky.

Did you not hear the bell? I asked.

Yeah.

Why'd you not answer it? I asked.

I wasn't sure who it was.

What's the matter?

Nothing, I just don't feel like getting up.

Oh, I said.

I sat on the bed and checked out her dressing table. It was covered in make-up and perfume and hairbands. Galileo was in the mirror. He smiled at me.

Ask her if she misses you.

I half turned.

Do you?

What?

Miss me.

She didn't say anything so I looked back in the mirror. I heard her blow her nose.

See, said Galileo, she does.

How would you know? I asked.

He nodded to her.

Look at the poor cow.

I turned back again and she was wiping tears from her face. I leaned over and stroked her.

Are you OK baby?

No, she said.

What's the matter? I said in a baby voice.

I want my Gary, she said.

I lay down beside her and touched my nose to her cheek. I pulled my fingers through her hair. I kissed her on the ear.

See? said Galileo.

I know, I said.

What? she asked.

I shook my head and rubbed the back of her neck.

Oh nothing.

Is it him? she asked.

Him she calls me, said Galileo.

Yeah, I said.

Oh poor baby, she said.

You'd think I was a bad influence on you, said Galileo.

But you are, I said.

She smiled through the tears.

You're weird.

I know we are, I said.

Ask her what's going on, said Galileo.

I've got plenty of time for that.

For what? she asked.

It's just him, I said. He's starting to get on my tits.

She struggled up out of the mess of duvet.

Would a smoke help?

I thought you were getting clean?

Yeah, said Galileo. Fucking lying bitch.

She reached to the side of the bed.

They're taking me in Tuesday morning, she said as she straightened up with the foil.

Likely fucking story, said Galileo.

We had a couple of lines each and Galileo seemed to relax. It was good to sit there without him shouting and carrying on. Like I could speak to her without him butting in and getting me all mixed up and flustered.

★

Nigel lay back on his pillow. He stretched his arms and folded them behind his head. The smell of frying bacon filled his nostrils. He thought about Gary and Charlie. It was like a game of chess, he reflected. He'd lost a rook last night but the queen was still in play. By Tuesday he'd have her tucked away in the treatment centre. Then he could sort out his other pieces and checkmate the black king by the end of the week.

He was sure the worst influence on Charlie was Gary. If he could split them apart it would give her the best chance at a new life. Gary's detention was necessary so another human being could escape slavery.

Not professionally ethical, he realised, but when examined through the standards of a higher moral code, surely the right choice.

Gary was irredeemable because his illness could not be cured. It could only be managed. That meant close supervision and a tight medication schedule. If these conditions were not adhered to, members of the public became at risk. When that happened, the law stated he had to be detained. It was a real shame because Gary was probably one of the brightest patients he'd ever had.

But that was where Nigel earned his money. Making tough decisions.

Nigel was fairly sure these judgements would turn out best for Gary. He would most probably have a course of intensive therapy and then be offered rehabilitation in a different county. This episode may become the turning point in his life. A fresh start with some insight into his condition may mean that he accepts his illness and has a chance of moving on.

As for Charlie, Nigel knew that his motivations were complicated by the nature of their relationship. If he was a robot, he was sure he could deal with her in a balanced way. But no man could look at her and not be affected by her beauty and sexuality. She oozed it.

And anyway, sex was the closest two people could get to one another. He truly had feelings for her. If he wasn't a mature man, he could easily mistake them for love.

For the moment she might not be able to see or accept that, but her mind was befuddled by drugs, so if he kept showing her what she meant to him, and she was in the process of getting clean, surely it was only a matter of time before his feelings for her were reciprocated.

His contemplations were interrupted by the arrival of Sarah. She carried a tray. He sat up in the bed and pumped the pillows against his lower back. He put his arms up to receive the food and she kissed him on the cheek as she bent over.

'There you go, sweetheart,' she said.

'Thank you,' he said and straightened the tray on his lap. 'It smells delicious.' He picked up the knife and fork and started eating. 'Lovely,' he said as he chewed.

'I've hardly seen you since I got back from camp,' she said.

'Mm,' he nodded. 'We've both been busy, I guess.'

'Would you like to go to Holkham beach today?' she asked. 'We could make a picnic.'

'Or have a long walk followed by a pub lunch.'

'Yeah,' she said. 'Let's do that.'

*

We went into the living room. I sat on the couch. She opened the curtains and stood there, then she tugged at the belt of her dressing gown and turned round. She walked over to me.

She sat on the coffee table and faced me.

Oh Gaz, I don't want to leave you.

I put my hand on her knee and patted it.

You've got to though, I said, philosophical with smack.

She nodded. A tear escaped from her eye and rolled down her cheek. I reached for her chin.

So where are you going?

Mundesley, she said. It's in North Norfolk.

How long?

She sobbed.

They say up to six months.

I felt like crying myself.

I'll miss you, I said.

She put her hands on my shoulders and leaned forward.

I don't want to leave you Gaz, but he's making me.

Who's making you?

She sniffed a gurgle of snot up her nose.

He is.

Who the fuck is he?

Nigel.

I pushed her away and frowned into her face.

What are you talking about?

He said he'd get me treatment if I stopped seeing you, she said.

I stood up and pointed at her.

I'm going to fuck him right up.

She shook her head like an epileptic.

Don't. Not yet. Let me do the rehab first.

I walked up and down the living room, breathing hard through my nose. If Nigel had walked into the room at that minute I would have stripped my clothes off and killed him. Man on man. No weapons. Just brute force. I would have bit lumps of meat from his body and pulled his eyes out with my fingers.

I walked up to the door and for a second I saw his stupid social worker smile. The one he gives you when he thinks he's helping you. I hate that smile and everything that stands behind it. All the files he's read that makes him think he knows me and the police and the courts that support his skinny little frame.

I clenched my fists and gave the door a right-hander. Bang. It split the panel and shards of wood and paint fluttered to the carpet. I turned to Charlie and she was wedged in the corner of the couch. Her knees high up and her hands across her stomach. For a second I felt like jumping on her. The stupid fucking whore letting cunts like Nigel control her. I raised my fist and looked at her. I tried to tell her what I thought about the whole fucking business. But only a bit came out. I couldn't even think the thoughts through, never mind speak them. I just stood there shaking my fist and breathing hard.

It was like I was balanced on a tightrope. I could fall on the side of peace and talk. Or I could fall on the side of screaming rage.

I looked again at the body I could easily break, and I felt terrible. I sat on the floor and leaned against the opposite side of the couch to her. I put my hand out.

Give me a fag.

We sat in silence. My heart beat slower as I puffed.

Please wait for me, she said.

She moved closer to me.

It'll be worth it Gaz. I promise it will.

★

Nigel rolled his window down as he stopped at the kiosk.

'Busy today,' he said to the attendant.

'There's been a whale washed up on the beach,' the man said as he counted out the change. 'Tom, Dick and Harry have come to see it.'

Nigel put the coins in the tray under the stereo and drove into a spot fifty yards from the path. They climbed out and he locked the doors.

There were people everywhere. A variety of dogs mingled with Wellington boots. The legs streamed towards the wooden pathways that were built just above the sand.

Nigel didn't like to walk on them. Even though they'd been built to save the beach from the erosion of thousands of footprints, he preferred to step away from the crowd and feel his feet connect with the earth and the grass.

He took Sarah by the arm. 'This way,' he said and they moved between bushes of lavender and blackberries towards the woods. The only person they passed was an old lady with a Labrador.

They walked round a marsh and up a hill and were alone in the trees. The wind in the boughs sounded like the sea.

'You won't believe this,' said Nigel as his hands swept round the emptiness of the forest, 'but when it's dark, this place is really busy.'

'Why's that?' she asked.

'It's a cruising haunt,' he said. 'Apparently people come from miles.'

'Nice pun,' she said.

'Very good, darling,' he said.

'Have you been here before?' she asked with raised eyebrows.

'Yeah,' he said, 'but only at night.'

They arrived at the edge of the woods and stepped into an expanse of undulating sands. The sea was in the distance. It had a cloud-strewn sky moving above it.

They piled down one mound and panted up the next. Nigel's thighs started to ache. The wind whipped at his ears and odd pieces of grit seemed to tear at his cheeks.

'Beautiful,' he said when they reached the last of the dunes. He stood at the top and put his arm out for her. She cuddled up beside him. They watched a trail of people march along by the side of the water.

'It's like a scene from the Bible,' she said. 'Or Europe after the war.'

'Come on then,' said Nigel as he grabbed her hand. They both called 'Wee' as they went stumbling down the slope and slowed to a walk as they reached the flats.

★

I left Charlie's in a fucking rage. I walked towards Nigel's house. I stomped along paths and roads with my eyes on the ground. I kicked an empty can into the middle of a road.

I'm going to kill him, I said.

You should calm down, said Galileo.

Shut up you cunt, I said.

Fucking idiot, he said. I don't know why I bother with you.

I pointed up the street.

Well leave then, go and find somebody else to live off. But there was no way that was happening. He started talking like someone on speed.

You should realise how lucky you are to have me. Most people don't have the benefit of a wise voice that can give them advice when they're in a hard spot. They have to do this life on their own. But not you. You've got me, watching everything around you, and making sure you don't do anything stupid.

You'd be fucked if I wasn't looking after you. You'd be sitting in a ward, snivelling to some cunt-faced shrink about the voices in your head. Please doctor, he's telling me to hurt people, please doctor he's telling me to wank myself in public, please doctor please doctor please doctor please doctor please doctor please doctor.

Shut the fuck up, I screamed.

For a moment there was a silence that seemed to extend from my body to the street. A man walking on the opposite pavement stopped and looked at me. Then he got on with his life.

I stood there and felt the emptiness gradually fill with cars and buses and people, beeping traffic lights, passing music and pinging shop doors.

The whole world swirled round me in a giant cake-mix. I scanned the mess and the only fixture was the sign for the Cricketers.

I ran for the door and pulled inside. I went to the bar and ordered a beer. As I swigged it the Sunday afternoon crowd seemed to swell and take up more of my room. I could feel them push against me and I got closer and closer to the wall, every little contact making me retreat into myself.

The atmosphere was so hot I thought I was going to explode and end up killing some cunt.

Go to the toilet son, said Galileo.

When I got in there, I splashed some water onto my face, then I examined it in the mirror. It seemed as if there were maggots crawling under my skin. Four of them. One wriggled under my eyes and my vision twirled in another massive whirlpool. I had to hang onto the sink in case I fell to the floor.

You're in a bit of a state, said Galileo.

I'm going to kill that cunt, I said.

Don't be stupid, go home and have a sleep.

He only lives round the corner.

Don't go round there, said Galileo.

Why the fuck not? I asked.

You'll go straight to jail.

So fucking what?

Would you like the world to view you as the father of modern psychology, or just another nutter that wanted to kill his social worker?

OK, I said. But I'm going to burst.

He pointed at the condom machine.

Headbutt that.

I walked over and banged it.

Harder, he said.

So I did. Again and again I hit it with my head, till the metal started to fold in on itself.

Come here, he said, and I went back to the mirror. I saw myself with blood running from my forehead down my face.

Go home, he said. Have a sleep.

I walked back into the pub. People turned around as I passed, and I saw them nudge each other. One old man asked if I was all right.

I stopped and stared at him. His lips moved up and down his teeth and his tongue wriggled like a snake.

Ignore him, said Galileo. Just get out of here.

*

The tide was out and the shore seemed to stretch for ever. They stuck their heads down and put their hands in their pockets. Nigel wrapped his scarf tight around his neck. In the distance he saw a concentration of people.

'There it is,' he said as he pointed.

They walked with renewed vigour. Sarah hooked her arm into his. 'This is nice,' she said and leaned against him. 'We should do more things together.'

'Cold though,' he said to her watery eyes.

'We can keep each other warm,' she said as she pulled herself closer to him.

As they got nearer they could see the clothes people were wearing and the big black hump they were walking around.

'Can you smell it?' she asked.

They joined the crowd and Nigel circled the whale.

Fluid oozed out of its orifices. He pressed his foot into its hide. He could feel the meat give. It felt kind of hollow. A great inert beast he could kick at will.

'You wouldn't do that if it was alive,' said Sarah.

He turned to her and put his foot on the carcass and his arm on his hip. He felt like a great hunter without a rifle.

'Me bring food to wife,' he said.

'Only if animal accept debit card,' she said and there was a titter from a woman in the crowd.

Nigel dropped his arms to his side and walked to the water's edge. Foam travelled in with the waves and was left in crescents on the beach. He stood and looked far out to sea. Towards Europe and Scandinavia. He breathed the air in and out. Deep and slow.

Gulls soared above the shallows. They held themselves still in the air and flew in and out of each other's wakes. Sometimes they settled for a float on the water.

'Shall we get back?' asked Sarah's voice behind him. He turned and she grabbed him by the arm.

When they finally reached the parking lot, she went to the toilet and he waited in the car. He checked his mobile for messages. There weren't any. He wrote one to Charlie.

How u doin?

He pressed send just as Sarah arrived. She pulled on her seatbelt.

'Are we off then?' she asked.

★

I wasn't long home when there was a knock on the door. I opened up and there was two people standing there. A man about forty and a girl. She was so tasty I was tempted to let them in.

Have you heard the good news? asked the man.

The girl smiled. She looked bored. I stared at her teenage tits and she stopped smiling. I felt warm in my pants and would have touched my dick if I wasn't holding a knife. They couldn't see it. It was hidden behind the half-open door.

I focused back on the man, the religious maniac who exposes his child to devils like me.

What good news? I said to him.

You are going to hell, but the Lord Jesus Christ can save you and give you everlasting life.

So where is he? I asked.

The maniac looked confused.

Jesus is everywhere.

I can't see him. Can you? I asked him.

I looked at the girl.

Can you?

Both shook their heads but the maniac wasn't finished with me.

You seem pained brother. Maybe we can help you.

I took a direct hit there and pushed the point of the knife into the door. I heard it scrape through the paint and into the wood. A couple of flakes of gloss fell on the carpet.

How? I asked.

By showing you the way, the truth and the light.

The girl smiled at these words and I felt the light. My cock also felt the light.

The maniac passed me a leaflet.

We are all sinners, but thanks be to Jesus we are saved. I watched his tongue flick out and lick the crease of his lips. He kept talking. All I heard was one phrase.

He died on the cross for all of us.

The rest was covered by Galileo going.

Blah, blah, blah. Bullshit, bullshit, bullshit.

He wanted me to look at the girl.

Ask them in, he said.

No, I said.

Smell her tight little cunt, he said.

No, I said louder.

The maniac stopped talking. He focused on me and frowned.

Come to our service this afternoon, he said and passed me a pamphlet.

I'll think about it.

I closed the door and re-did the locks. I could smell the girl. Delicious it was. A vision of her floated through my mind. She looked happy and good. She had a skirt on and no tights. I went hard thinking about her. I kissed her and rubbed her legs. She moaned and licked her lips. I went on my knees and kissed her shins. I lifted her skirt and kissed her fluffy thighs.

She whispered no, please God no. She put her hand on my head and pulled me close. I went up her legs and sniffed her pussy through her pants. It smelled lovely. Just a hint of piss. Warm it was. I put my tongue under her knickers and tasted salt. She moaned and gripped my ears harder.

I wanked till I came on my hand. Then I went to the bathroom and cleaned off on paper. I flushed the toilet and washed myself.

Galileo watched from the mirror.

You're a dirty pig, he said.

I couldn't hold his stare and my eyes wandered to the floor.

*

There was a girl on the street corner when they got home from the beach. Nigel noticed her skinny white legs and his heart thumped in his chest. He tried not to stare as he passed but his eyes kept flicking back.

'How any man could pay to have sex with that poor woman, I don't know,' said Sarah.

Nigel had another glance and realised it was Charlie. He locked eyes with her and she nodded like a defiant child.

His life was sucked into a sewer laden with shit and condoms and semen-crusted toilet paper. He coughed and focused on Sarah.

'Yeah, shameful,' he stuttered. 'That's what drugs do to you.'

'Do you know her?' asked Sarah.

'No,' he said, trying to control his shaking hands. 'How would I?'

'I don't know,' she said with a shrug. 'From work?'

Sarah unlocked the front door and went in. Nigel had a last look at Charlie and felt helpless in her smile. He stepped into the house. He went to the toilet. He heard Sarah put cutlery in the sink as he checked his mobile phone. He tapped out a message.

What u doin?

When he came out of the toilet Sarah was changing the bag in the bin. He lifted out the full one and placed it by the side of the back door.

He felt his phone buzz. He slid it out of his pocket and opened the message. It was from Charlie.

Mind ur own business.

The phone buzzed again as he had it in his hand.

Duz ur wife no bout us?

He replied.

Can I come and cu 2moro? I got u a present.

He put the rubbish bag in the outside bin and went back into the kitchen. He reached past Sarah and washed his hands in the dishwater.

'Do you have to do that?' she asked.

'Sorry,' he said and dried his hands on the tea towel. He was about to kiss her on the back of the neck when he felt his phone vibrate in his pocket. He went into the living room and sat on the couch as he read the text.

Yes. 1pm at mine.

'Do you want a cup of tea?' asked Sarah from the kitchen.

'Yes please,' said Nigel.

*

The church had a ragged hedge round it and a notice board with a sign saying, Surrender and be Saved.

I had timed it just right. They were going in for the seven o'clock service as stated in the pamphlet. I'd taken a couple of Valium, so following the herd into the building was easy.

When the crowd settled itself down the maniac came onto the stage. I didn't realise he was the minister. He was well dressed and charismatic. If I was one of the congregation I'd wonder where he got the money for the suit, but this lot seemed charmed by the easy smile and the biblical quotes.

The meek will inherit the earth, said Galileo with a laugh.

As the maniac chanted, some of the audience stood up with their arms outstretched.

Praise be, they called.

I was on the verge of leaving, when the angel appeared. She looked even more virginal than when I saw her at my doorstep. A vision in white she was, and an advert for God's heaven. I relaxed back into my chair. This was not the moment to go. Not when redemption might be forthcoming.

She was reluctant to come onto the stage. She shook her head but the maniac waved her on.

I believed at that moment there was something beautiful running this world. I could feel the heartbeat of baby Jesus at one with mine. I almost stood up with the fools shouting hallelujah brother I have been saved. But I was too self-conscious for that.

The maniac grabbed the microphone.

I'd like to introduce my daughter, who has just had her A-level results.

The girl blushed and bent her head towards the floor. The maniac went on.

We're pleased the Lord Jesus has blessed our house with such an intelligent young lady. And we will make sure she uses this God-given talent to spread the message of hope to the unfortunates of this world.

The crowd shouted some more sycophantic rubbish. I hardly heard them though. I was staring at the beauty on the stage.

I'd ride that in the arse, said Galileo.

Don't be so fucking filthy, I said.

The woman on the next seat heard me. I could feel her shuffle away from me.

The maniac ushered his daughter off the stage, then he did a lecture on backsliding. We need to be constantly vigilant because the devil sneaks in upon us by degree. First it might be the dishonesty of keeping something that we've found on the street. Then a cashier gives us too much change and we don't say anything. A few white lies to the wife about a late evening's work and we're on the road to perdition. Next thing we know we're robbing banks and the devil's stoking up the fire because he knows he can burn our arses for ever.

The maniac slammed the lectern.

How would you like it if you'd lost your wallet, and someone found it and didn't hand it in?

The crowd nodded to the stage and each other as if they were learning a new philosophical concept. Honesty.

Like most of them weren't honest anyway. These were the sort of people who wouldn't dream of keeping someone's wallet if they found it on the street.

Now me, I'd have it spent on drink before the day was out.

A different philosophical concept called responsibility. If a man loses his wallet and gets it handed in, then he's not likely to learn anything. But if he loses it and doesn't see it again, perhaps the next time he'll take better care of his possessions.

The ranting maniac brought me back to the sermon. He reached a bellowing climax and there was a thunderbolt silence. Then he wiped his sweaty brow and the crowd stood on their feet and went mental with frothing adoration.

Hah-leh-fucking-luja, said Galileo.

They started to file out and I slotted myself into the flow. I got to the door and felt a tug on my arm. It was the maniac.

Good to see you brother.

I nodded and tried to smile.

Likewise, I said.

He put his hand out and we shook. He told me his name.

Frank.

And earnest, said Galileo.

Gary.

Did you enjoy the service?

It was all right, but I'm not sure I belong here.

He cocked his head like a bird.

Why is that? he asked.

I don't believe in God.

The maniac smiled and glanced around as if he was afraid of eavesdroppers.

Shall I tell you a secret?

He's a paedophile, said Galileo.

I didn't believe, said the maniac. But I kept coming and the love of Jesus Christ our saviour just wrapped me up till I had to acknowledge there was a miracle working in my life.

Fuck off, said Galileo.

The maniac inspected me with an intensity I hadn't been aware of before.

Well keep trying brother. Someday soon you'll notice the difference and then you'll wish you'd seen it years before.

I worked my way through the happy mass. A few of them smiled at me as I squeezed past the front door. I stepped down onto the pavement and walked till I was alone. I wondered if the love of Jesus had entered my body and I was now under his protection.

Don't be fucking stupid, said Galileo.

As he spoke, a car came racing along the road, and I knew I was as vulnerable as ever. A youth was driving and he had a girl in the passenger seat. They were talking and he was going too fast for the attention he was paying to the street. I backed into a gate as they flew past. All it would take would be a bump on the road and he could swerve onto the pavement and kill me.

Just like that, said Galileo and clapped his hands together.

Dead.

At that moment I knew no one was looking after me but me. I hunched my shoulders up and walked home, keeping my eye open for troublemakers.

*

Galileo and Chastity stood in the middle of the lights. The sound of ladders being climbed got louder. Sometimes it was like it came from their left. Then from their right. Then behind them and in front of them.

Galileo realised they were being surrounded. He stood closer to Chastity.

Turn off the lights, he said.

She touched his elbow.

That's not the solution.

The clamour increased until it sounded like the marching of a victorious army. Hands gripped the tops of the ladders and pulled men from the tunnels. Big ugly men with bad teeth and warts on their faces. Twenty or thirty of them and more pouring out of the holes. One stood taller than the rest. He walked towards them.

It was Gaston.

Long time no see, Legionnaire, he called.

He came closer and Galileo could see veins pulsing on his forehead.

The others came in different directions until they formed a solid wall of staring eyes and broken noses. An unbreakable circle of ugliness.

What do you want? shouted Galileo.

Gaston stood over him as a man to a child. He raised his hand and struck so hard Galileo was knocked to the floor.

As he lay on the concrete he heard Chastity scream. He looked up. Two of the thugs had grabbed her by the arms and a third was feeling her breasts.

Lovely titties, he said through broken teeth.

Another brushed his hand between her legs.

Sticky cunt, he said and a few of them laughed.

Fuck, fuck, fuck, they shouted.

Galileo tried to stand, but Gaston put his foot on his chest and sent him back to the floor. Galileo could only stay there and wait for whatever happened.

Take her away, said Gaston, pointing to a distant ladder.

Chastity was dragged off between two of the men. Her heels left lines on the floor. As they bundled her into a hole, her ankle caught on the edge and one of her shoes was clipped from her feet. It was left behind like Cinderella's.

Gaston and Betts stood over Galileo with their hands on their hips.

It's been a long time, said Betts, bending over.

Galileo tried to sit up.

Why are you doing this? he asked.

Gaston kicked his hand away so he fell back down.

We ask the fucking questions.

What about Chastity?

Gaston kicked him in the side.

She is not your concern. She belongs to us now.

The two men set about Galileo with boots to the head and body.

Next time we see you we'll fucking kill you, said Gaston, between grunts.

When they'd hit him enough, they left him alone with his head against the concrete.

The beating showed him how small he was. Like a microbe in the middle of the dark sphere that was his home. It was while lying there that he realised there was no escape. If he walked for days, or weeks, or years, he would eventually come back to this place, the lights, and the table and chairs.

A tear ran from his eye down the side of his cheek. He felt it tickle as it reached his neck. He wiped his hand over his face and sniffed. He sat up and the pain in his head thumped hard before easing into a steady beat. He looked across the floor and saw her shoe, laid on its side, a half-torn price tag on the instep. He crawled over to it and picked it up. He sniffed it and held it close to his chest.

Chastity, where are you? he asked and sobbed like a child.

He sat there, holding the shoe, rocking back and forward, trying to work out what to do next.

*

I snatched the cans and inspected them as Hitler ranted in the background. Chris looked at me a bit strange.

Search him, said Galileo.

Sit down, I told Chris.

Search the cunt, he might have a knife.

What do you want? I asked Chris.

He blinked at me like a rabbit.

You told me to come over.

He's lying, said Galileo.

Shut up, I shouted.

Chris flinched and sat on the floor.

See what you're doing? I said to Galileo.

Behave, said Galileo.

I glanced round the room then back to Chris.

Sorry mate, I'm not feeling very well.

I handed him one of the beers and opened one myself. We swigged from them as we watched the telly. Von Paulus had surrendered the sixth army at Stalingrad. Hitler slammed his fist on a map-covered table. Russian trains brought one hundred new tanks to the front.

I picked up another can and opened it. Chris didn't take his eyes from the screen. He was like a dead person who drank beer and smoked fags and sucked in images from the telly. Maybe he took the odd shit but dead people have shits, and snot, they even grow hair and nails.

Chris had long fingernails. Dirty they were and yellow with nicotine and God knows what else. I asked him when he'd last been with a woman and he told me back in the eighties.

Probably wanks a lot though, said Galileo.

Out of the four cans, I drank three of them. By the time they had worked their way through my system, I felt easier. Like the pressure was off. I wasn't so aware of where the knife was. I even looked at Chris and thought he wasn't such a bad guy. Not bad company really.

Then I spotted a drip of snot on the end of his nose. He fumbled in his pocket for his hanky. Pulled it out and opened it like a well-stuck envelope. And he didn't blow his nose. He just wiped it and sucked most of the snot back up.

He had a swig of beer. I prodded him on the shoulder.

Have you got any more?

No.

You sure?

Yeah, he said. Honest.

Stalin smiled from the telly.

I'm choking for another one, I said.

Sorry mate but I've none left.

That was what I hated about beer. You have two or three and all you want is a load more.

I picked up the knife and turned the point into the coffee table. I chiselled away at the hole. Then I cleaned my nails with it. It was a delicate operation using such a big knife. Chris started to fidget. I flicked the blade and it pinged like a sword or a bell. And he flinched with the noise. I felt an impulse to run it into the soft part of his side. Just under the ribs and into his kidneys and liver. Then twist it round to do the maximum damage. Every time he flinched the impulse got stronger.

I stood up quickly. Chris jumped back to the wall.

What's the matter?

Have you got any money?

He glanced at the front door.

I've got some.

Just take it off him, said Galileo.

Where? I asked.

Chris reached for his back pocket. He pulled out two tenners.

That's all I've got, he said.

Shall we get some gear? I asked with my best smile.

Don't beg him, said Galileo.

I didn't have to. Chris nodded like a child promised sweets.

I turned the telly off. He stood up.

Do you mind if I go to the toilet first? he asked.

He left the room and I rummaged around for a piece of paper. I found an old letter from the DSS. It was a statement about an increase in my payments. I tore a corner off that had no writing on it. Big enough for what had to be done. The envelope was a bit crumpled but I smoothed it out on the coffee table.

When Chris came back I pointed to the paper.

I want you to write a letter for me.

Who to? he asked as he approached.

Never mind that, I'll dictate and you put it down. OK?

He started writing. When he was finished I pointed to the envelope.

Address it to Mrs Sarah Paston, I said.

He did it.

Put it in your pocket, I said.

We went outside. It was quiet on the streets. Most people were in bed. Maybe they weren't sleeping too well because they knew the weekend was over and in the morning it was up for work.

Fuck that.

I'm glad I'm mad at two o'clock on a Monday

morning. While everybody else is struggling with the knowledge of impending slavery, I'm prowling the streets spying in their daughter's bedroom window.

We headed into the night, me and Chris.

★

The spider had almost crossed the ceiling. The man groaned and came inside her. Charlie turned from him as he climbed off the bed. He pulled the drooping condom from his dick and held it in front of him.

What shall I do with this? he asked.

She pointed at the bin.

Just wrap it in tissue and chuck it in there.

He pulled his trousers on and she wrapped a dressing gown around herself. He looked flushed and pleased and shamed by what they'd done. She walked him to the door. He reached into his wallet and gave her another tenner.

I'll phone you next week, he said.

As he passed she gave him a kiss on the cheek.

OK. Drive safe on the way home.

She closed the door and locked it. Then she went into the bedroom and put the tenner with the rest of her money. A hundred and fifty quid. Enough to give Gaz a going-away present.

★

Clive handed me a wrap.

Thirty nicker, he said.

I gave him three tens.

Cheers. All right if we have a smoke before we go? He gave me an ugly grimace but nodded his head. I put some skag on the foil and heated it with the lighter to melt it. As I sucked it into my chest I could feel instant relief. The world and all its shit receded from my mind like waves from a beach. Galileo shut his mouth. I was becalmed on an island without a thing to bother me.

Nice gear, I said.

Clive nodded, smug as a Christian.

It's the best around at the minute.

I passed it to Chris, who got straight in there, his head bent and lungs going like bellows.

The boy's taken to it like a duck to water, I said to Clive.

He nodded and rubbed his hands together.

Looks like I'll be seeing plenty of him.

I laughed.

You should give me a commission on everything he smokes.

Monday, 17th May 2004

Nigel produced a box of chocolates from behind his back. She looked at them with her lips twisted. 'I can't eat those,' she said.

'Why not?' he asked.

'I'm fucking sick, you idiot,' she said as she ran to the toilet. He heard her retch.

'Have you got a bug or something?' he asked when she came back out.

'No,' she said as she drew the back of her hand across her lips. 'I wish I did.'

'What's the matter then?'

'I'm fucking rattling,' she said and rubbed her red eyes.

'Ah well,' he said, moving forward to give her a reassuring hug, 'you'll be OK tomorrow.'

'Get away from me,' she said as she jumped back from him.

'OK,' he said, holding up his hands.

'Just don't touch me,' she said, shivering. 'I don't like being touched. Especially by men.'

'I'm sorry,' he said. 'I didn't realise you found me so repulsive.'

She didn't reply. She tightened the belt of her dressing gown, turned round and walked to her bedroom. He stood and watched her disappearing back before he realised he still had the chocolates in his hand. He went into the kitchen and put them on the worktop. Then he went after her.

She was sitting on the edge of her bed. He looked at the pile of clothes on the floor.

'How's the packing going?' he asked.

'I'll do it later.'

'Do you want any help?'

'You just want to get your hands on my pants,' she said.

'You need to get it done for tomorrow.'

'I know,' she said, scratching deep into her scalp. 'I know,' she repeated.

Nigel took a breath and sat beside her on the bed. She didn't move or say anything. He put his hand on her shoulder.

'What do you think you're doing?' she asked as she shrugged him off.

'You seem to be forgetting,' he said as he got up and walked to the window, 'that I'm doing you a big favour.'

'Now we're getting somewhere,' she said lighting a cigarette. 'You want a fuck before I go.'

He turned round and she lay back on the bed. She undid the belt of her dressing gown. She pulled it open to show her stomach and a little bit of hair. 'Is this what you want?' she asked as she rubbed her hand down through her pubes.

He felt disgusted and horny at the same time. She

parted her legs and slid her finger between the lips of her vagina. She had a puff on her fag, and then dropped it in an ashtray. 'Come on then,' she said, blowing smoke, 'be man enough to take what you want.'

Nigel went to the bed and lay down beside her. He tried to kiss her but she pulled away. 'Just put your dick in me,' she said with her hands on the buttons of his trousers. She opened them up and stroked it as she manoeuvred him onto her.

He went to push inside her but she struggled out of his way.

'Put a rubber on, you dirty cunt,' she said as she reached for her bedside cabinet. She threw a package at him. He tore it open and rolled it on.

He got back between her thighs.

'That's it, Nigel, fuck me,' she gasped. He jerked in and out and came within seconds.

He felt his heart beat as he lay on top of her.

'Get off me,' she said.

She got up and left the room. He heard the bathroom door closing and the lock clicking. A couple of minutes later the toilet flushed.

He pulled his trousers up before she came back into the bedroom.

'I'm not well,' she said as she lay down and cuddled up to one of her pillows.

'You'll be going into treatment tomorrow,' he said. 'It's not long to wait.'

'You don't understand,' she said. She sat up and looked into his eyes. 'If I don't get something soon, I'm out the door.'

He looked at the rumpled sheets and a cigarette end on the carpet. 'It's just one day,' he said.

'You don't fucking care,' she spat through her teeth, 'that's what the problem is.'

'Of course I care,' he said. 'Why do you think I've organised the rehab?'

'But that's no good to me today,' she said. 'I'm a fucking junky. I need my medicine.' Her voice changed and she sounded like a public information film. 'I might go into a fit. Or have a heart attack.'

He didn't say anything. She started to cry.

'I'm sick, I'm fucking sick,' she said as she reached up and held his hands. 'Please help me, Nigel. I'm begging you.'

'OK,' he sighed, 'I'll take you to the dealer's.' He pulled his car keys out of his pocket and fiddled with them. 'You better get dressed.'

'But look at me,' she said, holding her stomach. 'I'm not well enough to go out.'

'What do you want from me?'

'If I phone him and give you the money,' she pleaded, 'could you get it for me?'

*

Chris stood in the middle of the death room with his arms out.

Wow, he said.

He went up to the writing and started to drag his finger along it as he read.

I didn't know you were in the Foreign Legion, he said.

Just for six months. They gave me a discharge because I went mental.

Chris looked at the sphere.

And what's this?

It's a model for the human psyche.

That shut him up.

I sorted through the pipes we got from Homebase. They were all jumbled up like a plate of multi-coloured spaghetti. I grabbed the end of a rubber hose and jerked it free of the pile. I cut off a six-foot length. Then I inserted one end through a spring and into a hole in the globe. With a pair of pliers I gripped the wire and squeezed it so the hose was firmly attached. The other end I lifted as I climbed the stepladder. I held it up as I pointed to the corner.

Pass me that hammer, I said.

Chris picked it up and handed it to me. With a couple of bangs the tube was attached to the ceiling.

I got off the ladder and stood on the floor, looking up. The hose hung there in a curve.

Not bad, I said and Chris nodded.

I turned to him with the pliers.

Do you think you could do that?

He frowned and nodded like a teenager.

Yeah. Easy.

I pulled out another length. A yellow one. I cut a four-foot span of it and handed it to him.

Here, do this one.

I stood back and watched him. He was a bit clumsy but managed to fix it to the sphere.

Well done mate, I said and patted his back.
He gave me a smile.

Do you want me to clip on any more? he asked.

I cut another length and told him where to fasten it. As he plugged it into the hole I grabbed my hammer and a nail. I picked up the other end of the hose and attached it to the wall.

We inserted one after the other and before long the model had hoses coming out from all the holes. They were intertwined with each other, and hanging loose or fixed to the ceiling and walls.

Chris sat on the floor and leaned against the wall.

It looks like an octopus, he said.
He spun his hands around like a hippy dancer.

With its tentacles twisting through the sea as it swims, he said.

I nodded at him, but I thought it was more like a tarantula, with its legs laced amongst its web. As if it was waiting for the vibration of an insect as it bumbles into the sticky weave. And there it would panic and coil the threads around itself until the spider walked from the middle and inserted a paralytic poison into its neck.

Chris buzzed like a fly.

Do you want me to roll you a fag? he asked.

Yeah, nice one kid.

As he got his tobacco out I examined the hole at the bottom of the globe. It needed expanding so I went into the kitchen and fetched through my nine-inch knife. I sawed into the paper and made it bigger.

Could you get your head in there? I asked.
He came over and tried to stick it in but it caught him

round the ears. I pulled him out of the way and sawed some more.

Try again, I said.

He managed to get it in this time, with room to spare.

I went into the living room and opened the cupboard. Inside was a biscuit tin filled with electrical equipment. One of the bits was an old Bakelite adaptor that you could plug into a light socket and get a power supply. Attached to it were two wires with insulated crocodile clips at the end of them.

I went back into the bedroom and turned the light on and off. When I was sure it was off I took the bulb out and inserted the adaptor. The wires dangled but with the insulation they would be quite safe, even if the electricity was turned on again.

I looked at Chris.

I'm going to need your help here mate.

He bobbed up and down like a nervous beggar.

I want to attach these clips to your ears and stick your head up into the globe, I said.

He shook his head.

Fuck that, he said.

I was surprised by the strength in his voice.

I won't turn the electric on, I said.

No chance. It might kill me.

I walked closer to him.

Don't you trust me?

His voice started to quiver.

Yeah but.

I stood under the model and picked up the clips.

There's no power on, I said.

I don't know, he stuttered.

I attached them to my own ears.

See? I asked.

He was still frozen, so I spoke gently.

I just want to see if the model appears balanced when someone's head is in it. Come on Chris, help me out here.

He couldn't meet my eyes, but he kept shaking his head.

No, I'm not doing it.

I pulled the wires off and walked up to him. He backed against the wall. I leaned my hand above his shoulder. I tried to sound disappointed.

Fuck sake Chris. I can't believe you don't trust me. I thought we were mates.

I'll stick my head in, but you're not putting the clips on my ears.

I smiled.

OK, I said.

As he walked over to the model I spoke in a soft voice.

I mean it's no problem mate. It would be a lot better if you could put them on but if you can't do it, you can't do it.

I could see he was wavering so I hit him with the trump.

I've got some gear left.

His eyes brightened at that.

If I wear the clips will you promise not to turn on the electric? he asked.

What do you take me for? Of course I won't.

His face fell back to the floor.

I don't know Gaz.

I went through to the living room and brought out the tin foil.

Why don't you have a smoke and think about it?

He grabbed the drugs like he already had a habit. I watched him puff away and the nervousness leave his body as he relaxed into the heroin. When he'd smoked half a dozen lines I cleared my throat. He looked at me, holding his breath.

Are you ready then? I said.

He nodded and walked over to the sphere.

You're not going to turn the electric on? he asked.

I looked into his eyes.

Of course I'm not. You should trust me. We're pals, aren't we?

He nodded. His face was covered in sweat. Stupid really, because that makes the electric conduct better.

He ducked down by the globe and I clipped the wires to his ears.

Right, stand up, I told him.

He pushed his head up and it slid inside. His body was shaking.

That's it, I said. You stay right where you are.

I walked over to the light switch. I put my hand on it and pressed it a little. Like it was a gun and I was squeezing to find the point just before it fired.

And it amazed me how far I could push. It was like the last couple of millimetres were the ones to click the gate that released a torrent of electricity. It would come gushing up the wires and into his brain, flooding his senses with everything he'd ever seen until he drowned in a pool of his own being.

I let the switch go and went back to the sphere. I pulled him from underneath and he popped his head out. He smiled and blinked his eyes. It was like he wasn't sure if he was alive or dead.

All right mate? I asked.

Yeah fine.

That wasn't so bad, was it?

He didn't say anything so I pointed to the gear.

Do you want another smoke?

*

Charlie walked up and down the living room. She picked her phone off the coffee table and found his number.

What's going on? she asked.

He's just nipped out to get it.

Did you give him the money?

Yeah, of course I did.

She almost threw her phone at the door.

He won't come back you stupid cunt.

I'm in his flat. Where's he going to go?

She couldn't be bothered explaining.

Just hurry up Nigel. I'm not well at all.

She ended the call and fell back into the couch.

She stood up and lit a cigarette. She stared out of the window. She glanced at the clock. She flicked the ash. She picked up her phone and dialled.

Hello?

It's Charlie.

There was a pause.

What do you want?

I need to see you.

He didn't say anything.

She started to cry.

Gaz?

What?

I really need to see you.

I thought you were going to the rehab?

She rubbed her eyes and sniffed up a load of snot.

That's tomorrow. I want to see you before I go.

She could hear him breathing.

Gaz?

What?

Can I come over?

When?

The call waiting sound came on her phone.

I need to hang up. I'll call you back in a minute.

Char –

She clicked the button to swap the call.

Hello?

I've got it.

Well get over here.

He wants another twenty.

Just give him it.

I've only got a tenner.

Put him on.

The phone rustled and Clive spoke.

All right, Charlie?

Let him have the gear, she said. I'll give you the cash later.

I would darling, but according to your boyfriend here, I'm not going to see you again. Am I?

I've spent thousands with you Clive.

That's yesterday's news. You know that.

She wiped the sweat from her forehead.

For fuck sake.

Swearing at me won't help.

I'm sorry.

Clive laughed and she knew what to do.

I'll get Gaz to give you the money.

Last I heard you were finished.

I was just speaking to him. He asked if he could sort anything out for me.

Did he?

She didn't say anything.

OK, Charlie. I'll let you have it this time.

She hung up and phoned Gaz.

Hello it's me again.

So you can talk to me now?

She tried to sound sweet.

Sorry. I'm not well and needed to sort out a message.

I thought you were getting clean.

Starting tomorrow I will be.

I hope so.

Can I come and see you later?

*

Galileo wiped the tears from his face and the snot from his nose. He sat up and looked around the dome. There was nothing left to do but climb into the hole where they had dragged Chastity.

He took it slowly so the ladders didn't creak and nobody would know he was there. He came into a tunnel that was high enough to walk along. Occasionally he felt a strong wind and the sound of an electric motor whining past and away into the distance.

He stepped into another tunnel that was well lit. It was filled with people moving along. He followed the crowd and came to an escalator. He mounted it and stood behind a woman in a suit. She carried a brief-case. He tapped her on the shoulder. She wheeled round and blinked at him.

Yes?

Where are we?

She studied him, as if he was crazy or something.

King's Cross, she said and walked through a turnstile.

Galileo squeezed through the exit of the tube station. He moved across the pavement till he was against a street barrier. Then he stopped and glanced up and down the road.

A man with a bent back approached.

Galileo, he said in a hoarse voice.

The man smiled. He had two front teeth missing and a scar across his dead left eye.

Don't you recognise me? he asked.

Galileo leaned closer.

What are you doing in these parts?

Raphael brushed his lank hair from his forehead.

Begging.

Galileo frowned at the former soldier.

What happened to you?

The crack got me.

That's terrible mate.

Could you spare me a tenner?

Galileo peeled one from a wad and held it out.

Have you seen Chastity?

Raphael's eyes glinted at the money.

Forget about her.

Why's that?

She's fucked.

Where is she?

She's working at Gaston's.

Show me, said Galileo.

Raphael looked scared. He shook his head

That cunt can fuck a man up.

I'll give you the rest of my money.

Raphael picked at a scab on his face. The skin on his cheek twitched. Then he nodded.

Follow me.

They crossed Euston Road and walked up Argyle Street. On the other side he saw a line of men. Mainly young, they looked like well-off builders having a big spend on wages night. Some of them were boisterous with drink.

At the head of the queue there was a doorway with a neon sign above it. It said Gaston's.

Raphael led him into an alleyway. Galileo looked at him.

What was going on there?

You'll see.

They came to a set of iron stairs. Raphael pointed.

You'll find her up there.

Galileo gave him a few notes.

You said you'd give me it all, said Raphael.

Don't be so fucking greedy.

Raphael scuttled off muttering and Galileo climbed the steps.

When he got to the first floor he walked along a ledge before he came to a window. Light shone through parted curtains. He put his face close to the glass so he could see inside.

Chastity was lying on a bed with her nun's habit on. It was pulled up over her waist and there was a fat man pumping between her legs. A younger man watched from the doorway. He was pushed from behind and came into the room before retreating back.

Fuck off you dirty cunts, he shouted.

Fatso worked faster till he came to a shuddering stop. He lifted himself from her and pulled his trousers up as he left the room.

Chastity reached for a pipe that sat on the bedside table. She lit it and had a long puff. Then she lay back and beckoned. As the youth mounted her she turned to the window. Her eyes were glazed. Her head nodded to the rhythm of thrusts.

Galileo pulled his eyes from the scene. He swallowed a couple of times and took a breath.

He looked around the alleyway, at the gutters and the drainpipes and the blackened brickwork. He tried to think of a way to get her out of there.

He climbed down onto the street. He walked past tramps begging spare change and girls looking for business, men in grey suits and women with expensive shoes. He didn't make eye contact with any of them. He watched the cracks in the pavement disappear beneath his feet. He filtered plans through his brain like a German general trapped in Stalingrad.

He eventually came to a Jet garage. He went to the cubicle and tapped on the glass.

My car's run out of petrol.

A man with a gold tooth sneered at him.

What do you want me to do about it?

Sell me a plastic carton.

They're five pound fifty each.

Galileo dropped a tenner in the tray.

And fill it up.

The man didn't speak till he had the money in his hand.

You'll need to do that yourself.

Galileo walked back with the petrol container tugging on his arm. On the way he called into a newsagent. He bought a bottle of milk, twenty fags and a box of matches.

★

Charlie's heels left dents in the carpet as she walked into my living room. I gestured to the couch. She peeled off her jacket and I got a whiff of perfume. She flicked her eyes round as she sat down and crossed her legs.

So the decorating isn't finished?

I shrugged.

Nearly. Just got a bit of glossing then I can move the bed back in there.

Can I see?

Maybe later. Do you want a cup of tea?

She nodded and I went into the kitchen.

By the time I brought them back she was smoking a cigarette. She held the pack towards me. I slid one out and lit it. Then I sat down beside her. Really close. My leg touching along the side of hers. I turned and gazed into her eyes.

What's happening?

She glanced at her fag as it brushed against the ashtray.

I'm going away tomorrow.

Yeah you said.

She picked her handbag up from the floor and rummaged around in it.

I've got something for you, she said.

What?

She smiled as she handed me a folded wad of tenners.

I won't need this where I'm going.

She put her hand on my shoulder and pulled me towards her.

I love you Gaz, she said.

*

Nigel went through his front door. Sarah was sitting on the couch watching the television. He found it difficult to look anywhere near her eyes.

'Where have you been?' she asked with a frown.

'Just round the shops and that.'

'Until this time?' she asked as she glanced at her watch.

'Then I went to the pub for a drink.'

'Hope you didn't drive.'

'I only had a lemonade,' he said as he walked to the kitchen. He stopped and turned to her. 'Have you had a good day?' he asked.

She patted the cushion next to her. 'Come and sit down,' she said. 'We need to have a talk.'

'What about?' he asked. His eye was distracted by a crumple of paper on the coffee table. He remembered the receipt from the bank withdrawal.

'Us,' she said. 'Among other things.'

As he moved towards the couch he brushed his hair back with his hand. He stopped when he realised he could smell a trace of Charlie. He stammered, 'I'll just have a pee,' and nodded to the back of the house.

She folded her hands across her chest.

He walked into the toilet and whipped his clothes off. He turned the shower on. He got under and gave himself a good scrub. Then he dried his body and headed for the bedroom.

'Did you just have a shower?' she asked as he sneaked through the living room. He ignored her and jogged straight up the stairs.

As he got dressed he wondered what she wanted. Was it the ticket from the auto bank? Had she seen texts on his phone? He bent down and got it out of his jeans. He flicked through the folders till he opened Charlie. There were three messages halfway incriminating. One was unambiguous. He deleted them all and then the folder.

He pulled his pyjama bottoms up his leg and tried to think of what he could have spent the money on. A drink problem? Gambling? He contemplated drugs and laughed.

'New tyres,' he said as he put on his slippers. He smelled his fingers. They seemed clean, so he took a deep breath and went back down to the living room.

He sat on the couch next to Sarah.

'I really needed that,' he said, smelling his armpits. 'Forgot to put deodorant on this morning.'

'Oh,' she said. She sniffed at him, but didn't seem to notice anything out of the ordinary.

'What do you want to talk about?' he asked.

'When I left for work this morning,' she said as she picked up the piece of paper, 'this was on the mat.' She waved the scrap in the air. 'What's going on?' she asked.

He was trying to say something when she said, 'Are you having an affair?'

'No,' he gasped. 'I love you, I wouldn't even dream of having sex with someone else.'

'So what's this about then?' she asked as she waved the sheet again. 'What were you having a shower for?'

He opened the paper and it wasn't the receipt. It was a note. He started to read.

'Your husband is fucking a prostitute.'

He looked at his wife. He tried to be outraged, but not too much. 'What the hell is this?' he said, holding it up.

She snatched it out of his hand. 'What do you think it is?' she asked and pointed at the words.

'Your husband is fucking a prostitute,' she said slowly, a syllable at a time.

Nigel put his hands together, like he was praying. He took a breath, through his nose and out of his mouth. He studied her face, the wrinkles in her forehead, the hurt in her eyes, and the tightness in her lips.

'Sarah,' he said. 'Somebody is playing a cruel joke on you.' He paused and watched her shaking head before adding, 'On us.'

As he spoke he kept his voice unemotional. At first it seemed as if she didn't believe him, but he kept talking. 'We've been together for ten years,' he said and paused. 'Do you really think I would risk that,' he asked as he frowned at the window, 'for one of those girls out there?'

'There are other things,' she said.

'Like what?'

'You're home late every night.'

'I've got a lot on at work.'

'Showering.'

'So when I stink I'm not allowed to have a wash?' he asked. 'Now you're being ridiculous.'

'It's the combination,' she said. 'You've got to admit it does seem suspicious.'

'Do you trust me?' he asked. 'Because if you don't – '

'But the note,' she said with a shrug. 'Who would do that unless there was an element of truth in it?'

As she asked the question, he saw a glimmer of confusion, or doubt. He interlocked his fingers and placed them on his lap. He spoke with the same measure he used as a witness in court. 'It might have been one of my patients,' he said.

'But why would they do this?' she asked with the note in her hand.

'You know the sort of people I work with,' he said. 'They're damaged, and I really feel for them.' He put his hands out to show his sincerity. 'But sometimes they react to their treatment by blaming the people who are trying to help them.'

He paused.

'You must remember that incident with Doctor Frederick,' he said. 'The young girl who accused him of interfering with her?' She nodded. 'That nearly destroyed his marriage,' he said as he put his hand on her knee. 'Don't let the same sort of thing finish ours.'

He cleared his throat.

'I'm going to break confidentiality here,' he said. 'Are you listening? This is important.'

She nodded again.

'The reason I've been home late is that I've been working with a patient,' he said and folded his arms. 'He's very dangerous and we're in the process of having him detained. I don't want to frighten you, but he's resourceful, and it wouldn't surprise me if he'd managed to gain access to our address.'

As Nigel spoke he noticed her glance at the possible entrances to the room. 'I'm sorry for subjecting you to this,' he went on. 'But I think it might be best if you didn't answer the door until you know who it is.'

He put his hand on her shoulder. 'Maybe we should

make sure you're not in the house on your own,' he said. 'At least until he's under lock and key.'

Sarah moved along the couch as he spoke.

'You're frightening me,' she said.

'We'll be all right,' he said as he let her cuddle into him. 'We just need to be vigilant.'

Tuesday, 18th May 2004

They drove along roads that became increasingly narrow. Hawthorne bushes arched over them and occasionally clipped the side of the car. Charlie stared straight ahead, but turned when she heard Nigel cough. It was a sticky one that made her feel sick. She looked at his big nose and receding chin and a shiver went down her spine.

I need to speak to you, he said.

What about?

Have you told anyone about us? he asked with a frown.

No, she said. Why would I do that?

Someone sent my wife a letter.

Well it wasn't me.

Have you told Gary?

I haven't told anybody.

Are you sure? he asked.

I swear on my mother's life.

They didn't say anything for a few minutes. Charlie reached for the stereo and turned it on. She sucked her tooth at Radio Four and clicked the channels until a drum and bass tune came on. She turned the volume up and banged her knee in time to the music.

The hedges thinned and they were presented with a large white building. It had a lot of windows. Nigel turned the radio off and pointed.

There it is.

Charlie felt her heart leap.

Great.

He patted her leg.

It'll be OK, he whispered.

All right for you to say. I'm the one facing a detox.

You'll soon be leaving here for a new life on the straight and narrow.

Can't wait, she said.

A large sign appeared.

Elizabeth, the Queen Mother Treatment Centre.

As they got closer Charlie noticed that the building needed painting. Nigel drove into the car park and stopped beside a minibus. It was like one from a special school.

We're here then, he said.

Charlie lifted her handbag and held it in her lap. She looked at him.

I'm scared Nigel.

He patted her leg again.

Don't be. It's a good clinic.

Will people be able to come and see me? she asked.

Not for a while.

Why not?

They worry in case people have drugs brought in.

He smiled like a shark.

I'll be able to come though, he said.

That's good, she said.

I'm an official, you see. They assume I'm above reproach.

He pulled his keys out of the ignition and opened his door.

Come on you, he said.

She climbed out and stood by the side of the car. He lifted her case out of the boot and they walked to the entrance.

A couple of blokes stood on either side of the door. As Charlie approached, one of them nodded to the other. He whistled softly as she passed. She smiled at him. He dropped a cigarette and stood on it.

When they got inside Nigel turned to her.

You want to stay away from him, he said.

I'm sure he's all right, she said.

Nigel opened his mouth as if he was about to say something, but he was interrupted when a fat nurse came out of an office. She waddled up to them with a smile and her hand outstretched.

Nigel, good to see you.

He shook her hand.

And this is Charlie, he said.

The nurse smiled and showed them her teeth.

Welcome to the start of your new life.

Charlie felt like gagging but shook the hand.

This place is nice, she said.

Yes we think so.

It used to be a TB hospital, said Nigel.

That's right, said the nurse. It was the sea air.

She started to walk back along the corridor.

Follow me and we'll get you signed in.

They went into an office and she grabbed a clipboard with a form on it. She clicked her pen and asked Charlie where she lived and how old she was. Then she turned over the page.

Who's your next of kin? she asked.

Gary Johnson, said Charlie.

Nigel coughed.

You better have me for that, he said.

Yeah OK, said Charlie.

She pointed at Nigel.

Put him down.

The nurse glanced at them both then wrote down what they said. When she was finished the form she took them to a bedroom. It already had her name written on the door. And opiate detox, and blood-borne virus.

Charlie pointed to the sign.

What's that? she asked.

Nothing to worry about. We say that for everybody with your history. High risk, you see. We'll give you a test when you're clean.

Charlie looked over the back of the door.

Is there no lock? she asked.

Yes, said the nurse as she left the room. It's on the outside.

When the door closed Nigel lifted her case and put it on the bed. He started to put her things away.

Charlie gazed out of the window as the drawers went in and out. Some trees surrounded a piece of lawn. A wooden shed with a wire cage attached to it housed some budgies. She turned to watch him fold her clothes.

Nigel?

He looked at her.

Yeah?

Why did I have to put you down as a next of kin?

He frowned and hesitated.

Who else have you got?

She folded her arms over her chest.

Gary.

He leaned on the wardrobe.

We've already spoken about this. I thought we agreed you weren't going to see him any more?

No, you agreed.

He seemed to grow taller.

Do you want to do this treatment?

She nodded and stared at the floor.

Well I suggest you forget about Gary Johnson and concentrate on your recovery, he said.

She started to cry.

But I love him.

The fact is, Charlie, he's not going to be around when you get out.

Why's that?

His eyes flicked round the room.

You know he's not been well, so we've decided to admit him to hospital.

You mean lock him up.

He shook his head.

It's not like that.

Yes it fucking is, she said. Yes it is.

*

I arranged to meet Chris in the city centre. When I got there he was standing by the market. I spotted him through a gap in the shoppers. He had the fidgety appearance of someone who's been there for a while. I moved towards him, pushing people out of my way. He saw me and smiled.

All right kid? I asked.

He nodded but didn't say anything.

I pointed to a bench.

Shall we have a sit down?

Yeah, he said.

There was room between an old lady and a man with a dog. When we were settled I handed two tenners to Chris.

There's that dosh I owe you.

Thanks, he said, like he wasn't expecting it.

I got a touch last night, so there you go.

He tucked it into his back pocket.

I opened my packet of fags.

Smoke?

He slid one out and I gave him a light. Then I had one myself.

Are you doing anything? I asked as I puffed.

He scratched the back of his neck and shook his head.

No, he said.

Shall we get some gear?

His eyes lit up at that. He'd only being at it for a few days and already he was behaving like a junky. If he wasn't careful he'd be selling his arse in no time.

I stood up.

Come on then.

We went round Clive's and I bought two grams. We didn't have a smoke there. I thought it would be best to go to my house, so I put the smack in my pocket and we went straight down the stairs.

The journey back gave Chris plenty of time to get himself worked up over having some. When we got in the car he drove like a lunatic.

Easy tiger, I said.

He looked at me as if he'd just noticed I was there.

Sorry, he said. Then before long he was bent over the steering wheel and driving fast again.

We made it back to mine without crashing.

What you doing now? I asked.

The realisation that he might not be invited seemed to pass in a crease over his forehead. His leg jumped up and down, his knee hitting the edge of the door. He coughed.

Coming in yours.

Oh do you want a smoke? I asked.

He nodded fast and sucked saliva off his tongue.

Yes please.

I jumped out the car.

You should have said. Come in.

He was out and by my side in a couple of seconds. We piled up the garden path and into the flats. He held the door for me and we went up the stairs.

When we were in the living room I sorted out the foil and gave him a line. Then I took it off him. He seemed disappointed. I smoked a couple of lines myself then looked at him.

There's something I want you to do for me.

What's that? he asked.

I sat the foil on the coffee table.

You trust me, don't you Chris?

He nodded.

Of course I do, he said to the drugs.

★

Nigel fumbled with his hands-free kit as he drove out of the treatment centre. The car skidded slightly on loose gravel when he turned into the main road. When he was safely en route, he dialled a number. He listened to it ring on the loudspeaker.

'Norfolk Mental Health Team.'

'Hello, this is Nigel Paston,' he said. 'Is Doctor Frederick around?'

'Hold the line,' said the receptionist and there was a pause filled with light rock music. She came back on. 'I'll just put you through,' she said and the line crackled before the doctor answered.

'What can I do for you?' he asked.

'It's about Gary Johnson.'

'What's he done now?'

'To start with,' said Nigel, 'he sent my wife a note saying I use prostitutes.'

'And do you?' asked Frederick with a laugh.

'That's not funny.'

'Sorry,' said Frederick. 'Couldn't resist it.'

'It's frightened Sarah,' said Nigel as he scratched his ear. 'She's scared to be at home on her own.'

'Did Gary sign the letter?' asked the doctor.

'He didn't,' said Nigel. 'But it was him.'

'How do you know?'

'It was written on a torn piece of DSS paper,' said Nigel. 'Half of his National Insurance number was on the back of the note.'

'Oh.'

'And his girlfriend works the streets.'

'No need to call in Sherlock Holmes then,' said Frederick. 'Have you confronted him about it?'

'Considering his state of mind,' said Nigel, 'I've been a bit hesitant.'

'I understand.'

'I do think we should section him.'

'If that's your considered opinion,' said Frederick, 'I'll put the wheels in motion.'

'Thank you.'

'Is tomorrow too late, or would you like to lock him up this afternoon?'

'There's no need for sarcasm,' said Nigel.

'I was being serious,' said the doctor.

'I think we can wait until the morning,' said Nigel. He brushed his hand through his hair. 'I'm sorry to get worked up but I'm really concerned.'

'It's tricky working with cases like Mister Johnson,' said Frederick, sounding like a kindly teacher. 'Don't give yourself too much of a hard time about it. Perhaps he will change after another course of medication.'

'Einstein said the definition of insanity was repeating the same mistakes and expecting different results,' quoted Nigel.

'Have you got any better ideas?'

'There must be some other course of treatment.'

'Maybe there is,' said Frederick. 'I'll look into it.'

*

I brought Chris into the death room. The stepladder was sitting under the sphere. I stood next to it and took a deep breath.

It won't be long now, said Galileo.

Come here, I said to Chris.

He walked over.

Remember when you put your head in there? I asked him.

He twitched like a frightened little rabbit.

Nothing bad happened. Did it? I asked.

No, he whispered.

I pointed to the equipment.

I want you to lean on the steps, and do exactly what we did yesterday.

Now? he asked.

I nodded at him as I walked over to the door.

And I want you to do it yourself, I said.

He glanced at me and the sphere.

Do you think you can manage? I asked.

You won't turn the electric on?

Of course not, I said in a soothing voice.

He started to put the clips on his ears.

We'll have a nice smoke afterwards, I said.

I went into the bathroom. Galileo stared at me from the mirror.

I think he might be the one, he said.

I hope so.

Give him another couple of minutes then check him out.

OK, I said.

And be nice to him.

I had a quick piss and walked through to the death room. When I opened the door I could see Chris had climbed onto the ladder. He was resting his bum on one of the steps and his hands were gripping the sides.

That's it mate, I said. I'll be with you in a little while.
He mumbled something. I'm not sure what.

You're doing well kid, I said.

He's just the man, said Galileo.

Do you think? I asked.

What's that? said Chris.

Nothing mate, you just sit there and relax.

Let him out now, said Galileo.

I led him out of the sphere and into the living room. I sat him on the couch and gave him some foil.

Smoke that, I said.

I left him chuffing away and went into the kitchen. I made him a bacon sandwich and a cup of tea. By the time I brought them through he was nodding on the couch.

Chris, I shouted.
He jerked upright.

What? he asked.

Here's a butty and a cup of tea.
He slurped them down and then I gave him a chocolate biscuit.

These are really nice, he said.

I was saving them for special.

He looked at me with the openness only the stoned get.

Thanks mate, he said.

I fetched through another.

There you go son.

He smiled as he opened the wrapper.

You're a real pal, he said.

When he'd drunk his tea I gave him another couple of lines. I turned the telly on and a bit of boxing came on.

I raised my fists.

Stick them up, I said.

I punched him a few times for fun. I even let him get one or two into me.

When the match was finished I clicked the remote and the sound went off. I pushed my hands on my knees and stood up.

Listen Chris, I've got things to do, I said.

He got up from the couch.

OK, I better get home myself, he said.

As he walked through the door I patted him on the back.

Thanks for helping me out with my model. It means a lot to me.

No problem, old mate.

*

Charlie walked along the green-carpeted corridor. A youth in a tracksuit top was leaning on the wall next to the phone. She smiled as she approached him.

Excuse me mate, she said.

He looked at her and mumbled.

What?

Could you spare me fifty pence to make a call?

He didn't say anything but jingled in his pocket and dropped the coin into her outstretched palm.

Cheers love, she said.

You're not allowed to use it without permission, he said.

She gave him a wink.

I won't tell anybody.

She went into the booth. It stunk of cigarettes. There were a few numbers written on the walls, with girl's names next to them. She picked the handset up, dropped the money in, and dialled.

*

When Galileo got back to Argyle Street he hunched over the gutter and opened the milk. He had a long drink. It was cold and he was thirsty. Then he poured the rest away. It flowed down the drain like pollution. He filled the empty with petrol. He glanced up and down the street before tearing a strip of material from his shirt. He stuffed it in the neck of the bottle and shook it till the rag was wet and inflammable. Then he sparked a match and lit his grenade.

He ran up the street. As he got closer to Gaston's he started to cross and approached it on a diagonal. He ran faster and shouted like a warrior.

Fire, fire.

As he closed in on the entrance and the confused faces of the queue of men, he launched his missile, over their heads and into the hallway of the establishment. It exploded in a loud flash and a bubble of flame and smoke escaped outside. The queue panicked and scattered onto the road. A black-suited bouncer screamed as an inferno clung to his face and hair. He ran outside patting his head before falling to the ground. A circle of patrons beat him with their jackets.

Galileo made his way to the fire escape at the rear. He climbed to the window where he'd seen Chastity. He pulled his elbow back and slammed it into the glass. When it cracked he kicked the shards clear and climbed inside. Men were struggling to get down the stairs and out of the building. They had left her on her workplace. She looked unconscious but her eyes were still open. He grabbed her by the shoulders and she flinched.

It's me Chastity, he said.

Galileo? she asked.

He pulled her habit down over her legs. Then he lifted her to a sitting position at the side of the bed. She was floppy with drugs. He squatted on the floor beside her and pulled her over his shoulder. He stood up and flexed his legs. He bent as he stepped through the window in case he caught her on the glass. It was difficult getting her along the ledge and down the stairs, but he managed it.

He walked along the alleyway, listening to the sounds of pandemonium. In the distance he heard a siren, then another, and another. As he moved they seemed to get closer. He came to a main street and turned left towards King's Cross. He walked past terraced houses. By the time they got to the station, police and fire engines flashed lights up and down Argyle Street.

Galileo got a ticket from a machine and went to the entrance. He couldn't get past the automatic barriers so a man in a blue uniform let him through the side.

The man nodded and pointed at Chastity.

She's had one over the eight.

Yeah, said Galileo. She's always getting pissed and I have to pick up the pieces.

Women eh? said the man.

Galileo saw his smile change to a frown as he looked at Chastity's habit.

Fancy dress party, he said and the man smiled.

He carried her down the escalators and through the tunnel. A train passed them as he climbed a set of ladders. By the time he got into the sphere, he was sweating.

He dropped to his knees and let her slip gently to the floor. He made a pillow with his jacket and rested her head on it. He searched around till he found his bag. He dragged it over beside her and unbuckled the top.

Would you like a drink? he asked.

Yes please, she croaked.

He opened the water and kneeled over her. He supported her neck and put the bottle to her lips. She drank slowly.

That's my girl, easy does it, he said.

When she'd had enough he lay down beside her. She rested her head on his chest. She cried softly.

I didn't think I was going to see you again.

He stroked her hair and thought of a future in safety.

They lay quietly as the candle burned.

When it reached the floor, he eased himself from under her and went to his bag. He pulled a box of them out and lit one. He was picking at the wick of another when she stopped him.

Don't, Galileo. We should only burn one at a time.

He began to speak.

But it's –

She interrupted him in a whisper.

If it glows too bright, they may come back.

He looked over her and into the darkness.

I should find them and kill them.

She reached her hand and touched him on the forearm.

No, stay with me.

OK, he gulped through tears.

He put the box away and searched through the rucksack.

Are you hungry? he asked.

Yes.

He dug out a packet of biscuits. He passed them in pieces she could put straight in her mouth.

Thank you, she whispered.

He watched her eat, her teeth glistening with the candle flame.

She glanced at him.

I'm sorry, she said.

What for?

She spoke like a tired old lady.

Demanding light, and more, and more.

You only wanted to show me what we were living in.

And what good did it do us? she asked.

Galileo peered into the darkness.

Sometimes when you see everything, you realise you want what you've already got.

And what have we got?

Each other, silly.

She didn't look at him as she spoke.

Are you sure you still want me?

He broke another biscuit.

Of course I do.

I'm glad.

Now eat, he said.

*

I stood naked in the death room. The walls were lovely and white, and on them I had scored the stains of the world that would mark them forever.

The sphere hung from the ceiling, covered in the phone numbers of all the people of the city, every address and name and number, their identities absorbed in the globe of my life. The wires hung ready with the clips for the ears, and the current of those who watched could zoom along and into the brain at the centre of the circle.

I went to the kitchen for my knife and cut a nick

into my wrist. The blood flowed down my hand to the tip of my fingers. I painted the red onto the phone numbers. I made patterns of me on top of the patterns of the people who lived in the city.

When they were complete I went into the living room and switched the telly on. I tuned it out of the stations until all I could hear was the hiss of dots sparkling on the screen.

I turned the volume up as high as it would go. I sat on the couch and stared at it. Just stared until the Messages started to appear, the odd flicker of words interrupting the hiss.

Buzz.

Judas and Jesus were two sides of the same consciousness.

Buzz.

The hollow in the middle is where we think and make decisions.

Buzz.

Fear is the saviour of the lonely.

Buzz.

Creation is Shit.

Buzz.

I got off the couch and fetched an old newspaper out of the cupboard. I took it into the bedroom and laid it on the space under the globe. I squatted and squeezed till my bowels moved and It fell onto the paper.

I picked It up and held It in front of my face.

The body of Christ, said Galileo.

I tasted It with the tip of my tongue.

The smell of the start of life, and of the end of life, said Galileo.

I held It high in the air and closed my eyes.

Show me the way, I asked.

I squeezed It in my hands and It flowed between my fingers, releasing colours and smells and a picture of a flower.

I inhaled the sweetness then I spread It into the hairs on my chest. I made finger lines down my arms and my legs. I put three stripes on my cheeks.

I held my arms out like Jesus on the cross.

For I am the resurrection and the light, said Galileo. I touched the sphere, and left handprints of Creation amongst the swirls of blood.

Tell me what to do, I asked.

You know what to do, said Galileo.

Wednesday, 19th May 2004

Charlie was woken at 8 a.m. by the nurse. She got out of bed and stumbled along behind the blue clad bum.

This way, she said every time she turned a corner. They eventually came to what looked like a cupboard.

Is this it? asked Charlie.

Yes. Everything we need is here.

The nurse pulled some liquid into a syringe and held it in the air and flicked it. She squeezed it till a teardrop formed at the end of the needle.

If you'll bend over that desk, she said.

What about my Valium?

The nurse picked up Charlie's file. She flicked through the charts then looked grim for a second.

We haven't prescribed you any.

I can't detox without downers.

The nurse spoke in a soothing voice.

Everything will be fine, dear. Just bend over.

Charlie did as she was asked. She felt the cold metal pierce her skin and the ache of the liquid as it entered her flesh.

She rubbed her bum as she was walked back to her room. The nurse nodded at her bed.

You should lay down love, it won't be long now.

She left and Charlie heard the door being locked. She sat on the white sheet and tried to get herself comfortable. Her nerves were stretching already and the room was getting bright. It wouldn't be long before the sickness attacked her like a raging man.

★

I looked around the room. It was a mess. Bits of shit on the carpet, old newspapers scrunched in the corner, bent beer tins lying by the side of the couch and cigarette ends overflowing from the ashtray.

I got out of bed and turned the telly off. The noise disappeared like water leaving a bath, and my head was emptied of everything except what I had to do.

I tore the sheets from my bed and put them in a bin bag. I searched through the flat and found dirty socks and pants and stuffed them in too. When it was full, I tied a knot in it and left it by the front door.

I checked to make sure there was enough credit in the electric meter.

I went into the bathroom and turned the shower on. I stepped into the hot flow and felt its hands on my skin. I rubbed soap into myself and the dried shit became sticky before dissolving in brown liquid, leaving bits of undigested food that finally fell away with the water.

I had a shave and put some fresh clothes on. I looked in the mirror on the way out of the door.

Not bad, I said to Galileo.

He winked at me.

You know what to do.

I bent down and picked the bag up.

Won't be long now.

The laundrette was empty until I walked in. The old lady gave me change for a tenner and I stuffed the washing into a machine. Because of the state of the sheets, I put it on hot. I sat on the ledge and watched it go round and stop, go round and stop.

The old lady mopped the floor.

Nice day out, she said.

It certainly is.

She got close enough that I could see the sweat on her forehead. I lifted my legs so she could do under my feet.

Thanks love, she said, and moved along the bench. Bits of chewing gum wrapper were flicked out by the mop.

I pulled my phone out and buzzed Chris.

What you up to? I asked.

Nothing.

Do you want to come round for a smoke?

I'll be about five minutes.

I wasn't surprised by his enthusiasm, but that was too early.

I'm out and about at the moment.

Oh, he said, disappointed.

Get round mine about eleven o'clock, I said.

I put the phone away as I gazed out of the window. People walked past on their way to work, or the shops.

The machine gave a final whirr before it stopped. I waited for the green light to come on and opened the door. I took the washing out and was going to put it in the dryer.

You'd save some money by spinning it first, said the old lady.

Where is it?

She pointed to the corner.

I filled it up and put a fifty-pence piece in.

When the washing was done, I took it back home and dumped it just inside the front door. I got an old plastic bag from under the sink and went round the living room picking the rubbish up. Some of the shit was hard to get out of the carpet, but I managed to get most of it up, just leaving a couple of small stains by the couch.

I put the bag in the kitchen and dragged out the vacuum. I took my time with it, making sure I got into all the corners.

When I was finished I opened up the laundry and put the fresh sheets on the bed. I put the rest of the stuff in the airing cupboard.

I looked at the clock.

★

Galileo climbed down the ladder. It was a long way. More rungs than any climb so far. He took it slowly so he wouldn't lose her, and was always aware of her presence. Every time he heard her slip or swear, he braced himself in case he needed to catch her. When they'd descended for three hundred rungs, he stopped.

Do you need a rest? he asked.

No, let's keep going.

He put his hands on the sides of the ladder and went on.

It took another three hundred steps before his foot touched the ground. He could hear the sounds of insects and water flowing. They were in a huge dark cave that seemed brighter in the distance.

He led her towards the light. As they got closer he could see the blue was tinged with green caused by huge leaves that curled into the entrance of the cave. He turned to her.

You wait there, he said.

He walked to the hole and poked his head out. Just a bit.

What he saw was a jungle, trees shooting up to the sky with creepers hanging from them. The sound of monkeys flicking from branch to branch. A parrot flew past in a blaze of red and blue.

He looked back into the cave.

Check this out, he said.

She walked slowly to the hole. She held her head to one side like a fragile little bird.

Wow, she said.

He took her by the hand and they walked into the forest. He kept one eye on the path and the other flicking around the scenery. They came to a river and decided to follow it downstream. It was shallow, burbling over stones, with runs in the middle that showed the occasional glitter of fish. They walked round a long curve until a tree appeared. Its branches drooped like a willow, and made a roof over a pool.

Chastity sniffed herself.

I stink, she said.

She tiptoed over the vegetation like a deer. She hunched by the water. She lifted a double handful and splashed it over her face. She turned and gave him a smile he hadn't seen for ages.

Get in, he said.

She watched the surroundings with suspicion.

Won't somebody see me?

I'll make sure you're all right.

She stood up and undid her belt. She wriggled her habit off her shoulders and let it drop, down her body, to the riverbank. He saw she still had welts on her back and dark stains on her bum cheeks. She stepped into the water until it covered her nakedness.

Do you need any help? he asked.

She looked over her shoulder and her eyes reflected the green of the jungle.

Yes please, she said.

He took off his clothes and paddled slowly in. The water was cool. He sighed as it climbed up his legs and over his belly. He waded until he stood behind her. She leaned against him.

This place is beautiful, she said.

*

Nigel was pacing up and down when his phone rung.

'It's Doctor Frederick,' said the receptionist. 'Shall I ask him to come through?'

'I'll be right out,' said Nigel.

He went to the lobby. As he pushed the doors and entered the room, the doctor stood up with his hand out.

'Hi,' said Nigel as he shook it. 'It's all go today.'

'Would you mind if we had a word,' asked the doctor, 'while we wait for Margaret?'

'Follow me,' said Nigel.

He walked down the stairs and into the kitchen area. When they were seated the doctor coughed.

'I've been thinking about our patient since we spoke yesterday,' he said. He had a sparkle in his eye. 'I think I may have a solution.'

'Let me hear it then,' said Nigel.

Frederick brushed his hand down the arm of his suit. 'We've tried medication,' he said. 'And we've tried talking cures.' He hesitated and Nigel nodded.

'Yeah?'

The doctor finished in a rush. 'The only thing we haven't attempted is electro-convulsive therapy.'

Nigel grimaced when he heard that. 'It's a bit extreme,' he said.

'And unusual,' said Frederick as he retrieved a folder from his briefcase. 'But I could justify it.'

'What about side effects?' asked Nigel, 'Is there not a danger of permanent damage?'

'Of course there is,' said Frederick.

'Is it worth the risk?' asked Nigel.

'I think so. But I would need the support of you, as the Care Coordinator, and one other psychiatrist.'

'It's a bit radical,' said Nigel. 'I'd really need to think about it.'

The doctor looked at the file and tapped it with his finger. His eyebrows moved and his forehead crinkled. He dropped the papers on the desk.

'Have you called Mister Johnson to make sure he's at home?' he asked.

'I was going to do that just before we left,' said Nigel.

'You better get on with it,' said Frederick, nodding at the clock.

*

I stood in the bathroom with Galileo. I had the phone to my ear.

I hope you can make our appointment, said Nigel.

I'm waiting for you, I said.

Galileo made a face and repeated my words. Then he snarled.

Tell the cunt, he said.

I know what you've been up to, I said.

And what would that be? asked Nigel.

Fucking my girlfriend.

Galileo nodded.

That's it son, he said.

Nigel didn't say anything.

He's thinking up an excuse, said Galileo.

She told me all about it, I said.

Nigel still didn't say anything.

Trying to get me locked up, I said.

Shut up, said Galileo.

Still Nigel didn't speak.

What have you got to say then? I asked.

Do you seriously believe I'm having sex with your girlfriend?

I can prove it, I said.

There was a moment of silence.

That shut him up, said Galileo.

How can you do that? asked Nigel.

I've got Charlie's word on it, I said.

Good boy, said Galileo.

I wouldn't call that proof, said Nigel.

I bashed the phone against the sink then spoke into it.

Proof? I shouted. You've been fucking my bird you dirty cunt.

Nigel spoke softly.

Gary, I'm a professional social worker and a married man. Do you really think I would risk all that?

Galileo tightened his lips.

He's trying to flannel you.

Shut up, I said to the mirror. I can't think.

I'm here to help you, said Nigel, softer.

Are you? I asked.

Don't listen to the cunt, said Galileo.

Shut the fuck up, I said to the mirror.

Gary, it's important you calm down. Try to think rationally. Can you do that?

Yes, I said.

Galileo shook his head.

Stupid prick, he said.

Have I ever been untruthful with you? asked Nigel.

No, I said.

Well I can put my hand on my heart and say to you that I have never been unfaithful to my wife. Do you believe me Gary?

I shrugged my shoulders.

I don't know.

Charlie's not always been honest with you, has she?

I couldn't look at Galileo.

No, I said.

He's fucking with you, said Galileo.

You need to examine her motivations for telling you this, said Nigel. If she were really having an affair with me, would it be in her interests to let you know about it?

I don't know, I said.

Maybe she told you to cause problems in your relationship with me and other services.

Why would she do that? I asked.

Yeah, said Galileo.

Because if she can isolate you from your support network, it becomes easier for her to manipulate you. Is that what you want from your girlfriend?

Don't listen to him, said Galileo.

Shut up, let him speak, I said to the mirror.

Gary, I know you love Charlie but she's done this before, hasn't she?

What? I asked.

Used you as a pawn in her power games.

I can't handle this, I said. It's doing my head in.

Gary, I care about you and will do everything I can to help you. I'm going to be at your flat in a few minutes.

Please calm down. Don't do anything silly. Wait until I get there and you can tell me all about it.

Galileo looked from the mirror.

Do you think he spoke so softly when he was fucking Charlie? he asked.

I started to shout.

Come round you cunt, and I'll fuck you right up.

You're not helping yourself, said Nigel.

Fuck off, I screamed.

I threw the phone against the bathroom wall. It bounced and fell clattering into the bath.

I slammed the door open and barged into the living room. Chris was on the couch having a smoke of my gear.

Give me that you cunt, I said.

Is everything all right? he asked as he handed it to me.

Tell him to shut the fuck up, said Galileo.

My hands shook as I held the foil.

Fine, I said.

Yeah OK, said Galileo.

I sucked up a line.

That's it son, you hide in drugs, said Galileo.

Shut up, I said.

Out of the corner of my eye I could see Chris fidget in his chair. I turned to face him.

What? I asked.

He looked away.

Nothing.

Do you want a smoke? I asked.

He nodded.

Wait till I've had one, I said with a growl.
I puffed another line and felt Galileo relax.
I passed Chris the foil.
Best get that down you, I said. It might be the last for a while.
He didn't pay attention. He just sucked on the tube till his head began to flop.

*

Nigel drove his car to Gary's house. Frederick was in the passenger seat and Margaret was in the back. They'd been arguing about the merits of ECT since they'd left the city.

'It's barbaric,' she said. 'There's no place for it in modern psychiatry.'

'But don't you think it would be worth trying?' asked Frederick.

'Not in this case,' she said.

'We've exhausted the other options,' said Frederick. He half turned in his seat and spoke over his shoulder. 'It's in the patient's best interests that we try and find a solution.'

'What if it makes him worse?' she asked. 'And anyway,' she added, 'it's not appropriate for personality disorders.'

The doctor held his finger in the air. 'But the paranoia is becoming severe.'

'Is this true?' she asked.

'It's a shame,' said Nigel with a sad nod. 'I really

thought we were making some progress.' He paused before going on. 'The ECT might be an idea,' he said with a shrug.

He glanced in his rearview mirror at Margaret. 'I mean, we should keep an open mind. Gary's in a lot of pain. If we could ease that, we'd be halfway there.'

As Nigel drove into Gary's street, Margaret pointed at the police car waiting by the flats.

'What are they doing here?' she asked.

'When I spoke to Gary earlier,' said Nigel, 'he seemed fairly angry, so I thought it might be a good idea to have some support.'

'But it's asking for trouble, taking them to his home,' said Margaret.

'Come on,' said Nigel. 'We all know how dangerous he can be.'

'You might think so,' she said, 'but I've always found him open to suggestion.'

'There are protocols,' said Frederick, 'and in this case we need to follow them to the letter.'

'But that way doesn't work with Gary,' she said. 'He'll fight fire with fire, it's the only way he knows.'

'What would you suggest?' asked the doctor. 'A weekend in a sweat lodge with some earth mothers?'

'Very funny,' said Margaret. She reached for the door handle. 'Shall we just get this over with?'

The two policemen joined them at the garden gate. 'All set?' said the sergeant and the constable nodded. He touched his fingers to the implements dangling from his belt.

Nigel watched Margaret. 'I'm sure everything will be

relaxed,' he said to her. 'Let me speak to Gary and he'll come with us without much of an argument.'

'It's your call, Nigel,' she said as they pushed through the door and started walking up the stairs.

The boots of the policemen echoed around the hallway.

*

When I looked through the spy hole, I knew it was all over for me.

Who is it? I asked.

My social worker pushed his big nose near to the door.

It's Nigel.

OK, I'll get the key, I said.

I watched him nod to one of the coppers.

I told you, said Galileo. But his voice was mellow with smack, and it didn't make me jump.

Chris was dozing on the couch.

What's happening? he asked.

I went over and took him by the arm.

You better hide.

As I drove him through the hall and into the bedroom, he turned to me.

It stinks in there.

He wafted his hand in front of his face and tried to walk out.

What is that? he asked.

I pushed him back in.

Never you mind, I said. Get in there.
He tried again to come out.
Come on Gaz.
Just stay here, I snarled.
But it's dark, he said.
I grabbed him by the front of his shirt and shook him.
What did I fucking tell you?
I felt him sag.
OK, he said.
I raised my fist to his chin.
And don't come out till I give you the word.
He nodded, meek as a lamb, and I pulled the door closed behind him.

*

Nigel noticed the smell of shit as he walked into the flat, but it seemed exceptionally clean. 'The place is tidy,' he said.

'I like to keep it that way,' said Gary as he picked at a piece of skin on his neck.

'Why don't you sit down,' said Nigel.

'After you,' said Gary.

Nigel and Frederick sat on the edge of the bed. Gary settled into the couch with Margaret beside him. The policemen stood by the door.

'So how have you been keeping?' asked Margaret.

'I'm perfectly all right,' said Gary. He looked at the people in his flat one at a time before bringing his eyes back to her.

'Are you sure?' she asked. 'I thought things weren't going too well,' she said as she glanced at Nigel.

'You can tell Margaret,' said Nigel, but Gary didn't say anything.

'You should tell us the truth,' said Frederick in an assertive tone. 'We're here to help you.'

'It's true,' said Nigel, trying to sound soft and gentle.

Gary stared at him and opened his mouth a couple of times as if he was going to say something. Then he turned to Margaret.

'Don't listen to them,' he said and paused as if he was gazing into another world. Then he looked back at Nigel and the doctor. He pointed at them and nodded. 'You can't believe what they say.'

'But you know you can trust me,' she said. 'Don't you?'

'Yeah,' said Gary. 'You're OK.'

'I'm really worried about you,' she said as she sat forward in her seat. She leaned on her lap and looked at Gary. 'I've got a feeling you might be coming to a crisis, and I don't know how safe you are living here by yourself.'

'I'm all right,' said Gary.

'That's not how it appears to me,' she said. 'Don't you think it might be better if we arranged for you to go back into hospital?'

Gary flinched at the word, and his head turned to the window.

'No,' he said, very quietly. Then he said it again, louder.

'Only for a little while,' said Margaret.

'I'm not going there again,' said Gary. He got to his

feet and his body appeared bigger with every breath. 'It's just not happening.' He faced Nigel and the doctor. 'You can't fucking make me.'

'That's just where you're wrong, I'm afraid,' said Frederick as he stood up. 'Under Section Two of the Mental Health Act we can detain you for a period of seventy-two hours.' He nodded to the sergeant.

The policemen stepped closer to Gary, but Margaret put her hand out to stop them.

'Gary, please listen to me,' she said.

'What?' he asked, appearing more and more dangerous.

'You're going to have to go to hospital,' she said. 'I don't like it, and I'm sure you don't. But that doesn't change the fact that you have to go.'

'He only wants me locked up' said Gary, pointing at Nigel, 'so he can have my girlfriend.'

Nigel didn't blush. His heart beat a little faster, but he managed to give incredulous looks to his colleagues.

'I think we've heard enough,' he said.

★

I backed towards the wall and they all closed in on my space.

But you did fuck my missus, I said to Nigel.

He looked at the others like I was crazy.

Don't make this any harder on yourself, said Margaret.

My eyes searched around the room for a way out. A gap in the line of jailers.

He said he'd get her into treatment, I said.

I pleaded with Margaret.

Honest to God he did. I swear on it. My mother's life.

She turned to Nigel.

We need to go gently here.

He didn't blink. He even seemed sad.

I'm sorry Gary, he said. You must be in so much pain. But these accusations need to stop.

I looked at the faces and all I could see was a wall of disbelief.

Hit him, said Galileo.

You're a dirty fucking cunt, I shouted at Nigel. I tried to punch him in the face.

I didn't even get him once. The police jumped me and I fell with their bodies on top of me. They pulled my hands behind my back and I heard the rattle of handcuffs.

*

Charlie twisted the sheets round her wrists and arched her back like a woman about to have a baby. She turned on her side and held her stomach as cramps hit her. She stood up and walked from one side of the room to the other. She tried the window but it was nailed closed. She tried the door but it was locked. There was a red string hanging above the bed.

Only to be pulled in emergencies, said the sign next to it.

Charlie yanked it so hard it came out of the switch on

the ceiling. She counted to thirty before she heard the sounds of footsteps on the corridor.

Keys rattled, then the door opened and the nurse came in.

What's the matter?

Charlie brushed her sweaty hair from her face.

I need something.

What do you want?

A sedative.

The nurse manoeuvred her to the bed.

Come on love, sit yourself down.

Charlie struggled free.

I don't fucking want to sit down.

We're not going to give you anything, said the nurse as she left the room. You just need to go through it like everybody else.

Charlie sat on the bed. Then she got on the floor and leaned into the corner. Then she paced the room. Then she sat back on the bed.

I can't do this, she said.

She screamed and ran at the door. She beat her hands against it.

Let me out, she shouted. Let me fucking out.

No one answered.

*

As the policemen secured Gary, Nigel looked around the room. 'Where is that smell coming from?' he asked.

'It's somewhere through there,' said Frederick. 'Why don't you investigate?'

'No,' said Gary. 'Stay out of there.'

Nigel and Margaret exchanged glances. He walked to the hallway, but when he got in there he noticed the bathroom door was open and it appeared clean and tidy. The smell was stronger though. He popped his head back into the living room.

'How's the decorating?' he asked Gary, who was now sitting on the couch between the policemen.

'Mind your own fucking business,' said Gary.

Nigel walked to the bedroom. He opened the door. The smell was intense. He heard Gary shouting, 'Don't turn on the light.'

Nigel heard someone snoring in there, but he couldn't see anything except a shadowy outline in the middle of the room. 'There's someone in here,' he said over his shoulder.

'Don't turn on the fucking light,' Gary repeated.

Nigel reached for the switch and pressed it. There was a flash and the image of a body falling to the floor.

Wednesday, 2nd June 2004

After breakfast I had a walk in the grounds. It was like going about in a big plastic bubble made from the anti-psychotics. I rolled across the grass and sat on a bench by an old chestnut tree. I took in some deep breaths to try and blast the fog out of my head. But it didn't work, I felt as dopey as ever.

It was nice to have a rest from Galileo though. I could sit still and have quiet in my head. I could watch crap telly shows in the day room without getting angry. I could even talk to the nurses without him saying things about them, or trying to get me to stare at their tits.

But I knew he hadn't gone away. All I was getting was a holiday while he was hiding from the shrinks. He could wait for ever in there. When the time was right he'd prowl back into my life like a cat from under a tool-shed.

I sparked up a fag and gazed into the valley below the hospital. Except for the fence and the barbed wire, it could have been the view from a holiday cottage. Green rolling downs with a couple of red-roofed barns.

A fly buzzed my head, attracted to my sweat. The noise of it gave me a shudder. It made me think of doctors standing over me with electrodes in their hands. Not that I was conscious when they did it.

But it left its mark.

And then sitting in a room with dribble running down my chin and some nurse reading from my file, telling me about my life, trying to prod my memory back into action.

I swatted at the fly and went back to the view. Taking nice drags on my fag and waiting to see if anyone walked in the countryside, or if it was populated by animals and empty houses.

I heard a rustle behind me and turned round to see who it was. A nurse had appeared on the lawn.

You've got a visitor, she said.

Who?

She shrugged.

I don't know. All they told me was to collect you and take you over to the centre.

★

Nigel and Sarah left the house. As he unlocked the doors of the car there was a whistle from the end of the street. He looked and a prostitute was waving to her friend.

'Just get in,' said Sarah.

As he drove past he didn't glance at the girl. He kept his eyes on the road ahead. He coughed and rolled the window down.

Sarah turned in her seat.

'I am so embarrassed,' she said.

'I'm sorry,' he said. 'What more can I say?'

'Just tell me you didn't fuck her,' she said.

'How many times do we have to go through this?' he asked and looked round.

'Till I'm satisfied you're being honest with me,' she said with her chin jutting out.

'I've been interrogated at work, and by the police,' he said. 'Do I have to suffer from you too?'

'Don't give me that shit,' she said. 'If it was the other way around, you'd want to question me.'

He didn't reply. He concentrated on the traffic. He switched the stereo on. Drum and bass battered round the car and against his head. He turned the volume down and pressed the button for Radio Four.

'And,' said Sarah, 'there's what happened to that poor man.'

'How do you think I feel?' he asked. 'I was the one who killed him.'

They drove in silence for a while. He was dreading the visit to the therapist, but Sarah had said it was either that or she was leaving. It didn't seem like he had much choice.

His thoughts were interrupted by her next outburst.

'And there's the cash you gave her,' she spat.

'It wasn't that much,' he said.

'It was three hundred pounds,' she said. 'Now that you've lost your job, it's me that has to replace it.'

'I'm sorry,' he whined.

'What did she give you for the money?' she asked, throwing her hands up. 'A blow-job?'

'She didn't give me anything.'

'Why did you let her have it then?'

'She was trying to get clean. I thought it would help her stay off the streets.'

'You fucking idiot.'

'I just tried to help the girl,' he said, like it was a litany. 'I made a couple of calls to see if she could be admitted into rehab. That's as far as it went.'

'Why didn't you tell me about it when it was happening?' she asked. 'Why all the secrecy?'

'I knew what it looked like,' he said as he braked for a red traffic light. 'I didn't want to upset you.'

'I'm fucking angry about this, Nigel.'

'Don't let her do this to us,' he said and turned to her. Her eyes creased as they connected with his, but she but didn't say anything.

'When will people start to believe me?' he asked and rested his head on the steering wheel.

'I'm sick of your manipulations,' she said. 'If you don't realise that, I can't see much of a future for us.'

The threat and its implications silenced him.

*

I moved through the corridors with my shoes squeaking on the linoleum and the smell of carbolic in my nose. The nurse walked beside me. She was an old dear from up north.

Did you enjoy yourself in the grounds love? she asked. I nodded.

Yeah. It's nice to get off the ward.

Make sure you behave yourself and there should be plenty more.

It was like being with my mum.

OK, I said. I'll try my best.

Good boy, she said.

We arrived at a door made out of steel bars. We stopped and the nurse rang a bell. A well-built black man appeared from a side room.

I've got one for a visit, said the nurse.

He cast his eyes over me before he pressed the buzzer. I pushed through the gate.

Thanks, I said.

When it closed behind me I realised I was in a length of corridor six feet long. There was a camera scanning from the corner.

The man pointed to a seat.

Put your bum on that, he said.

I looked back down the corridor. The nurse waved.

I'll come and collect you when you're finished.

She walked away and I faced the man.

What happens now? I asked.

He pulled a fluorescent jacket out of a cupboard. It was like the ones the binmen wear.

Just slip this on, he said.

When I had, he started walking towards a door with a window in it.

Follow me.

On the other side was a room with a coffee table and two easy chairs. I sat down. He kept standing.

After a couple of minutes, I heard the squeak of a door. Then heels clipping down a corridor. I turned to the man with a question in my eyes, but he didn't show any expression. Just stood there like a soldier outside Buckingham Palace.

The heels got louder, with a slight echo, and a scrape every couple of steps. I kept my eyes on the wall and the rules for visits.

A door banged and a nurse came into the room. She led someone in after her.

It was Charlie.

She glanced from one nurse to the other. Her eyes were bright and her clothes were clean. Her teeth seemed to sparkle when she smiled at me.

Hi babe, she said.

I stared at her for a few seconds.

Hiya, I said.

A NOTE ON THE AUTHOR

Mark McNay was born in 1965 and brought up in a mining village in central Scotland. He graduated from the UEA creative writing course in 2003 with distinction. His first novel, *Fresh*, won the Arts Foundation New Fiction Award and the Saltire First Book of the Year Award in 2007.